# Love Like Crazy

ALSO BY MEGAN SQUIRES

*Demanding Ransom*
*The Rules of Regret*
*Draw Me In*

# love like crazy

MEGAN SQUIRES

First Kindle Edition: 2014



Cover art by Tiffany Willett at On The Spot Studio
Editing by Tiffany Tillman of Redhead Book Services

For the three people I love like crazy. *Incurably.*

Brad,
Jacob
and Abby.

# ONE

I jumped out of a second story window when I was eight.

There weren't any white-hot flames licking up the walls, forcing me to resort to a twenty-foot free-fall escape route. There was no masked predator slinking into my room, under my covers, and into my nightmares. It wasn't even the fantastical childhood desire of flying that propelled me out of that window and onto Mrs. Tompkin's wax myrtle hedge, thick and padded with evergreen.

You couldn't always blame these sorts of things on others. Sometimes the blame landed squarely on your own shoulders. Even if they happened to be those of a boney, freckle-faced, third-grade girl.

No one really looked at you the same after doing something like that, as would be expected. Some might call that a tragedy. For me? It was sort of a relief, because now they were giving me the very same gawking stare the mirror had reflected most of my adolescent life.

*What on earth is wrong with her?*

Good question, truly.

In fact, this question was my proverbial elephant in the room, and that imaginary pachyderm had been hanging out in our house for far too many years. I was really beginning to hate elephants.

I also didn't love mirrors, but that was likely a result of today's reflection not looking too different from the girl of days ago. Sure, I was slightly older. A little curvier, but just barely. Breasts where a shallow, concave chest used to be. Hair a bit thicker—longer—with a burnished luster. Not quite black, not truly brown. Somewhere in between, nearly mahogany.

I *almost* looked like the adult I would legally be in just a few short months, but something was still off. The exterior appearance had some catching up to do, though my interior mindset had made that swift transition years ago.

For most kids my age, taking ownership over your own life often happened when you turned eighteen: flying the nest, embarking on a college adventure, being empowered through your patriotic vote and all that jazz. But in my case, it had been years since someone else held the title to mine. In fact, sometimes it even felt like I was the original owner, like I'd tacked on every mile.

And there were many miles in the long road of my short life. That might sound like a cheesy paradoxical metaphor, but in my seventeen years, I'd witnessed a lot of life. That's what the counselors always said, at least: "You've seen so much for such a young girl." It struck me as ironic that this was a phrase reserved for those who'd mostly experienced the ugly side of things. Death. Sickness. Sorrow. Betrayal.

I'd agree there was a lot of ugly out there. But there had to be an abundance of beauty to be found, and I made it my mission to seek that out and live it daily. Strangely enough, the easiest place for me to locate the beautiful was at school. Learning meant growing, and growing meant you were moving forward in life, which I considered to be a beautiful thing. Keeping the wheels in motion. One foot in front of the other. When you stopped moving, that's when the trouble settled in. That's when it got a foothold and shook things up. That's when the wheels fell off.

I planned to always keep moving.

Which was exactly what my own feet should've been doing with only five minutes left until the chime of that first period bell down at Masonridge High.

So I grabbed my canvas rucksack, threw it over my shoulder, and raced out the front door, the winter cold smacking my cheeks as I trekked down the street, not quite running, but faster than a walk. Like those grandmas that power-walked with their water bottles in hand, tiny hips swishing side to side. When I got to the light post, I dug my nail into the shiny metal knob, waiting for that geometric red man to flash. Almost there.

I had to admit, this part was most embarrassing, worse than looking like an elderly exerciser. The first block wasn't so bad because I was tucked into the camouflage of houses and fences and tree-lined sidewalks that sheltered me from view. But this last stretch toward campus was an exposition. Everyone could see me, and I could see them as they guided their parents' gently-used luxury vehicles into the parking lot, the motors so quiet they could sneak up behind you like a panther stalking its ignorant prey.

Since I lived less than a mile from school, it wasn't like I needed a car to get me there—that wasn't my issue—it was that everyone else had these boxes to hide inside. These pretty, expensively packaged exteriors, so captivating it didn't even matter what was contained within them. I didn't want a car; I just wanted an outer identity other than the transparent one my parents had wrapped me up in. Where my peers had these thick, solid facades with their pristine tract homes and hand-me-down wheels, I had clear cellophane wrap, wrinkled and torn that left me naked and undone.

I was the daughter of a woman I hadn't seen in roughly ten years and the spawn of an apathetic alcoholic.

And I was also the girl that everyone thought tried to kill herself when she was eight. I'd slapped that unfortunate title on myself. Maybe this was where those doctors got their whole "she's seen a lot of life" thing from. Probably the case.

My dad was on the receiving end of those same eyes that glued on to mine as we walked throughout town. But where I'd grown somewhat comfortable with them, he despised those stares. "*Who the hell do they think they are?*" he'd scream in a voice that used to rattle like thunder, but now had become so raw and gravelly from the four packs a day that he only sounded like an old man gurgling for air. He'd sputter when he spoke as he strangled the neck of a 40 and swayed side to side. He couldn't even keep his feet planted long enough to attempt the act of intimidation. He looked like reed, not a towering oak. Nothing about him was frightening, except the fact that this was what our existence had boiled down to.

Dad didn't bother to hide his drinking from me. You hid things you were ashamed of, I figured, the things you didn't want exposed by the light of day. Dad just wasn't all that ashamed. There was no wrong in it. Go ahead, turn the floodlights on. *They* all had it wrong.

*"They think they're better than us?"* he'd slur like his tongue was too thick for his mouth. *"Try walking a mile in our shoes and then they'll see how things really are."*

But I wasn't sure it was possible to walk a mile in the shoes of someone who was going absolutely nowhere. Dad wasn't a forward mover anymore, and as much as I'd tried to push him along the road with me, children just weren't meant to do some things.

In a way, that made me feel sorry for him, though I realized kids shouldn't feel sorry for their parents, either. That wasn't the way the world worked. But when that flimsy line between adult and child was blurred with the fuzz of alcohol and the coating of a lifetime's worth of mistakes, it was just one human empathizing for another. That, I figured, made it okay to feel just a little bit sorry.

I was still thinking about my dad's non-movement when the traffic lights finally changed and the WALK sign pulsed red like a beating heart drawing me across the street. I loved school. For me, it was my beautiful, golden ticket. School was the arteries and veins that pumped knowledge and information into me, giving me a real chance at a successful adulthood. Sure, the education system was screwed up, people would say. Public school was a joke. Maybe so, but I'd already had an education of my own within the four walls of my home. I'd take whatever lessons my teachers could offer me over that.

And I only had five more minutes until today's lesson would begin.

I might actually get there in time to talk with Sam before chemistry lab started. She had a date with some junior college guy last night and I was eager to hear the details. Sam never left anything out. Sometimes that was awkward, leaving my imagination very little to imagine. Most of the time it was refreshing.

The first warning bell sounded and I stepped out into the temporarily paused flurry of traffic. Two gangly senior boys slunk past me, one slamming into my shoulder as they traded a blunt back and forth, quickly attempting to get just one last drag before their feet crossed onto campus property.

I wasn't in a daze when it happened because I always tried to be aware of my surroundings. Having a parent with fewer than five lucid minutes per day put your senses on high alert permanently. You became their eyes, ears, and brain, too. Sometimes at school I would let that slip a little because I was only responsible for myself while I was there. But right now, I was still out in the open world. Still overly aware, standing at attention.

So when the locking of tires violently trying to grip the road like Velcro crashed into my eardrums, I heard it and picked up my stride to safely hop onto the opposite curb before I could even see the beater of a truck careening straight toward me.

Unfortunately, the dog that bolted out into the lane at exactly the same time didn't.

Maybe that was due to the fact that his eyes were on either side of his head, spaced too far apart to take it all in. Maybe it was because he was a dog, and dogs had dog brains. Whatever the reason, there was no mercy in the act, no softening of the blow of oversized tires and twisted metal and fur and bone that collided so brutally they almost became one, like some instant osmosis.

And there was also no mercy in the way the man—his thin yellow beard curling down to the middle of his chest, his cigarette sticking to the inside of his lip like it was attached permanently—looked my direction, locked remorseless eyes upon mine, and sped off as though the life of that furry and four-legged creature was somehow less important than his own.

The light hadn't even turned green yet, but he gunned it, disappearing from sight.

Then the school bell rang.

"No, no, no, no, no, no!" I gritted, staring at the unmoving animal ten feet away. Blood seeped from his mouth. His leg was a twisted hanger, bent and contorted. Blond tufts of hair floated through the air like the aftermath of a dandelion wish.

I made a wish of my own. A cruel one. One that hoped he was dead, for his sake. Maybe a little for mine. Probably *a lot* for mine, truthfully.

Expelling a breath that lifted my sweat-laden hair from my forehead, I held up a hand, acting as both crossing guard and guardian as I walked over to the crumpled mass on the road. I was amazed no one else stopped—not even slowed down to witness the train wreck unfold.

I wanted to close my eyes the closer I got, but that wasn't fair—to shield myself from someone's pain because it was too messy and real to handle. If I did that, it would make me no better than an animal. I was human. I still felt sorry for things.

I could see his chest ballooning, which meant he wasn't dead. In shock, probably, if animals also had the ability to do that—to shut down in order to sustain. There was no collar around his neck, and even though I was certain it was the accident that left him looking mangled and disheveled, the thick layer of grime that clung to his matted coat had to be several weeks in the making.

He belonged to no one.

*Double damn it.*

I crouched down onto my haunches and shoved my hair from my face with the heel of my hand.

"It's okay," I lulled, pressing a light hand to his ribs. He flinched, eyes flashing. They were dark brown, a cat-like rim of black lining their edges. "You're gonna be okay."

I didn't know that. But that's what you said, right? It wasn't like I could blurt out, "How are you not dead?" Even though that's exactly what I thought. How had the impact not killed him instantly? How had his small frame—his bones and muscle and flesh—withstood the unfair discrepancy in the size and weight of his opponent? Why hadn't someone, somewhere, in some universe or heaven or whatever it was, had pity on him? Why hadn't my cruel wish come true?

I didn't have time to ask those questions because the traffic light changed again, and now I was no more visible than the golden-haired dog as I sat, bent down next to him, eye-level with the bumpers and hubcaps that filtered past. It must've been one of those superhuman moments when endorphins laced with adrenaline fed strength to your muscles, because even though he had to weigh at least forty pounds, I lifted him from the asphalt without struggle, not even hobbling with difficulty as I carried him back to the curb.

And in that moment I was my dad.

And I wondered if he'd made the same selfish wish about me years ago.

# TWO

"My dog was hit by a car."

I didn't figure it was okay to drop his bloodied body onto the laminate countertop like I was making a return at a department store, so I continued clutching him to my chest. He was all dead weight now—limp, hairy legs and arms. A wet nose nuzzled into the crook of my neck. His air that puffed in and out of him matched my own struggling effort for breath and left a damp ring of moisture against my skin. But the space between the gusts had gotten longer, stretching out with each passing minute, and it allowed enough time for that wet patch of warmth to evaporate. I wondered if I would even notice the transition from him being a body to becoming a corpse when it eventually took place. That sort of freaked me out.

"Name?"

The gray-haired woman behind the counter didn't look up, but drizzled a generous helping of salad dressing onto what resembled rabbit food in a clear-blue Tupperware container. She unsnapped a plastic fork from its convenient place inside the lid and stabbed at the lettuce like she had a personal vendetta against the farm where it came from. It was too early for a salad, but maybe she'd worked the night shift. Not everyone lived their days in tune with the rise and fall of the sun.

"Name?" she ordered again. Her scrubs were a complete miss. Happy, cartoon-drawn puppies and kitties stood up on their hind legs, some holding balloons in their paws (even though the lack of opposable thumbs would obviously prohibit that), some holding lollipops, all swirling psychedelic rainbow colors. She was like one of those angry carnies that just didn't fit the energized landscape of a buzzing midway carnival.

"The dog's name?" I clarified.

"Yes." Another senseless slaying of romaine and cabbage.

My eyes tracked the room, landing on the dressing bottle as she shook out more of her anger, this time resorting to drowning the leafy greens in Italian Herb Vinaigrette.

"Herb."

"You have an appointment?"

My head sprang back into my neck. Herb shifted in my arms, noticing my falter, somehow understanding my human reaction on a primal level. Thank God he was still a body, not yet a corpse. "No." I narrowed my eyes at her question. "I didn't plan for him to get run over by a big rig today."

"You'll have to take a seat." She flicked her fork/weapon toward the lining of chairs positioned against the wall at my back. There was an elderly woman with a cat carrier. The Persian cat inside hissed every five seconds at the ticking clock on the wall, like it was conducting some type of countdown.

There was also a boy, all jean-clad, long legs crossed at the ankles, a dirty Cincinnati Reds baseball cap tucked low over his eyes, brown curls of hair peeking out from under the fabric rim. He had a hamster in a wire cage seated on the empty chair next to him. It raced around and around in its wheel, so fast that at points it flipped up and over onto its little back. Then it would start again.

"Before you sit, what form of payment will you be making?"

*Payment.* I hadn't factored that into this messy equation. The equation where one attempted-dog-murderer plus one guilty-feeling-girl equals five months of a nonexistent paycheck down the drain.

"Debit card."

My body recoiled at the startling sound of his voice and the pressure of his arm as he reached around me to flick a plastic credit card onto the waist-high counter. The pointed tip of my elbow fit into the hollow inside of his. I couldn't move out of the way with the half-dead dog in my arms and there was no other method for him to get around me. We were touching and it felt incredibly weird.

The stranger gripped the brim of his hat and swung it around. Where just shadows existed earlier, his eyes were now exposed golden irises, friendly, but with more lines in the corners than he should have for someone his age. He looked like a teenager, with boyish roundness clinging to his cheeks, and he had full lips stained the color of strawberries. No longer necessarily cute, but not quite handsome. Somewhere awkwardly stuck in between a boy and a man.

"Fine," the woman groaned. I figured it was her job to take our money, but you would have thought we'd just handed over a live grenade about to detonate. "Take a seat."

"Here." The guy stretched two long arms my direction, both hooked upward like he was carrying an invisible load of towels. "Give it here." He fluttered an impatient hand at me.

I knew he meant the dog, but something made me want to throw my arms around him and bear hug him for offering to pay for this other stranger currently in my arms.

I must've stuttered in my movements for longer than he liked because he shrugged under his navy blue hoodie and pulled Herb from my hands while my feet were still locked in place, and my brain still worked to play catch up.

"Go sit down." He nodded toward his vacant chair.

I did as told for some crazy reason, and heeded the direction and advice of this kid I didn't know from Adam. But I supposed he *did* just offer up his own money to pay for a dog that technically wasn't even mine. I guessed that earned him the right to tell me what to do. Plus, it wasn't like I'd be able to figure out what it was that I needed to do on my own.

I hadn't been operating on all cylinders this morning. It was all instinct.

*Get out of way of truck. Pick up wounded animal. Save wounded animal. Sit down.*

*Breathe.*

It took three full breaths, each one filling my lungs to capacity, then falling back out in a slow, counted exhale, before my head finally synched with my actions.

I had completely missed first period.

And now half of second.

This day was getting away from me.

And I also had a dog.

"Herb?" a man in the same jubilant scrubs called out over the top of a metal clipboard, his steel-toe boot propping the door open to the medical offices in back. "Is there a Herb in here?"

I glanced over to the guy with my dog, almost forgetting what I was doing posted up in this waiting area. *So much for being aware of my surroundings.* It was all fuzz and fog, like looking through a cup of water, beads of condensation clinging to the glass, obscuring your vision.

"Do you want me to take him?" He leaned over the rattling hamster cage separating us. "Or do you want to?"

"Oh. Yeah. I guess you can. I mean, if you'd like to. I'd appreciate it."

"You wait here," the man/boy said, standing up without struggle as he held Herb to his chest.

We matched in blood-speckled attire now, some morbid twinsie type of outfit. We had those dances at our school where the girl was supposed to ask the guy and then they'd buy these silly matching shirts to wear. I never went to those, but maybe this could count. I hadn't asked him to a dance, just to hold on to my bloody dog while I stared blankly at the wall, but I didn't imagine high school dances went much better than this, anyway.

"Wait here," he said once more, giving me a brief, heartfelt smile. "I'll let you know how it goes."

Again, another nod. I sure wasn't using my words well today.

Then the boy and my dog disappeared behind the door.

# THREE

*"End of discussion, Eppie."*

*Daddy's words were hard, just like his expression. Even though I could only see his eyes and fuzzy dark eyebrows above the folded-over flap of the newspaper, I knew exactly what shape his mouth took. It was a flat, tight line. No smiling. Daddy hardly ever smiled.*

*"End of what discussion, Mark?"*

*"Mama!" I spun around toward her voice. She hadn't completely entered the house and was still in the doorway to the garage. She dropped her large purse onto the kitchen counter and bent over to remove her black high heels, one and then the other. Unlike Daddy, she had a huge smile on her face. And it was just for me, I knew it was.*

*"Eppie, my sweet girl."*

*I ran to her fast, slamming into her waist as she stooped down to wrap me in her slender arms. The fabric of her suit was scratchy and it tickled my cheek. She squeezed me tight and it felt like rough whiskers against my skin. I didn't mind, though.*

*"Mama." I looked up at her with pleading, puppy eyes. "Daddy won't let me go to Sarah's birthday party tonight."*

*“Because you’re not even seven, Eppie. You’re too young for a sleepover.”*

*I glared at Daddy, but he couldn’t see me. His newspaper was back up again. “No, I’m not. Everyone in my class has been to a slumber party before. I’m the only one.”*

*“I’m sure you’re not the* only *one, sweet girl.” Mama lifted my chin with her thumb and finger. She still smiled, but this one looked different because there was a laugh behind it. She shook her head as she said, “But if Daddy says no, then it’s a no.”*

*“But that’s not fair!”*

*“Eponine, do not raise your voice to me!” The newspaper tore from his face and Daddy slammed a fist on the end table. His glass of water tipped over and ice cubes slipped across the wooden surface. I cowered back into Mama’s chest, shielding my eyes from him. Daddy was angry, and it was my fault he was yelling like this. I’d made him so mad. “I will not argue with you about this any longer. You are a child; you don’t get to have an opinion on this. You are* not *going to the party.” More calmly than before, he folded the paper in his lap, deliberately creasing it like he was in slow motion. “Now, go to your room.”*

*“But, Daddy—”*

*“Go to your room, Eponine!”*

*The tears didn’t waste any time. They flooded down my chubby cheeks and my nose also started dripping. Mama gave me one last squeeze, but nudged me forward like she wanted me to go away, too. I thought she was on my side. That hurt my feelings even more than Daddy yelling at me.*

*Without looking at either of them, I stomped my way up each of the stairs, counting them as I went. There were twenty-two, and each time I planted my foot down, I made it just a little louder. Once I got to the top of the stairs, the bottoms of my feet tingled, even through my shoes.*

*I didn't slam my door, but I wanted to. Daddy would spank me if I did that, so I just shut it softly and slipped under the covers of my bed with my shoes and play clothes still on.*

*I could hear Mama and Daddy talking downstairs. I knew it was about me. I kept hearing my name. Their voices were loud even though they were in the same room. Sort of shouty. They didn't have to talk so loudly to each other.*

*I pulled the quilt all the way up over my head and jammed my thumbs into my ears, humming quietly to drown out the yelling. My heartbeat was louder like this, and I tried counting its beats, just like I'd counted the stairs. It sounded like a drum. If I added my own made-up words, I couldn't hear Mama and Daddy talking quite so much. I did this for a long time. So long that I fell asleep.*

*When I woke up, there was no more yelling.*

# FOUR

Three hundred and twenty four hamster wheel rotations later and the boy and Herb were back from their visit with the veterinarian.

"C'mon. Outside." He motioned toward the door with the tip of his straight, thin nose. This kid sure did a lot of nodding—and even less talking—but he'd communicated more than I had, so for that I was grateful.

I grabbed the yellow plastic handle of the cage next to me and swung it at my side as I followed him into the parking lot.

He carried my dog with him to an old, teal and white VW campervan and fished his keys out of his worn pocket, sliding them into the lock on the back passenger side once he'd located them. It was one of those long doors that sounded unreasonably heavy based on the clunks and creaks it made as it slid open on its track.

Herb was still dead to the world, but not actually dead. I hoped not, at least.

The boy raised a foot to the running board and lowered Herb over the 90-degree angle of his knee, balancing him there as he slithered out of his sweatshirt, his white ribbed undershirt also slinking out with it. I'm sure he felt the instant cold, because his lungs sucked in tighter, pulling in shallower breaths that carved into his chest and ribs.

I did the same type of breathing, but not from the cold.

"Just got Trudy reupholstered," he winked, making me suddenly feel like my stomach had its own heartbeat tapping away at my insides. Of course he'd named his van. Of course he'd be that kind of guy.

This kid wasn't necessarily built, but his lean body displayed the corded muscles of his chest, his abs, and his hips more definitively because he lacked that extra body weight most guys his age carried. I didn't pin him as a swimmer or a soccer player even. Maybe someone on track. Someone who did a lot of running.

He hugged Herb back to his body and laid his sweatshirt on the middle row backseat, smoothing out the wrinkles before he settled the dog onto its cotton surface. Then he replaced the white tank on his body. I almost wished he hadn't.

"Hop in," he instructed, popping open the front passenger door. I settled the hamster cage down on the floorboards in the backseat, the space between the cushions and my passenger chair. I had to shove three empty 7-Up 2-liters out of the way and move a small, metal toolbox to the other side before it would snuggly fit in the space allowed. Despite the new improvements to his vehicle, man/boy was a bit of a slob. "I have some bad news," he said.

*Really?* I thought. *Try me.*

"So," he began once we were both secured into the space of the cab. Today was riddled with firsts for me: adopting a dog and willingly getting into a stranger's van. Maybe I could add something exciting like bank robbery or jewelry heist to the list, just to keep things interesting.

The boy grabbed the bill of his baseball cap and flung it onto the dashboard so it slid down to the place that met the windshield, sandwiched in the groove there. His hair fell in longer strips down to his ears. It was a disheveled cut that wasn't quite a cut, but more a show of procrastination and priorities. He didn't care what his hair looked like, or so it appeared, and I bet he wouldn't even bother getting a trim until those waving brunette strands fell completely into his eyes. Even then, part of me thought he might just tuck them up under the brim of his cap. I liked that. A lot.

"I can't pay for your dog and the repercussions of his unfortunate incident." He turned to face me. One hand was wrapped around the keys in the ignition, the other draped over the top curve of the steering wheel that wore one of those fuzzy alpaca covers like it was cold and needed a sweater. He had long, strong fingers and calluses on the heels of his hands. He rotated his wrist over and the engine rumbled—thunder, low and hollow, vibrating against the pavement. "His leg is broken and apparently that needs surgery. To the tune of $1200. I have $800 in my checking, which will get us close, but not quite. In the Vet's words, that would cover opening Herb up, realigning his bone, but not stitching him back together. I don't know about you, but I'm a terrible seamstress. Like, utterly awful." The boy swung his gaze over his right shoulder to angle the camper out of the parking space. We both rocked forward like on a boat as he flipped the gear back into *Drive*. "Oh," he added, pulling his honey eyes back to mine. "By the way, I'm Lincoln."

"Hi Lincoln." I smiled. "I'm Eponine."

"As in the needle that kids with allergies have to carry around to keep from dying?" Even when he drove he looked at me, which made me nervous, because operating heavy machinery was kind of a full focus sort of thing.

"You're thinking EpiPen," I laughed, not that I hadn't heard that a thousand times already growing up. It just sounded different coming from his mouth, wrapped up in naiveté. It was spoken as an honest question. That was a nice change. "Eponine as in Les Mis. The girl with the loser parents who ended up with the hole in her chest."

A Cheshire grin spread across Lincoln's lips. There was a thin, white scar on the tip of his chin, not one I would normally be able to notice, except for the fact that I was sitting so close to him—practically breathing him in. He smelled something like a worn, leather baseball glove and mint. Maybe an Altoid. There was a dented container of those in a cup holder in the makeshift center console. They rattled and slid in their metal house each time we turned a corner.

"I'm Lincoln. As in the famous president who freed the slaves and ended up with a hole in his head. So not *too* different from Eponine, actually, since they're both kind of holey." His mouth tugged upward again, crinkling his eyes. "Sorry, but I don't know a lot about Les Mis."

"That's about the extent of my knowledge regarding American history, as well."

"Makes two of us," he winked, keeping the vehicle dead center between the white and yellow lines that flanked us. "So...," he hummed. I liked the sound of his voice. A rasp accompanied each syllable like it should be lower than it was, but he didn't know how to push the tenor down far enough yet. Like someday he would have this deep, sexy adult voice crooning out of him, but for now he was just halfway there. He was nineteen. I was absolutely sure of it. "Where's home for you, Eponine? Where are we headed?"

I played with the inseam of my jeans, my legs tucked up underneath me in crisscross-applesauce fashion. My nail traced up and down the ridge of fabric, a methodic, senseless busying of my fingers and mind. When I was a littler version of myself, I would rub my yellow receiving blanket between my index finger and thumb, treasuring the paper-thin velvet touch as it kissed my skin. The blanket could soothe me, hug me, and wrap me up in confidence like a loved one should. That fabric had life within its threads.

I remember the day I finally wore a hole through it. All the ceaseless friction had weakened the cotton, and in an instant, something that once provided so much comfort and calm was reduced to scraps—an oversized rag.

The next day, I saw my mom with it in the family room. She was using it to wipe out the blood encrusted under her acrylic fingernails.

She moved out for good that day.

I glanced down to the jeans I now wore, and they were speckled with drying spots of a similar red liquid. I shuddered.

"Well, I guess we're headed to my house," I spoke, finally. My thin voice quivered slightly, though Lincoln didn't let on. I forced myself not to look at the blood on my pants anymore. "Not sure I've quite found home, yet."

"Oh, Eponine." Lincoln's voice fell like the sudden dip on a roller coaster, all reckless and raw from the surprise. "*Namaste.*"

"My soul recognizes your soul," I translated out loud for his benefit. I didn't want him to get embarrassed in thinking I didn't know what he meant. Plus, it was a weirdish thing for him to say.

He smiled, not at all feeling awkward. "The spirit within me salutes the spirit within you."

"I'm not sure there's a spirit within me to salute."

"I'm not really sure there's one in me, either." Lincoln shrugged. "By the way, I'm still looking for home, too."

We were wordless for a few minutes.

There really was only one main road through our town, so Lincoln took it, and I didn't have to redirect his course because my house was located just four more blocks away at the end of it, like the juncture of a T.

"I'm up here on the left. Off Juniper."

He knew where that was, and like his camper had even heard me, it obeyed and turned at the next intersection.

"I'm really sorry about Herb, Eponine."

Most people wouldn't laugh about a maimed dog, but I did. Not at Herb necessarily, but at everything in the situation wrapped around him.

The made up name. The unfathomable vet bill. The day lost in a waiting room and in a stranger's VW bus and in thought.

This all had to be a joke.

"Don't be sorry," I explained as I shook my head, letting Lincoln in on the sordid humor. "He's not even my dog. Herb's not even his real name."

That was a shocker, I supposed. Two hands flew to Lincoln's forehead and Trudy moved forward without anything guiding her wheel for a moment. He tugged the strands of his hair behind his ears and laughed, almost maniacally. "Of course he isn't."

I waved up toward my house and Lincoln edged closer to the shallow curb. He got out first, then pulled Herb from the back, who was still unconscious and unmoving. I wasn't one to invite a stranger into my house—just like the whole not riding in a stranger's vehicle thing—but Lincoln wasn't really a stranger anymore. Our non-existent spirits had met or something.

He bathed Herb in the downstairs bathtub while I made sandwiches in the kitchen with peanut butter and apricot jam from a jar with a label that said it had expired in 2011. I cut the crusts off of mine because Mom used to do that. I left them on Lincoln's.

When he emerged, he was wet, and walked on the tips of his toes like that would keep the water from slipping down his legs and onto our carpet. It was the first time I'd seen Herb on all fours—or threes because his right hind leg still couldn't bear any weight—and for a moment he didn't look like a broken creature, but an actual dog that could have passed for a beloved member in someone's family. He was completely adorable.

And so was Lincoln.

"What do you want me to do with him?" Lincoln asked, running one of our pink hand towels over his scalp, front to back and then once more. Water flicked from the strands and landed on my cheek. "I can't have pets of his size at my duplex, but I can try to help you find a place for him."

"I've found him a place." I tossed a sandwich toward Lincoln. He seemed to both catch it and take a bite all in one swoop. "He'll stay here."

"Do you know how to care for a dog?" he asked, his words glued together with the tackiness of peanut butter. He swiped his mouth with the back of his hand and my eyes hovered a little too long on the bottom lip that drug across his skin.

"Honestly, not a clue. But I feel like I owe it to him, to offer him a second chance, you know?"

There was scrutiny in Lincoln's eyes as he looked at me. He was studying me. Eyeing me up and down. Taking in my hair, my mouth, my eyes. His gaze fell on the ring pierced through my nose. He stopped at the small, leftover drawings illustrated on my wrists from yesterday's English class doodlings—reading me like I was a book that had been on a shelf so long dust embossed the title on the spine. He read me as though he was the first to crack open that cover in over a decade. I felt him blowing off the pages.

"You are shockingly refreshing, Eponine."

I'd feared he'd opened a tragedy when he plucked me from the bookcase, but this was turning into a downright comedy. What could he see that was refreshing in me? Other than the impromptu shower he just took in my bathroom, I couldn't offer much in the way of refreshment. Even the jam that coated the bread had gone bad back when I was a freshman.

"Eppie."

"What?" he asked, downing the last bite of his sandwich.

"My friends call me Eppie."

"That's a relief."

"That I have a nickname?" I wondered aloud.

"That you have friends."

I laughed.

His eyes laughed. "I'd like to be your friend, Eppie."

"Oh, no," I said, a teasing lilt to my voice. "Don't tell me you're a loner that sits in a dark basement all day playing video games with virtual people that have made-up names like DeathSquadron420 and PrinceLucifer. Because I honestly don't have a whole lotta extra time to devote to being someone's BFF right now."

"Right. Saving the canine population of Masonridge from utter turmoil is a full-time job."

"That part's easy. It's the high-school-student-slash-daughter turned mother-slash-trying-to-be-a-decent-human-being thing that takes up a good portion of my days."

"Then I'll settle for your nights," Lincoln quipped. His Adam's apple danced up and down in his long throat. He really was exceptionally tall.

"I'm seventeen." Wow, that was fast. I surprised even myself with how quickly I threw up that barrier of age. It didn't always work because some guys were into jailbait, but I didn't take Lincoln for one of those guys, campervan aside.

"Get your head out of the gutter, Eponine."

"I told you to call me Eppie," I corrected.

"So you're saying I'm a friend?"

Lincoln managed to spin me around in a full circle with his words, a tornado of double meaning and quick wit. Dizzied, I retorted, "Okay, friend. I'll need dog food."

"I'll bring some by tomorrow afternoon."

"And a collar and probably some tags."

"Consider it done."

We faced one another, a breakfast bar between us, but not much else.

"You said you didn't know how to take care of a dog, but look at you asking for help. Not everyone is able to do that."

"I've made that mistake before. The mistake of trying to do it all on my own," I sighed.

"And how'd that turn out for you?" he asked, head cocked, brown eyes slanted.

I paused. So did Lincoln.

"It ended with three broken ribs and a dad that drinks himself into oblivion every night."

Lincoln's expression was a vacant front. Poker face.

"I'll be here tomorrow at 3:00. And the next day at 5:00."

I hung my head languidly before looking up from under my dark hair at this boy who I'd only met just a few short hours ago. "Thank you." I felt like I owed him more than that, but for now, it was all I had.

He shook his head and smiled widely. "It's nothing."

# FIVE

*"I'm so sorry, Mama," I said, the lipped rim of the bowl pressing into my abdomen. The washing machine tumbled in the room next door and I could hear the cycle switching and the water swishing into the tub to rinse my bed sheets. "I didn't mean to make a mess again."*

*"Sweet girl." Mama pressed a warm palm to my cheek, cradling it almost. "You don't ever have to apologize for getting sick." Her celery green eyes sparkled as she shook her head. I loved how her red hair puffed out around her chin, the natural curls coiling the ends up just under her ears. She was so pretty, like a doll almost. Daddy said I wasn't old enough to have one of those porcelain kinds because I'd probably break it, but I didn't need one. I had Mama. "It's my job to take care of you."*

*"That doesn't sound like a very good job," I laughed, but my stomach muscles hadn't recovered from the latest bout and the laughter only made them hurt more. Mama noticed. She was such a good Mama.*

*"Lie down, sweetie." With one hand at my back and the other on my shoulder, she helped me lower onto the twin mattress. I didn't want her to go. I wound my arm through hers to tug her close so she could lie next to me.*

*She smelled good, like roses. I took a really deep breath, like the ones you do with those Scratch and Sniff stickers. She even smelled so much better than those. "Believe me, it's the best job in the world."*

*"To clean up throw up?" I made sure not to laugh again.*

*"To look after my child." Her face pressed against the pillow. Bringing her hand up to my hair, she dragged her manicured fingernails over my scalp. It felt so good and helped me relax. For a moment, I forgot about the twisting feeling in my tummy. "When you have a daughter someday, you'll know exactly what I mean."*

*I closed my eyes and pulled my blankie over my shoulders. The chills kept sweeping through my body. I hated those.*

*"Will you stay with me?"*

*Mama's smile looked so big this close up. "Of course, sweetie."*

*"For how long?"*

*She continued playing with my hair, never once stopping, even when she spoke through her smile fixed on her lips. "I'll be here for as long as you need me, Eppie."*

*I scooted closer into her. She was much warmer than my blankie. "I think I'll always need you, Mama."*

*With her lips pressed to my forehead, she spoke softly, a promise that sounded like a prayer, "Then I'll always be here for you, my sweet girl."*

# SIX

Lincoln came by the next day just as he said he would, toting the stash of items I'd requested: three different types of dog food—the forty pound bags—a collar, and some tags.

One selection of food was for large breed dogs, one was gluten-free, and the other was specially formulated for mature canines. There was a sad image of dog with a salt-and-pepper gray muzzle plastered on the front of the last one, like he was the AARP spokesperson of the canine world. Lincoln said he knew little about Herb, even less about the eating habits of dogs, which was the unfortunate case for me, too.

So he decided to cover his bases, and we decided to keep them all, mixing our own cocktail of kibbles that Herb seemed to thoroughly enjoy. But 120 pounds of dog food wouldn't fit in a simple storage container, so Lincoln went out later that evening to buy one of those metal trashcans like the kind Oscar the Grouch lived in to dump all the food into. Herb and I waited expectantly at the front bay window, him with a wagging tail and me with a racing heart, as Lincoln pulled into the driveway this time rather than against the curb.

We made the mistake of emptying each dog food bag into the canister in the middle of the family room, and had to balance the garbage pail on its bottom rim in order to get it out onto the back patio, like rolling a tire on its side toward its destination.

Lincoln was close to me as we maneuvered the can and navigated our way around Dad's leather recliner and the end table stacked high with old copies of *Field and Stream* that didn't serve as reading material anymore, but instead as canvases for the sweat rings of bottles and a snuffing place for the tired red embers of a used cigarette.

Our hands brushed each time we rotated the garbage can. Eight times total, because I'd counted. The first time I wrote it off as accident, the second occurrence a lucky break, and the third and fourth as an intentional, but still innocent, gesture. By rotations five, six, seven, and eight, I felt like we should be making out on the couch.

We watched Herb eat three bowls of our mixed-brand food out of a bent Marie Calendar's pie tin I'd scrounged from the pantry, and we added a proper dog bowl to the list of his housewarming gifts.

We sat on the kitchen barstools, and though our eyes were on the dog, everything else was focused on each other. Lincoln's leg was two inches away, the tip of his shoe pressing into the rubber tread of my Converse sneaker. His long thigh ran the length of mine, creating a triangle that didn't quite meet up at the top, leaving a gap just by our knees. I leaned my right shoulder toward him for no other reason than the fact that I wanted to see how close I could get without pushing him away.

We laughed when Herb finished off his meal with a burp bubbling out of his throat, and Lincoln suggested we cut tomorrow's serving size in half, just to be sure that Herb kept it all down. I agreed and giggled, but since we'd been sitting in this precariously balanced pose, my arm brushed into his, and I know we both felt it, because the roll in my gut and the flash of his eyes matched, even though the reactions were different. It didn't necessarily matter what form your impulses took, they were all felt the same.

Lincoln left quickly after that. Said something about how he wasn't even supposed to be here, but I knew the "here" in his speech didn't necessarily mean my house. It was a word that could encompass so many things, from a moment in time to life as a whole. "Here" was relative.

I wanted to know what Lincoln's "here" was.

The next day was Friday. I began my morning race to school like all other days, and managed to cross onto campus without becoming responsible for an injured creature. I counted that as a big win.

Sam was already waiting for me with a toothy grin and a story when I lowered myself into the chilled metal seat in our chemistry lab. I slung the arms of my canvas tote over the back of my chair and then dropped my elbows onto the desk; fists balled up under my chin as I eagerly awaited her greeting.

She always had good stories. *Really* good. For the most part, her life encompassed an excitement I wasn't ever sure mine would achieve when it came to intimate interactions with the male gender. Plus, she was eighteen already, and for some reason, that one month difference seemed to matter so much. She was an adult, and even though I'd had to play that part for so many years already, my numbers didn't match up just yet.

Mr. McMillan was at the front of the room, scribbling some assignment on the blackboard. He was a man of tradition, even though the room was outfitted with enough technology to retire his pack of chalk. He was decidedly old school in the purest, most refreshing sense. I found that really endearing. His slim mustache, curled upward at the corners in a loop-de-loop, helped with that, too.

"How's Herb?" Sam's hair was blue today, green yesterday. Tomorrow it would be indigo, Sunday violet. This week, Sam was working her way through the colors of the rainbow. I think she mentioned metallics for next week, but I couldn't remember correctly. Whatever it was, it would be a statement. Everything was when it came to Sam. She was crazy that way, and I appreciated it so much.

"He's as good as one could expect for suddenly losing one fourth of his mobility."

She tilted her head back in laughter. Her slender neck was so pale, her skin like alabaster. She was the marbled beauty of Venus de Milo brought to life, but with arms and hands and an actual shirt draping over her upper body, though many times Sam didn't even feel the need for that.

That's what I figured today's gossip would be about. She'd gone out with that college boy again. The first time they had a two-hour make out session, complete with lots of clothes-covered groping in her pool house bedroom. Sam still had her Hello Kitty comforter from when she was a kid, and she'd told me that the guy—Brian I think his name was—called her "Kitty" throughout the whole thing. I found that creepy, but she apparently got off on stuff like that.

"Ryan and I had sex," she whispered matter-of-factly, and the first thing I noticed was that I'd had his name wrong. *Ry*an, not *Bri*an. Did it make me weird that I was more focused on the semantics of things than on the fact that my best friend just admitted to sleeping with a guy she'd only known for just four days? And one she met at her court mandated, monthly community service down at the food bank at that? Sam had made some pretty decent-sized mistakes in her past, and though I didn't know the details of all of her transgressions, I knew it was enough to make her cover herself in rainbows and drape herself in men, so I didn't hold any of that against her.

Mistakes weren't measured on a sliding scale, I didn't think. How did it go? All sin was equal or something all-encompassing like that? Some people covered their sins with prayer, others with distractions that hid them away so deep, you couldn't detect them on the surface. I was still trying to figure out what to do with mine.

The first warning bell dinged.

"And how was it? The sex?" I whispered as I slid out my notebook and began transferring the information from the board onto the paper. The Periodic Table of the Elements. Lots of boxes with a couple numbers and letters squished into them. All I could think about was *Breaking Bad.* I wondered if Mr. McMillan had a little bit of Walter White in him. Now *that* would be something.

Sam twirled a shiny blue strand of hair around her index finger and popped her gum loudly. She always had a pack of Chiclets in her backpack. Her dad owned the only candy shop in town, a small one over on the corner of Third Street and Maple, and it kept all of the sweets in these big wooden barrels like they'd been rescued from a pirate ship. Today it looked like Sam had separated each individual Chiclet by color, as I could only see faded red sugar each time she opened her mouth.

Leaning closer like she didn't want anyone else to hear, but loud enough that anyone within a six desk radius of us would be able to make it out clearly, she said, "Best thirty seconds of my life."

I'd never had sex before, but I assumed that was short.

Chemistry lab flew by, as did my five other classes, making the school day feel pretty short, too. But time, like the meaning of the word *here*, was also relative.

Those two hours before Lincoln was supposed to come over, though? Those dripped by like molasses, oozing down each minute in a slow, sticky *tick-tock*. That wasn't relative. That was just a fact. Time practically stood still.

Since it was the weekend, I didn't have any homework to busy myself, and the English assignment due next Thursday on the symbolism of the Eggs in *The Great Gatsby* had been completed weeks ago. I'd even rewritten Sam's paper after she'd shared her original thesis with me. Scrambled versus Over Easy wasn't going to help her get any closer to graduating come June. I didn't want to walk alone. Sure, there would be about a hundred of my other peers, but without Sam, I'd be alone.

I wasn't alone as I waited for Lincoln.

Herb had been glued to my side as much as proximity and ability would allow since the day I brought him home. When I'd go upstairs, he'd wait at the bottom, one hind leg sitting, the other jutting out like it didn't even belong on his body. He wouldn't whine for me to come back, but would wait patiently. His blond feathered tail would swish against the carpet like a windshield wiper as I got closer. That tongue would hang out of his mouth, every once in a while dripping with an excited pant.

I probably didn't look too different as I waited for Lincoln, actually.

I got excited about exactly three things in life: school, graduation (which, I realized, was an extension of school), and the apple fritters old Miss Ruby made down at the Golden Barn diner. I didn't get the fritters much since I didn't have a job. Dad was still scouting for one, but sometimes I'd meet Phil there for our sessions and he'd treat me to one and I'd forget about everything other than that donut. Just the first savory taste alone would get me to that happy place.

Funny thing was, I also felt that way as I stood at the window, looking out for Lincoln's camper. I didn't even have a donut to keep my mind off of things.

His vehicle rumbled into the drive at exactly 5:04. The two hours of waiting had been long. Those four extra, unexpected minutes were like going in reverse.

When his door clicked open, I plastered myself to the wall, just outside of view from the window I'd been spying from. I could still see him, though, and he flipped his cap off, smoothed down his unruly hair, and fit it back to his head as he did an awkward skip-jog up to my doorstep. I heard two feet plant loudly on the other side, and my heart rammed against my ribs in response, my breath sputtering.

I knew the knock was coming, but when it echoed through the door I still shot clear up to the ceiling. Counting *one, two, three*, I paused, and then grabbed the handle.

"Eponine," Lincoln smiled, all lazy and lopsided. There was an appearance of a dimple that I hadn't noticed before. "Sorry I'm late."

"Four minutes isn't really late." I just admitted to watching the clock as I waited for this guy. *Super pathetic.*

Maybe he wouldn't notice.

He smiled again. Crap. He did.

"I got caught up at the site and couldn't cut out as early as I'd hoped."

Hoped. Did that mean he was hoping to get here earlier? Maybe my recent comparative essays made me prone to the analysis of syntax, but *hoped* was usually considered a good thing, right? That was universal, I was pretty sure.

"Can I come in?"

I hesitated in my movements, and so did he—matching me as I shadowed nervously right, then left. After doing that three times, Lincoln grabbed onto my shoulders and physically slid me to the right so he could pass through. He didn't really need much room. He was crazy lanky.

"You make a better door than a window, my dear." Again with the smiling. Each time he did it, my stomach would tighten, like when you coughed and it contracted.

"You know a lot about windows and doors?" I teased, but that was a stupid thing to say. My words were clumsy and my fingers were suddenly extra body parts that I had no idea what to do with. I clamped them into a fist and shoved them into the front pockets of my jeans. I was still in the entryway and Lincoln was now in the family room, hunkered down over Herb. I thought he was assessing his leg, but I couldn't really tell. It looked sort of medical.

"Matter of fact, I do. Part of the job."

"And what's that?"

Still crouching, Lincoln swiveled my direction like those ice skaters do when they spin around all close to the ground. "I do construction. And I've had a lot of practice knocking on doors in the past, so I'd say I'm pretty familiar."

"Selling stuff?" I found a loose thread in my pocket and began to play with it.

"You could say that."

Yesterday, Lincoln came over to bring the things I needed for taking care of a dog. Today, there really was no *real* reason, only that he'd promised he'd show up. And he kept that promise. He was still a stranger, but already he'd done so much more than most people in my life had. I thought for a moment and wondered if I should tell him that. No. That was too heavy, too much too soon. We already had a dog that we were responsible for. He didn't need to know that he was now responsible for giving me such a gift in that kept promise, too. That would freak him out, as it rightfully should.

"You hungry, Eppie?"

"Yes."

I wondered if he was so lean because he didn't have the money to eat, too. But some guys were just built that way. Some guys our age could consume all of Aisle 4 down at the Winn-Dixie and still be nothing more than a splinter from a toothpick. I bet Lincoln was one of those guys. It made me want to have the chance to watch him eat, to see where he packed it all in.

"I'd like to take you to grab a bite."

My stomach did that cough/clench thing again. This felt like he might be asking me out, and I didn't know what to do with that. But if he truly was asking me out, it was the best feeling ever, to have someone ask to share your time.

I rocked on my heels, my hands still trapped in my pockets, my voice trapped in my throat. "I'd really like that."

Lincoln was standing now, his own hands slunk into the front pockets of his jeans. I wasn't sure what else we should be doing with our hands other than keeping them hidden in our pockets, but it felt like they could touch and that wouldn't seem weird. Since they were doing the same thing as they curled into our jeans, it almost felt like they were. He bent toward me and I felt his warm breath rush over my skin.

"That's a beautiful sound," he said, brown eyes meeting mine from under the shadowed brim of his hat.

"What sound?"

"The sound of you saying you want to spend your evening with me, too."

I wondered what sound he would call it if I told him that saying things like that made me want to spend forever with him.

A crazy sound, probably.

# SEVEN

"I want breakfast. You want breakfast?" Lincoln asked.

There were two places in town where you could get breakfast for dinner. One was Golden Barn, the other was Denny's, obviously. I'd opted for Golden Barn, hoping Miss Ruby might still have an apple fritter leftover from this morning's bakings.

She did, and as I ordered it, Lincoln's mouth turned up just at the left side, piercing that dimple into his cheek. "You look unreasonably excited about that donut, Eppie."

I wished for the menu back, just so I'd be able to cover my mouth with it. Smiling sometimes felt like such an effort, like I had to truly focus on the muscles and their individual strength to get them to move in the right way. It didn't feel that way now around Lincoln. It burst onto my face with reckless abandon.

"I love apple fritters."

The seats were a shiny red vinyl, the kind that looked like they had glitter strewn throughout the material. That wannabe 1950's diner decor. I ran my fingers nervously along the torn edge next to my leg and stuffing popped out from the slit in the plastic.

"I'm more of a cinnamon roll guy myself." Lincoln pulled off his Red's cap, chucking it across the silver tabletop that was flecked with the same glittery stuff in the vinyl. The hat rotated to a stop right in front of me like a spinner on a board game. "But I don't really discriminate when it comes to food. I'm sorta an equal opportunity consumer."

I bit the sides of my cheeks to try to hold the smile back, and it probably made me look creepy, but I'd look even creepier with my full-fledged clown grin.

"Hence the Lumberjack Platter," I nodded.

"You got it."

Lincoln's arms were long. Gangly, sort of, like the way a brand new foal's legs looked when they were freshly born. But there was still muscle wrapped around them, a little tone and definition. He stretched them out to full-length, his entire wingspan spreading across the back of the booth.

*I could fit right there,* I thought. *Right in that gap between the wall of windows and the groove of his body.* I bet it would be the most comfortable place in the world. I bet I could fall asleep there. I'm not sure I'd ever want to wake up.

I shook my head briskly. "So," I sputtered, one cheek still pinned in my teeth, warning it to stay put. "You used to sell things door-to-door?"

"Sorta." Lincoln slumped down further, crossing his ankles under the table, hitting my own feet when he did so. His feet were big, too.

"What kind of stuff?" Mindlessly, I reached out for his cap, wanting to touch the worn fabric of it. He didn't stop me, not even when I pulled it into my lap and turned it over, examining the *C* appliqué that curled at the edge.

"Religion."

Just then, Miss Ruby came over with two Cokes in those tall glasses that got wider up at the top. She pulled out a couple of straws tucked within her apron. That apron had so much grease on it there were portions that were practically see-through, made transparent from the many coatings of oil. Lincoln caught both straws and slid one my way.

"Selling religion?" I asked as I unwrapped my straw and popped it into my drink. It bobbed up and down against the bubbles and fizz a few times before settling in.

"You tell people your beliefs and they either buy it or they don't," he elaborated.

"Were you any good at it?"

His shoulders shrugged to his ears. "No," he said noncommittally. "I never bought into the particular brand I was peddling, so I sorta sucked at trying to get others onboard. Beliefs aren't something you can fake. I didn't last long."

"So how long *were* you successfully a fake?"

Lincoln chuckled. His eyes even closed, too, little slivers on his face. "I'm not sure you can ever be successful at being a fake, Eppie," he smiled with a sigh, wrapping his lips around the straw to take a sip. When he pulled them off and swallowed, he said, "I think that's the very definition of being a failure, actually."

"You don't seem like a failure to me," I spoke without thinking. There were too many reasons why I shouldn't have blurted out that analysis, but none of those came to mind quickly enough. Jamming the straw into my mouth, I sucked in enough soda to fill my cheeks and avoid any follow-up explanation.

"No, not in general. But I've failed my parents in more ways than I care to admit, my best friends, and even my country. So that kinda sucks."

I gulped down the cold liquid. "I know a bit about parental failures myself."

Lincoln just frowned.

Miss Ruby returned with a steaming platter of food—bacon curled into fatty ribbons, eggs over easy with their round yolks looking like suns, and about a pound of country-style potatoes, all seasoned and mounded into a huge pile of carbohydrates that made my mouth water at the sight and smell. Lincoln had a fork in his right hand, a knife in his left. He was going to slay this plate of food and take no prisoners, I was certain.

My apple fritter was on one of those plates they used as saucers under coffee mugs. It was way too big for it, and it made the donut seem five times its normal size. It was *Cloudy with a Chance of Meatballs* status, which made me self-conscious because I had plans to devour the whole thing.

"Enjoy that," Lincoln urged, tipping his knife toward me. "Looks delicious."

"Want a bite?" I tossed a piece into my mouth.

I could see the yellow egg in his mouth as it opened to speak. "Nah, you don't have to share your edible joy with me. It's all yours."

"Well, we already share a dog. A donut seems a lot less life altering."

"About that."

My stomach dropped. The apple fritter did somersaults within it.

"He's obviously going to need surgery." Lincoln leaned over his plate, his elbows pressed into the table on either side of it. Every time his eyes met mine it felt like they were looking into more than just my irises. That caused panic to settle in right around those bits of donut doing gymnastics in there. I was worried what he could actually see. "I've got a few more construction jobs lined up and think I can save enough money, but it'll be a few weeks before that and it's going to start healing wrong."

"You don't have to pay for him, Lincoln. He's not even your dog."

Smiling was clearly effortless for Lincoln. It looked so natural and welcome on his face, like he was born smiling while the rest of us entered the world screaming.

"He's not technically yours, either. Trust me, I don't mind," he said. "I just think it kinda sucks that by the time I can pay for his surgery, they'll probably have to re-break it to get it to heal right."

"I think it'd be better to be broken again if it meant he'd have the chance to properly heal."

His fork slipped from his fingers, clanging onto the ceramic plate, but Lincoln tried to play it off as some accidental falter. His telling eyes didn't do nearly as good of a job, though. "Because I think you're talking about more than just Herb, that makes me really sad." His lips were red, like they were stained with the jam from his toast, and they pursed into a decisive line. "Eat your fritter, Eppie. I want to see you happy."

I laughed quickly and pulled apart another section of the donut, popping it into my mouth dramatically for his benefit. I wished food could make everything right in the world. I wished there was some magic recipe to life that could turn everything bad into something good. Like how you could save a meal gone wrong with a little salt, or rescue a bland baked good with just a pinch of sugar. Life needed something like that.

So far the donut wasn't cutting it, but strangely, this boy sitting across from me was getting close.

"And put my hat on," he instructed with a wave of his fork my direction, pieces of food trapped behind his teeth.

"Your hat? Why?"

"Because that would make *me* happy." He smiled with his cheeks stuffed full of potatoes.

I pulled his cap from my lap and settled it onto my head cautiously. It smelled like him and was still warm from his body heat. My hair curled out from under the fabric and the back of it was slightly baggy, even with all of my hair stuffed into it. Lincoln was a lot bigger than me.

"How's that?" I spoke hesitantly, eyeing him from under the brim.

Snapping off a piece of bacon and chomping on it loudly, Lincoln flashed a toothy smile. "That, Eppie, is perfect."

...............

"I'm on *E*. Think your dad'll be upset I'm getting you home this late?"

"My dad?" I blurted. "Goodness, no. The Flying Stallion doesn't close until 2:00. I've got at least four more hours until he even sets foot in the house, and by that time, he won't even be able to see straight enough to even know I'm home. We're fine."

"So who puts you to bed?"

"Seriously?" I cocked an eyebrow as Lincoln slid the VW into an open stall and killed the engine. Orange haze from the lamppost funneled into the van in a cone of light. It made Lincoln's eyes harder to see, sunken into the deep hollowed-out shadows. I had to really search out his expression for once. "No one puts me to bed."

"Well, that's entirely unfortunate," he shrugged as he opened the door to hop out of the vehicle. Removing his wallet from his back pocket, he swiped a credit card through the machine and pulled the hose from the pump. I could smell the gasoline tainting the air and hear the liquid swishing into the tank as he inserted the nozzle with a click. "Jimmy Fallon puts me to bed every night."

"I can't decide if that's funny or creepy."

"Probably a little of both," Lincoln admitted on a laugh. His hand was clamped down on the lever and he spoke to me through the open window. "But he's hysterical and I like to go to bed in a good mood. I find it helps me wake up in one, too."

I couldn't imagine waking up tomorrow in any mood other than one that was utterly, unrealistically giddy. If I happened to fall asleep any time soon, that's exactly how I'd start my day, no need for Jimmy Fallon.

"I'm gonna grab a 7-Up." Lincoln hooked a thumb over his shoulder toward the minimart once the tank clicked full. I glanced to the gas gage on the dash. "Want anything?"

"I'm good."

"K. Be back in a jiffy."

I watched him skip—literally skip—across the lot to the store, and I followed his movements until I couldn't see him behind the shelves of snacks and chocolate bars. It was as though I didn't want to miss a moment of him. Even watching Lincoln interact with others gave me a rush. He seemed happy, even when he wasn't. I knew that didn't make sense to say, but that's just how it was with him. When he spoke about things that were inherently sad, he was still so beautifully joyful.

And it was contagious.

It made me happy that he was happy. That he'd figured out the secret to turning this life into something more. I thought that maybe if I spent enough time with him, he'd share that secret with me.

I mentally blocked out my calendar for the entire month.

There was a line of three people forming at the register in the minimart, and I could see Lincoln slink in at the end of it, his disposition cool, his composure relaxed as always. He had a 2-liter and a bag of Funions in his hands and he was also making small talk with the elderly man in front of him. The widespread grin on the old guy's face shot a pang of jealously into my stomach because, jeez, how I wanted to be a part of that exchange. I didn't even have a clue as to what they could possibly be talking about, but I was certain it would make me feel good.

*Lincoln* made me feel good.

And bad, too, as it would be. Because when he jumped back into the driver's seat and slammed the door into place, my gut wrenched so tight that, for a moment, I felt horribly nauseous. I figured it was all the butterflies in there that were making me sick, but then the thought of literal insects swarming in my insides made me feel like I was going to puke even more.

I was working on keeping the contents of my stomach in place when Lincoln's fingers brushed against mine on their way to throw his receipt into the small canister in the center console. All of those painful sensations culminated and exploded within me, butterfly guts everywhere. And can I just say, it was the best feeling ever. It fluttered in my stomach, against our skin and into the air like magic. Magical exploding butterflies.

In that same moment our eyes collided, and his were shifty and nervous, like he'd never made eye contact with a girl and wasn't sure how it all went. I didn't do much better. I looked at him, away from him and through the windshield, and then allowed them to land on my lap where my fingers twisted together, all woven and tangled. It might've seemed like I was holding my hands there to keep them from touching his again, but the truth was that I wrapped them together so tightly just to keep that feeling *in* them. Like I could bind up the moment and hold it in my palms. Never let it go.

Lincoln released a breath loudly through his mouth. "Ready to head home?"

"No."

"Where do you want to go then?"

"Not sure."

The engine turned over and Lincoln placed the vehicle into gear, but hesitated before moving it anywhere. "Like, do you want me to drop you off somewhere?" His inflection rose. "Or do you want to go somewhere *with* me?"

"With you."

"With me," he smiled, his head bobbing slowly.

I tried to smile back, but I doubted it looked half as good as his. I wanted to lick that smile off his face.

"I have four more hours with you?" he confirmed. "You said your dad'll be home at 2:00?"

I was going to tell Lincoln he could have all my hours—all of tonight and as much of tomorrow and even into next week—if he wanted them. They were his for the taking. But I held back and just said, "Yep."

Lincoln grinned, clicked his seatbelt across his lap and pulled out onto the street.

# EIGHT

"Are you sure it's okay we're here?"

I stepped over a two-by-four and tried to avoid the nails that littered the floorboards. There were hundreds of them—more than the actual number hammered into the walls, it appeared. Almost like someone decided to just throw a bucket of them into the air only to watch them fall, and then they forgot to clean them up. Since I figured I was due for a tetanus shot, I proceeded with caution.

"Relatively sure," Lincoln answered.

"Only relatively?"

The light from Lincoln's phone swung back and forth, illuminating a framed-in room that I figured had to be the kitchen. There was an island in the center and a wooden outline where cabinets would one day go. This house was just a skeleton, which made it all the more creepy. Just joints and bones.

"That was actually a failed play on words." Though I couldn't see him, I could hear the smile in his voice. "It's my uncle's property. Get it? Relative? So yeah, it's fine that we're here."

"And why *are* we here?"

Lincoln stopped short and I would've slammed into his back—my face planting against his pointy shoulder blades—if it weren't for his hand that jutted out behind him to halt me. It grazed my stomach, just above my waistband, and he recoiled the moment his fingers touched the flannel edge of my shirt. "Careful there. That beam isn't quite secured yet." I skirted around the column in front of us as instructed—tiptoeing almost—and followed Lincoln out of the kitchen and up to a rise of stairs at the back of the expansive home. There obviously weren't any railings, and it was dark out—just the moon and Lincoln's phone providing any light. I was definitely going to trip and fall.

"Take my hand."

He offered it to me, palm upturned, and I grabbed on. But it wasn't handholding because our fingers didn't interlock at all. This was the mitten-type grip. The one that you did with your mom or dad when you were little and crossed a busy street. The one where all of your fingers were Superglued together.

But my nerves didn't know the difference between the two types. Sweat slipped between our skin. I rubbed the palm that wasn't pressed to his against the thigh of my jeans, willing the clamminess to go away, but it didn't help much.

"Watch your step."

I did, and then suddenly we were at the top, like we'd floated there together through the dark, hooked hands and all. I looked up. Hundreds of stars hung above us, brilliant white pinpricks in the black paper sky. They glittered and literally twinkled like diamonds, just like the nursery rhyme said they would. Go figure.

Another song came to mind.

"And she's buying a stairway to heaven," I sang softly, my neck craned back to wash in their light. Mom used to play that tune on repeat, over and over, in the car every morning. An anthem of sorts. I knew this wasn't what the song meant, but I made my own meaning, because if I had been that woman trying to buy her way there, this was surely the heaven I'd want.

I let my hands drop to my sides, insecure in the fact that my skin was still on Lincoln's skin and that I was sort of singing to him.

"God, your voice is beautiful, Eppie."

"No."

"Yes," he paused. "It is." He walked backward until the hollow of his knees bumped into a waist-high pile of sheetrock, layer upon layer of chalky building material. It almost looked like a bed, though I wasn't sure what room we were even in, if it was a room at all. Could've been a hallway. It kind of resembled one. "I've never been a big fan of rock—more of a classical guy myself—but you made that sound so classically beautiful."

"You're being very generous."

"I'm being truthful. I'm generous with the truth." He dropped down to sit on the sheetrock, and then he patted his hand on the space next to him. "C'mere. You asked why we were here earlier. Well... this is why."

"You brought me here to... ?"

"Share something with you. Something that's all mine."

I chewed on my bottom lip. "You already shared the hat." My cheeks flamed with heat, and even though he couldn't see it, I drew my hands up to cover them. The nubby sleeves of my flannel rubbed against my skin.

"I like you in the hat. It's a good look."

"I sorta feel like a fake wearing it," I admitted as I walked over to Lincoln, careful for the nails again. His hand was still on the drywall, and I waited for him to move it so I could sit. He got the hint, I think, because he shifted slightly and I was able to lower down and leave about a foot of empty space between us. That felt like an acceptable amount of distance.

"A fake because?"

"Because I don't know anything about baseball."

"To be honest, I feel like a fake wearing it, too. Only 'cause it looks like I jumped on the bandwagon or something."

I fingered the tattered brim. "Did you?"

"No. I've been a fan since I was a little boy, but people don't necessarily think that when they see me wearing it." I was close enough that I could smell him again, and he was different this time. There was definitely some faint cologne clinging to his clothes tonight, some musky grassy scent. That thought made my fingers tingle, wondering if he put it on thinking it would be something I'd like. He was right. I did like it. "That's fine with me if they think that, though. I tend to find one thing and stick with it for the long haul." In one quick movement that brought his legs up to the sheetrock and his head back onto his arms crossed like a pillow, Lincoln laid down, his long body filling the entire space, head to toe. "But I digress." I fidgeted away from him, reclaiming that lost distance between us, but I had even less room to work with now. "I brought you here to show you this."

"The stars?"

"That *would* be really romantic, wouldn't it?" A brown lock of hair slipped across his forehead and over his temple as he spoke. I fought the urge to curl it around his ear, because although we'd held hands like we were Lego characters earlier, hair sweeping was definitely way, *way* down the line. "But no. I wanted to show you those beams and studs—" Jeez, I think I giggled out loud when he said studs, "—and roofing material. I won't be able to show it off for very long before it's all covered up, but that is all my doing. And I'm exceedingly proud over it."

"Over the studs and the beams?"

"Yes, over the studs and the beams," Lincoln said, as though it was an obvious fact. He wasn't looking at me, but instead gazed longingly overhead. "Do you have any idea how difficult it is to frame a house when you have a deep-seated fear of heights? It's like being an arachnophobic pest control guy. Or a claustrophobic spelunker."

"Spelunker."

"Spelunker: One who explores caves."

"I know what a spelunker is. I was just repeating it because it's a weird word. Rolls off the tongue in a funny way."

I could feel the vibration of the sheetrock underneath us before I confirmed it with my eyes, but Lincoln had shifted onto his hip, his focus no longer on the roofline, but completely transferred to me. That fallen hair from earlier dropped into his honey eyes, a brown fringe separating our stare. "You do that, too?"

"Do what?" I asked, unsure.

"Contemplate the auditory oddities of words."

I played with a hangnail on my thumb because nerves made me do stupid, self-mutilating things like cheek biting, lip chewing, and the infamous hangnail tearing. "Yeah, I guess."

"Goggles."

"What?"

"Goggles," Lincoln said. "It's a weird word. As are diatribe and marsupial."

I laughed. "I used to think diatribe was *diet*-tribe, and I wondered why anyone in their right mind would want to join a tribe full of dieters. That would have to be the crankiest tribe ever."

"Because of all the low blood sugar."

"Exactly. Who would want to be surrounded by cranky, starving people? But then I figured that was exactly what Weight Watchers was, right? That's got to be like some kind of hell."

"Does hell even come in kinds?" Lincoln slunk onto his back again, swinging his gaze upward once more. His chest jumped up and down as he chuckled.

"You tell me. You were the short-lived spiritual salesman, right?"

"*Failed* spiritual salesman. But if I'm making an educated guess, I'd say no. Religion tends to deal in absolutes, so I'd assume there is just one hell and one heaven."

I don't know what possessed me to do it, but I twisted my body down onto the remaining space next to Lincoln, my hair pillowing my head as I lowered onto the sheetrock. My frame suddenly felt too wide, like I took up more space than I usually would, and I bound my arms over my chest and endeavored to shrink within myself, if shrinking into oblivion was even a possible endeavor.

Lincoln was just the opposite—all lanky arms sprawled out at his sides and lean legs stretched to full length, taking up much more than his fair share of the world.

"But what I think doesn't really matter much," he continued, his voice lowering. "Because either way, I'll either be right or wrong, and it's not like my opinion on the issue will change the truth. That's already set."

"Right," I agreed. "But I still think it's worth having an opinion on it."

"Probably so. Opinions are usually good."

Lincoln's body shifted toward mine. I could feel his proximity in all of my nerve endings. I could hear his breathing; smell the heat of his skin. It amazed me that even my senses had somehow developed superpowers and now my nose was doing what only touch did before. Next I'd be hearing colors if I kept up with this craziness.

"Hey." That sound came out of him an octave deeper than all the others. "Can I ask your opinion on something else?"

"Yeah. Sure."

"What's your opinion on kissing me?"

I stopped breathing, aware that if I kept doing it, it would be all shaky and quivering. Utterly humiliating.

"I mean, not right now." I was so grateful Lincoln continued talking so his words could mask the nervous vibration in my exhale. I desperately needed another breath. Things were getting that fuzzy rimmed blackness that precluded passing out. "But, like, someday. Like, can I someday kiss you? Even if someday is really far off. Would that be okay?"

"I think that might be okay. Someday."

"Good," he smiled, crossing his legs at the ankles and his arms behind the nape of his neck. His mouth pulled fully up at the corners; his eyes crinkled into slivers. "I like to have things to look forward to. I'm very goal oriented."

"And you'd look forward to that?"

"I've *been* looking forward to it for the past three days, Eppie," Lincoln admitted. "And in my opinion, it's going to be really phenomenal."

"In your opinion, huh?" I asked, trying to keep in my nervous laughter. Insecurity took form in my racing pulse, beating so fast that I could feel it thick on my neck and hear it hammering in my ears.

"Yes, in my humble opinion, you kissing me is going to be out of this world."

Lincoln elbowed me in the ribs playfully, then raked his hands through his hair, gripping the strands at their roots.

"I can't believe I'm talking about kissing you to *you*! I shouldn't be telling you any of this nonsense. It makes me seem like a weirdo."

"No, not a weirdo," I consoled. "Honestly, I didn't even know that was something you thought about." I needed to just shut my mouth and let him continue talking because then I might be able to use my lips for something else if I just kept the words in.

"Oh, I don't."

My heart dropped.

"I'm totally kidding, Eppie!" Lincoln's hand collided with my leg, just above my knee and he squeezed it quickly. Everything in me went numb, frozen in place. "I don't just bring any girl up here to check out my wood."

"That is *so* wrong."

Lincoln snorted. His fingers flew up to his nose to stifle the spontaneous laugh. "I know, but I couldn't pass it up. It was just out there for the taking, so greedily, I took it." He shot out another gust of air. "But in all seriousness, I just really wanted to show this to you. I don't know why, but I did. Maybe because that beam right there is the paycheck that's gonna help pay for Herb. I thought you should at least see it before it's all covered up."

"I'm glad you showed me, Lincoln." I looked up at the rafters and tried to imagine Lincoln in a hardhat and tool belt, securing the beam into place. I imagined other things, too, like him getting so sweaty that he had to peel his shirt from his slick skin, which would obviously leave him bare-chested. I sighed pathetically at the soap opera-esque striptease I visualized. "I'm glad to see it. I really am." I figured I was still talking only about the beam.

His hand slid along the surface of the sheetrock, stopping just an inch or so way from mine. The space between us was charged, practically crackling with intensity. Liked if he reached into it, he'd shock himself or ignite the building around us, torching the whole place. It felt dangerous and exhilarating, just lying here next to him—just doing nothing at all—but doing it side by side. How was that even possible?

I closed my eyes longer in between blinks, and drew in deeper breaths each time. I could hear Lincoln's breathing, too, all intentional and focused. I purposefully made sure my inhales and exhales didn't match his. I tried not to fall into his rhythm just yet.

"I'm glad I brought you here too, Eppie."

Lincoln's pinky stretched out and tapped the edge of mine.

"Me too," I said again, leaving my hand right there, pressed lightly to his.

And we stayed just like that until it was time for Lincoln to drive me home.

# NINE

*"I'd like to get a second opinion."*

*The paper draped across the table crinkled underneath my thighs. I fiddled with the torn edge of the parchment, running the tip of my fingernail across it, careful not to get a paper cut.*

*"I don't think that's necessary, Ms. Aberdeen." The doctor sat in one of those metal chairs that spun all the way around. I imagined twirling and twirling on it until I got dizzy. Maybe he would let me after the appointment if I asked really nicely. "She's asymptomatic—"*

*"Until she isn't, which is much too often." Mama took a really deep breath, like the ones she did when she and Daddy weren't getting along. "Dr. Morgan, I value your professional opinion, but as a mother, I have to go with my instincts on this one, and my maternal instincts are telling me that something's not right here."*

*Dr. Morgan did a half turn in his chair and pulled up a calendar on the computer that had a bunch of notes typed onto it. He ran his finger over the screen as he read to himself. He was a very fast reader, it appeared.*

*"Eponine, tell me a little about school?" Pulling himself closer to the table, he walked his feet across the*

*floor. Thump, thump, thump. He wore an ironed white shirt with a tie, but had on sneakers. It looked kind of funny, especially since the laces were bright yellow. "Any favorite subjects?"*

*I thought for a moment. There were too many to list. "I love them all. Math especially. And science. I like learning about the way things work."*

*Dr. Morgan's eyes got smaller behind his glasses like they were at the other end of a telescope. His mouth turned into a super big smile, one that made his cheeks all puffy. "I like science, too, but I never liked the tests. Do tests bother you, Eponine?"*

*"They're okay." I shrugged my shoulders up to my ears.*

*The room was cold. It felt like the refrigerated room at that store where you had to buy twenty of everything. The one with the huge shopping carts and all those free samples from grandmas in hairnets. Mama took me there last week and let me get the biggest box of Lucky Charms I've ever seen. It was so large that instead of being a rectangle, the cardboard was shaped into a square. I'd already eaten all the shamrock marshmallows out of it for good luck.*

*"Tests used to make me really nervous. Sometimes so much that my tummy would hurt." Dr. Morgan rubbed the center of his stomach in circles as he spoke. "Do they ever make your tummy hurt, Eponine?"*

*I shook my head. "Not really."*

*"Do they make you nervous at all?"*

*I didn't know what answer I was supposed to say. It felt like maybe I wasn't saying the right ones. "I don't think so."*

*"It's not nerves, Dr. Morgan. This is something more than just childhood anxiety over school." Mama was standing behind him, her arms folded across her chest as she shook her head quickly. She looked kind of like a human pretzel. "I know my daughter."*

*The doctor stood up from his chair and leaned closer to Mama. I could hear him say something, but couldn't tell exactly what it was. It wasn't like when Daddy and Mama talked. He wasn't being loud like that.*

*"Eponine, will you please excuse your mother and me for just a moment?"*

*I nodded.*

*Mama followed him out the door and it locked quietly back into place behind them. The back of Dr. Morgan's shirt pressed onto the small window that separated us and it made the texture of the fabric look smooth like glass.*

*"We've exhausted every possible explanation, Ms. Aberdeen." He was speaking softly, but the door must not have been very thick because I could still hear him.*

*"I need answers, Dr. Morgan. I'm tired of all this run-around. That's my daughter in there." I could see Mama pointing her finger through the window. "Something's not right. It hasn't been for a while. There have to be more tests that you can run."*

*My tummy flip-flopped.*

*I must've lied earlier when I said I didn't mind tests. But these ones were different. I liked the ones they gave me at school. They made me feel smart. They were fun to take. I could study for those tests.*

*The ones I took in doctors' offices just made me confused. I was never prepared for the tests they gave me. I always felt like I got all the answers wrong.*

*"I'm not sure which ones we even have left to order—"*

*"Find some," Mama interrupted. She always told me it was rude to interrupt. I wasn't sure why she was being rude to Dr. Morgan. That didn't seem very nice. "I want my healthy eight-year-old back, Doctor. I* need *her back."*

*"I understand, Gloria. I'm a parent, too."*

*"Then you understand that she means the absolute world to me and every day she suffers, I feel like I'm failing her. I feel like* I'm *failing."*

*I could see Dr. Morgan lift a hand and drop it slowly onto Mama's shoulder. "You're not failing anyone, Gloria. I promise you that."*

*Mama sniffed. It sounded like she might be crying. I hated that I made her cry. "Just promise me you'll help her—that we'll get this figured out."*

*"I'll do everything I can."*

*They might have talked some more after that, but I couldn't hear them. Whatever noises they made weren't as loud as the ones in my head—the ones that echoed Mama's sweet voice saying everything was going to be okay. Everything would be alright. I'd feel better soon enough. I wouldn't always feel like this.*

*It was going to be okay. Dr. Morgan promised Mama that, and adults didn't lie, especially when it involved kids.*

*I breathed a sigh of relief and jumped down from the table, happy with the knowledge that maybe my life would be back to normal soon.*

*I owed Mama the biggest hug ever for bringing me to Dr. Morgan's office again. He was going to help me heal this time. He would make me all better.*

*He would make everything all better. I was sure of it.*

# TEN

"So this is the infamous furball?"

Sam folded her legs up underneath her and flopped down onto the porch stoop, right next to the faded welcome mat which never felt particularly welcoming at all. She swatted Saturday morning's newspaper out of the way, tossing it against the siding. Herb groaned in delight, completely pleased with her proximity, and flipped over onto his back to stretch his stomach out as far as he could, giving Sam maximum surface area to stroke his no-longer-matted belly.

"That it is. Sam, meet Herb. Herb, Sam."

The mutt was growing on me. Even when I'd come home in the dark hours of the night, he was still so eager to greet me at the door with a wagging tale and a lick on my cheek. Some of us were night owls, while others were morning people. Dogs, I figured, were 24/7 creatures. They were at their best at any given hour of the day. It was like they were just so grateful to be alive that they celebrated every waking moment with a slobbery kiss and a warm nuzzle. How much easier life would be to be able to operate like that, too?

"He's not so bad. A little scroungy, but sorta cute."

"That's not a very nice way to talk about me."

My eyes snapped up.

Lincoln was standing at the edge of the grass, right where it met the solid concrete line of sidewalk, where nature stopped and the city took over. His hands were deep in his denim pockets and he had a neon mesh vest hanging loosely on his body over a white undershirt with a V-neck that was stretched from wear. He'd been sweating at some earlier point because sawdust and dirt collected in dried lines that streaked from his sideburns down to his angular jaw. A circular indentation pressed into his hair, a ring from the hardhat he must've been wearing at the job site. He was definitely fresh—or maybe not so fresh—from work.

"What are you doing here, Lincoln?"

I stood up so fast the world around me spun. Blinking rapidly, I attempted to regain my bearings but the newly blossoming trees still pirouetted in my periphery.

"I thought I'd stop by on my lunch break to see if you needed any help with Herb."

Sam shot me a questioning look. A look that screamed, *'Who the hell is this?'* But not in a bad way—a really great way—because Sam pretty much spoke about everything in life with that same enthusiasm. Since I didn't think she'd ever witnessed an actual interaction between me and a guy before, the *hell* in her stare was a totally fitting inclusion.

"Sam," I said. "This is my friend, Lincoln."

"Your friend... Lincoln." She slowly used her legs to push up off the ground.

"Her friend, Lincoln." He'd made his way up the driveway now, skipping practically. He donned a smile and jutted a hand toward Sam.

"How come you have friends that I don't know about, Eps?" Her eyebrows furrowed over her light blue irises. The lids were caked with a painter's pallet of colors, and her lipstick was a deep metallic plum. And here we stood. Me and my two friends. Three if you counted Herb. And we couldn't look more unlike the other if we'd tried.

"I thought I was your *only* friend," Sam laughed, grabbing on to Lincoln's hand and giving it a firm, no-nonsense shake. "You've been *cheating* on me?"

"In all fairness, I'm just as surprised by this as you are," Lincoln said. "I was under the impression that Eppie had *lots* of friends. She was a bit misleading with that information."

"I told you my friends called me Eppie. I didn't specify as to the timeframe of when I had those particular friends," I defended. "My friends, *over the years*, have all called me Eppie."

"But your one current friend calls you Eps."

Sam batted at the air. "Oh, I call her all kinds of things. Eppie, Eps, Eeeps, Mullet Girl—"

Lincoln's head cocked to the side. He looked a little Herb-like when he did that.

"It was an unfortunate haircut."

He nodded with a grin.

"Homegirl. Homeslice. Chica. Chiclet. Bubble-Gummy."

"Her dad owns the candy store."

"Sounds like you've got all sorts of aliases," Lincoln laughed. "And all I have at my disposal is Eppie. Makes me feel a little slighted."

"*I'm* the one who should feel slighted. I had no clue Eps had a hot construction worker friend in her back pocket."

"Oh, I couldn't fit in her pocket. I'm crazy tall."

"You *are* crazy tall!" I nearly shouted. I'd noticed it the moment I met him, but wondered if he was aware of just how towering he probably appeared to the rest of the average height society. Like, did giraffes think their necks were unusually long, or did they just think everyone else's were too short?

"You noticed," he smirked.

"It's hard not to. I'm like eye level with your chest."

"And what a pity it is that those roles aren't reversed."

Oh man, my face scorched. I hadn't meant for it to come out that way. Or maybe I hadn't meant for Lincoln to interpret it that way because I thought the way I'd said it was just fine.

"I like this guy," Sam nodded. "He's funny."

"Not trying to be funny, necessarily." Lincoln bent down to rough up the top of Herb's head with his fist, sort of like a noogie. "It's the case for *my* one current friend, Dan. Damn bastard. It's boob vision for days with that guy."

"Dan must be incredibly short," Sam gathered.

"He is now." Lincoln popped back upright and stumbled off the porch step toward me. Like I said, I was staring straight at his chest. I flickered a glance up to the divot in his collarbone where his shoulders and neck met, and it was pooled with sweat, making my hormones go instantly haywire. "It's the lack of legs that will mess with your height."

"Dan has no legs?" I gasped, quickly covering my mouth. I was pretty certain that was the exact opposite reaction of what I should have said. It felt insensitive on the highest level. And stupid. It felt stupid, too.

"Yep, no legs for Danny-boy."

"What a trip!" Sam laughed, which made me want to retract my insensitive comment. Pretty sure Sam just beat me out with hers. "No legs, huh? Can I see?"

"Well, since they're not really there, they're pretty tough to see. But if you squint really hard and tilt your head to the left... nope, you still can't see anything."

I groaned quietly. "This is... just so wrong."

Lincoln dropped a hand onto my shoulder and squeezed it just a little. I knew there weren't any pulse points located in my shoulders—at least I didn't think so—but I still worried that he could feel my erratic heartbeat because it had to be evident even there. My body thrummed all over like some vibrating chord. "Oh, Eppie, don't feel bad. Dan knows he doesn't have legs."

"But does he really want everyone else discussing their nonexistence?" I asked, feeling bad for this Dan I hadn't even heard of two minutes earlier. I'd had years of people talking behind my back and knew the hurt of it firsthand.

"It's not like he isn't aware of the lack of legs."

"When can we meet this legless wonder?" Sam blurted.

I jabbed her straight in the ribs, starting to get a bit angry.

"What? What's wrong with that? I wanna meet him."

"Luckily, his worldwide tour just wrapped up and he's only doing local showings now. And I'm fairly certain he'll be at Roast House tonight for an exclusive, live, in-the-flesh concert!" Lincoln teased. "Also, he's my roommate. So there's always that connection."

"No way!" Sam slugged him directly in the shoulder.

"Yes way," Lincoln stated. "And no legs. But probably lots of caffeine-induced, long-winded reminiscence and an occasional expletive outburst about the glory days. You in?"

"Sounds outrageously incredible!" Sam said.

I wasn't sure I could say the same. It would likely be incredible in a way—incredibly awkward, incredibly uncomfortable—but not because of Dan at all. Because of the fact that hanging out in a group of four like this—two boys and two girls—had all the indications of double dating. And I wasn't sure I was ready for that. Or maybe I wasn't sure Lincoln was ready for that. For dating. For dating *me.*

"What about you, Eppie?" Lincoln nudged me with his elbow and simultaneously waggled his eyebrows.

We sure were doing an awful lot of jabbing, slugging, and elbowing. "It promises to be an evening unlike any other."

I smiled distantly.

I didn't doubt that. That had been the theme of all of my evenings with Lincoln thus far.

I was definitely in.

...............

"I'm going to climb in the back," I said, my shaky voice giving evidence to the unreasonable amount of nerves infiltrating my system. I fiddled with the hole in the knee of my worn jeans. A frayed, white thread snapped in two within my grip. "I should sit in the back."

"Not necessary. Dan doesn't need the legroom. You're fine as-is. Stay put."

Each comment about Lincoln's friend Dan made me increasingly hesitant to be participating in this double date that wasn't quite a double date.

"Just wait here and I'll be out in a few minutes." Lincoln left the camper idling as he slammed the driver's side door shut and jogged up the brick steps to their duplex. He had big tennis shoes on that took up almost the entire length of each stair, toe to heel. Then, like he'd suddenly remembered something that couldn't wait, he flipped around and skipped back our way. I rolled the window down on my side, cranking it open. "Just so I don't forget," he said, his hands hooked over the doorframe, "avoid making any Forest Gump references. Like, at all costs. Okay?"

"Well, shoot," Sam laughed from her place in the middle row. Her hands clapped loudly onto her thighs. "I brought him a box of chocolates and everything!"

"Oh, I'll keep the chocolates," Lincoln winked. "But seriously, no Gump stuff. Rubs him the wrong way."

"Got it," I assured, though admittedly confused. I waited until Lincoln was halfway back up the walk before I turned in my seat to face Sam. "I'm not sure how I feel about this."

"I know! It's an Academy Award winning flick! Who could have anything against that? And Tom Hanks. Love him. Even in *The Terminal,* and that entire flippin' movie took place in a godforsaken airport! Not the most stellar of performances, but notable nonetheless."

"Not about the movie." The thick strap of the seatbelt dug into my neck, and I pulled it loose with my thumb. Why were seatbelts constantly trying to strangle you? Wasn't their job to keep you safe? "About the fact that you, me, Lincoln, and Dan are all hanging out. It makes me uncomfortable. And it feels date-ish."

"Because it *is* date-ish." That didn't ease my worries one iota. "But look at it this way—at least you've *seen* your date. The only thing I know about my date is what he doesn't have. Does he have blue eyes? Maybe. Full, pouty lips that beg to be licked? Possibly. Sandy blond hair hinting at a beachy, surfer style and a laid back, no worries attitude? Could be. Legs? Nope." Sam shook her head. The fringe of her indigo hair stuck to the shiny patch of gloss smothered across her lips. "See? The only definitive thing I know about him is what he *doesn't* possess. So you really have a leg up on me in that department."

"You didn't."

Sam smacked her gum loudly. "Oh yes, I did. Good one, huh?"

"Shhh!" I fluttered my hand at her. My fingers got dangerously close to the sticky bubble ballooning from her mouth. "I think I see them!"

"They can't hear us, you know. Leglessness doesn't affect auditory function."

I shushed her once more. "Just shut up, your talking is making me more nervous."

"What do you have to be nervous about? You already know that your date is hot."

I blushed just hearing that. "You think Lincoln's hot?"

"In a too-tall, awkward man-boy kind of way, yes, he's hot." Sam crawled across the backseat to peer out the window on my side, her hands and knees pawing at the upholstered leather seats. Lincoln had the handles of Dan's chair in his grip and both guys had their backs to us as they maneuvered backward down the driveway. "Do you really need my validation on those kinds of things, Eps?"

"Yeah, I sorta do."

"Then you've got my notarized stamp of hotness approval." Sam pressed her index finger to the fogged-over glass, pointing almost. "Shhh, they're almost here."

"I thought you were just saying we didn't have to be quiet—"

"How's my hair?" She fluffed the back of her head with her palm and pressed her lips together tightly. Primping wasn't something I knew how to do.

"Purplish blue."

"Good. And my lips?"

"Kissable."

"Even better. God, I hope this Dan guy is hot. The anticipation is killing me!"

I giggled. Sam was consistently overly eager when it came to boys. She hadn't mentioned Brian—or was it Ryan? —in the past few days, and I assumed she'd flung that short-lived fling out of the way to make room for the newest flavor of the week. Sam ran through guys like one does Kleenex. Or toilet paper. Or whatever it was that served a completely necessary purpose, but also had to be quickly and appropriately discarded. She was a love 'em and leave 'em sort of gal, minus the love portion.

When the two guys we were impatiently waiting on got to the base of the walk, Lincoln spun the chair around so fast that it was all a blur of blond hair and tanned skin, a deep maroon t-shirt and glints of metal. It was like he was purposefully keeping Dan hidden from our view, only to ramp up the expectation.

"Please be hot," Sam whispered once more as a mantra. "Please be hot."

I faced forward, focusing my gaze straight out the front windshield.

Until I realized that was rude. And weird. It was weird to ignore someone when you were about to be introduced, obviously. So I peered slightly over my left shoulder, trying to maintain a cool, casual composure, but I'd never learned how to be either of those things. Instead, I devised a makeshift plan at attempting normalcy. I'd make the customary eye contact and then would swivel back into my assumed position. I wouldn't make things awkward for us all. Awkward was never fun.

Out of the corner of my vision I could already see Dan—a not at all unhot teenage boy—in Lincoln's arms, not so much cradled, just carried. The door opened and Dan lowered into the camper and immediately shot a heart-fluttering smile my direction, then passed the same one over to Sam.

Sam, clearly, was over the moon with this.

"Hello, ladies."

"*Hello,* Dan," Sam cooed.

Lincoln spoke up, still standing outside the vehicle. "I'm gonna throw this in the back real quick," he said as he motioned toward Dan's chair.

"Thanks, mate."

I didn't figure Dan to be an Australian, but oh how he had that beach vibe Sam had been craving. His skin wasn't merely kissed by the sun, but had clearly made out with it and taken it back to his duplex for a good old romp between the sheets. The evidence of its golden rays was all over him. He was gorgeously tan—

unrealistically so—with light eyes and silver studs in his ears, along with the brightest, whitest smile I'd ever seen. Though he had several visible pockmarks along his jaw and left cheek, if anything, they only added to his rugged, masculine aura. He truly was a sight to behold.

The back propped open and the entire frame jolted as Lincoln hoisted the wheelchair into the van and then slammed the door shut. I could hear his feet fall in loud claps as he jogged his way back around to the driver's side of the camper.

"Sam, I presume," Dan said as the vehicle began coasting down the street toward the coffeehouse, Lincoln at the helm. Even his voice was sexy and made my breathing stutter, which was weird for a sound to have the ability to falter something so normally routine for me. "Short for Samantha?"

"Yep. Dan, short for Daniel?"

"Short for Lieutenant Dan."

Sam huffed and gritted her teeth simultaneously. "You've got to be kidding me, Lincoln!" She jabbed at the back of his seat with a balled up fist. Still driving, Lincoln eyed her in the rear view mirror, giving her a *don't-you-even-think-about-it* glare. "Seriously? I can't say *any*thing?"

Lincoln shook his head so tightly it looked like a nervous tick.

"Listen," Dan interrupted. He seemed like a sharp guy. I doubted he'd be one to miss the underlying, very blatant nonverbal exchange occurring in the camper. "I don't have legs. I'd love to tell you the harrowing tale of just why I don't have said legs, but that will have to wait until we're in a location that has lots of paper products that can absorb the deluge of tears that will likely ensue."

"Coffee house it is. Then you're spilling the beans." Sam nodded with a playful smirk. "But just so you know, you're probably not the only one in this bus that has a sob-worthy story." Her gum crackled between her teeth when she spoke, almost giving her a kind of accent. "I just want to prepare you so you don't feel slighted and all when the sympathy is evenly dispersed around the table and doesn't solely land on your shoulders."

"You hear that, Linc?" Dan called out from the middle. He cupped his hands in a funnel around his mouth dramatically. "Sam thinks she's got you and me beat when it comes to pathetically tragic pasts."

Lincoln, still using the rearview mirror to communicate with the backseat occupants, shed a small, unwilling smile. It barely reached into his cheeks at all.

I glanced across the cab at him. I hoped to catch his gaze, and sure enough, within seconds Lincoln looked my way. That's when I reached over the console between us and rested my hand there, available. He must've seen me place it, because his ended up in exactly the same positioning, only two inches away. Every bit of what we were doing was intentional on the most honest level, testing one another's hormones like this.

I grinned. I wanted to dive across the cab and make out with his face, but figured grinning was probably more appropriate for this time and space.

"Just you wait, Sam. Linc's got a horribly pitiful past that would even make the toughest of grown men weep. It's really that atrocious."

Sam said something back to Dan, and Lincoln didn't offer any retaliation, but just leaned closer into the gap between us. His brown hair curled into his eyes like a sheepdog's when tilted.

"I hope you're not one to easily transfer your affections, because Dan's right, his story has been known to make women swoon."

"And what about yours?" I laughed. My hand stayed put where it was.

"Mine hasn't quite had the same effect," Lincoln admitted with a surrendering shrug.

"Well," I said. "Lucky for you, Dan hasn't had quite the same effect on me as you have, either."

"You're right," Lincoln said, slipping just his fourth finger and pinky under mine. My skin lit up and I honestly wondered for a moment how many degrees above 98.6 I could get before a trip to the hospital was warranted. Was a ten-degree increase something I should be worried about? Twenty? Lincoln grinned as he spoke only to me, "That does make me the lucky one."

# ELEVEN

We'd been sitting at the coffeehouse long enough for me to figure that even my hair would carry the burnt coffee bean smell until the next washing. It was dark and cozy in Roast House, and the four of us were curled into a back corner half-booth—Sam on one side of the table, Dan next to her, while Lincoln and I shared the padded cushion opposite them. Though the place didn't close for another hour, we were the only remaining patrons in the establishment, and I saw the baristas eyeing us every now and then, hoping for an early night off had we just gotten up and left already.

But we hadn't left already.

I'd nursed my white mocha the whole time we were here. I'm sure the rest noticed, though no one made mention of my aversion to coffee. But about a half hour ago, Lincoln excused himself from our table and returned with a glass of water for me, a gesture that both Sam and Dan didn't acknowledge, but one that still felt overwhelmingly significant. I'd always felt out of tune in this life, but even as off-tune as I was, Lincoln somehow matched it. *We* were in tune.

"You're not entirely out of the running," Dan said. "But that story didn't quite live up to the hype, Sam. Though I would have to say that you're lack of parental involvement and subsequent involvement with a literal traveling circus one-ups Lincoln's failed Army entry due to adolescent asthma." Dan rubbed his chin contemplatively, the way old professors do in offices adorned in polished leather and mahogany. "Sorry, buddy, but she's got you beat."

Lincoln sighed with more drama tacked on to the act than necessary. "Trapezes will outshine inhalers every day. It's a sad reality."

"It is, bro, it is. Though the fact that you technically took steroids could be construed as mildly controversial, the truth of the matter is that Sam effectively ran away with the circus. The friggin' circus!"

I took a sip of my water, swishing the cool liquid in my mouth. I held it there before swallowing it down. "I'm confused. Are we ranking based on patheticness or outrageousness? Because there's nothing pathetic about lions and tigers and bears."

"Oh my," Lincoln played along. Again, in tune.

"My vote is for outrageousness," Sam piped up. She was sitting so close to Dan now, practically in his lap. The more excited she got, the closer she'd inch his direction. I didn't think he minded much, though, because he'd also been sneakily rotating the wheels of his chair in quarter turns for the past half hour in a disguised effort to creep closer to Sam, too.

Apparently, they were hitting it off. "Only because I'm sure to win if outrageousness is the measuring stick."

"Hush," Dan silenced. He pressed a teasing index finger to her shiny purple lips. I think Sam actually blushed, though it was difficult to decipher under the muted lighting. But yes, pretty sure that was blushing. She pursed her mouth briefly before he removed his finger from it. "Do you not recall how I just told you that I had my legs blown off in enemy territory? What's more outrageous than that? Exploding bodies? Enemy fire?"

"Preventing an impeding elephant stampede on opening night, thus saving the lives of hundreds of well-dressed attendees out for a traditional—if not slightly animal-cruelty supporting—family outing under the big top. In a fuchsia sequined leotard, at that."

Dan wasn't letting up that easily, no sir. He swirled his coffee mug in circular motions, the contents inside slushing up and over the lipped rim as he readied his comeback. Then he fired out, "Hundreds of attendees? Oh, please. My gallant efforts likely saved the lives of millions of Americans, not to mention the freedoms of generations to come. I'm a future-focused life saver and freedom preserver. Beat that!"

"That's a bit unfair to cast such a wide net with that assumption. I don't think you can measure things based on *assumed* lives impacted. We need more concrete statistics here to fully make an informed decision as to who wins this little contest of yours, Danny."

This was their version of flirting, I figured. It was beyond quirky, though I wouldn't expect anything less from Sam. She excelled at quirk.

But I still hadn't quite figured out Dan. I'd never met someone who had been in a war—at least not someone so close in age to me. Sure, I had an uncle that fought in the Gulf War back before I was even born, but I'd never known anyone who was in such close proximity to the memories they held and their actual occurrences. Dan said that he was twenty-one, so I figured he could only be a year removed from battle, at the very most.

Which *did* sort of explain the flippant manner in which he spoke of his brief time in the military. I couldn't imagine that years from now, with the full advantage of hindsight, he'd be dismissing his experiences so easily, going so far as to toss them into the ring of a game that was completely made up and entirely politically incorrect on every level possible. He'd hold them closer, I was sure.

At least that's what I'd been doing.

Then, out of nowhere, Sam stammered, "Eppie tried to kill herself in the third grade. How's that for outrageous?"

The water in my glass was about as bland as drinks came, but the liquid sliding down my throat burned like acid. I was eating fire. I couldn't look up to see their reaction. I held my gaze, my composure, and my fingers so tightly that self-combustion seemed inevitable. *Ka-boom!* I could hear it already. But I supposed that's what I wanted to happen. To suddenly just disappear from this table and these people and these stories. It had been one thing talking about, examining, and dissecting each of theirs. It was different now it was my life that was suddenly thrust under the microscope.

"Eppie?" Lincoln's amber eyes fell wide open.

"Failed spelling bee," I joked, attempting to laugh it off in the way that Dan had so casually dismissed his own tragic near death experience just moments prior to this one. "I took it pretty hard."

Lincoln's eyes didn't falter. "Hey," he said in a soft voice.

"Who would've thought the word ambidextrous could lead to such ghastly outcomes?"

"Hey," he said again.

"It's a tricky word," Sam played along. Dan nodded in agreement, just for effect, I figured. He rotated one more quarter turn into Sam.

"I just couldn't make up my mind on how to spell it," I elaborated, never missing a beat. The story fabricated and tumbled from my lips, lies fresh and ready on my tongue. "It felt like it could be spelled one way, but then it seemed equally plausible that it could be spelled another. I just kept going back and forth."

The slight lift in the corners of Lincoln's mouth at least hinted at an appreciation for my efforts, though I knew he wasn't buying one second of it. He was pained.

Then he leaned closer. His mouth brushed into my hair. He parted his lips and the heat that fell from his breath skimmed along my neckline. "Let's go," he whispered. "I'm done with this. I don't want to do this anymore."

I nodded my agreement, thankful for an out.

"Guys, I think Eppie and I are going to head out," he said, jingling his keys in his palm. "Sam, can I drive you home?"

"Nah. I literally live three blocks from here. I can hoof it."

"Mind if I tag along?" Dan asked Sam. He swung his head to look at her.

Sam beamed. "I'd be offended if you didn't," she smiled, her chin tucked into her shoulder.

I slipped out of the booth and stood up, Lincoln following me.

Both Sam and Dan peered up and gave us twin smiles. It must've been code for *"Go on and get out of here, we have some making out to do,"* because Lincoln and I weren't even out the door and I could already hear the slurping of lips mashing against one another and saliva exchanging living spaces. I wanted to turn around and see, just to witness the act that made my own cheeks flush and heat up. But I didn't, and instead led Lincoln out of Roast House and into the parking lot.

It smelled like it was about to rain—thick, heavy air filled with the weight of moisture from clouds that felt like they'd come down to earth to wrap wetly around you. It wasn't quite a hug, nor a blanket, but some almost-oppressive layering. It made everything smell and feel different, even the pavement.

Taking longer strides than I was capable of making, Lincoln chased my steps and beat me to the passenger door first. His hand hung on the handle.

"Hey," he said again, this time louder now that we were alone. "I'm here, okay?"

"I see that," I laughed. "And I am here."

"No. I mean I'm *here.* However you need me, I'm here. You understand?"

I paused. "I don't really want to talk about what Sam brought up in there." I leaned against the camper and let the words out on a sigh. The frame was cold and slick with beaded water from the humid air. My skin clammed up upon contact instantly, making me shiver.

"So we won't. We won't talk about it."

"It's just that there's more to it than what she mentioned." *So much more that if I began expanding on it right now, it would be the beginning of next week before I'd covered the half of it.* I knew it wasn't fair to dangle that bit of information in front of him and then never give an explanation for it, but I just couldn't. Not yet at least. Maybe never. Probably never.

"Eppie, of course there's more. There's *always* more." Suddenly, Lincoln was closer to me, his body leaned in. As his hips pressed forward, he gripped on to my hands. His thumbs stroked over the soft flesh on the backs of them, ever so lightly. Then he stooped down to drop his forehead on mine. I failed to breathe. "You think Dan doesn't have more?" Lincoln's eyes flicked back toward the coffeehouse. There were boxes of yellow light cut into the building and the glow from these windows illuminated the parking lot, illuminating him. "God, there's so much more." He pulled his face back just a bit. "And Sam? My guess is that there's more there, too. We *all* have more, Eppie."

Right then, the first droplets of rain spilled from the sky, peppering down in a light mist across my face and arms. Lincoln's thumb fumbled out of my hand and he lifted it to my cheek, hesitantly. He was looking directly into my eyes as he ran the pad of his finger across my skin, and he kept it there against my jaw for a moment—a moment that didn't involve blinking, nor breathing, just staring. Just finding our tune again.

"Eppie, hold on to your more for as long as you like. I haven't earned my right to it just yet." The gap between us lessened again as he pulled closer, hovering over me. His eyes tightened and he said, "But believe me when I say, I sure hope that someday I will."

# TWELVE

*"You take this half of the list and I'll take this one." Dad ripped the paper in two, right down the middle, and shoved it my way, along with a red wire basket. There was an old price tag stuck to the bottom of it and it curled at the edges, making the barcode look wavy and swirly. "Meet me at check stand three in fifteen minutes. And don't forget the waffles. I didn't add those."*

*I skimmed over the list. Dad probably got the better one since mine was filled with veggies and beans and frozen dinners. The supermarket was nearly empty today, which made me happy. I didn't want to run into any of my friends from school. I doubted their parents made them do the shopping. It would be so embarrassing for them to see me.*

*With the list in my hand, I headed to the produce section. The music that played through the intercom was a wordless melody that repeated the same several beats over and over. The sound was hollow, and the speakers crackled at the high notes. This grocery store was really old, I figured.*

*Bananas were the first thing to get. Mom liked them green, when they almost tasted sour and they were super hard to peel. Dad liked them really yellow with even a few brown dots on them. Those always looked like freckles to me. I didn't like bananas much, but apparently lots of people did because the store's display was running really low. Only a few bunches were left on the square stand in the middle of the department. I stood and analyzed each one, lifting them up and turning them around right in front of my eyes. The music flipped to another song as I continued to compare fruit, but there still weren't any words in this one, either. I hummed along, making up the verses in my head.*

*"You need some help?"*

*A red-haired teenage boy stood across from me, transferring shiny green apples from a cart filled with boxes to the other side of the display. He was wearing an apron and had a pin on his shirt that said RICK. He also had tons of pimples; so many that I began to connect their dots in my head.*

*"Need help reading what's on your list?"*

*"I can read," I said, gripping the paper tighter between my fingers. Maybe some kids would have a hard time with it, but spelling was easy for me. I was really good at it, and sometimes I even found typos on my Dad's lists. I never told him about them, though. I didn't want to make him feel bad. He was usually a good speller. "I'm trying to pick out bananas."*

*"Not much to choose from today, unfortunately." Rick stacked the apples like a pyramid. What if some little kid came and took one from that bottom row? Then they would all fall onto the floor and be wasted. It seemed like a better option to arrange them in a way that wouldn't be*

*so easy to ruin. "Our truck that brings the shipments overturned on the 80. Boxes everywhere, all over the highway."*

*"That's bananas," I said, deadpan.*

*"Funny, kid." He swiped his hands across the front of the apron and then went back to transferring the packaged apples from their original box. "Should have more here by Thursday, though."*

*That didn't do me any good. I was supposed to meet Dad at the front in fifteen minutes, probably more like twelve by now. I surveyed the available bananas in front of me again. This was bad. How was I supposed to make a choice? If I chose the green ones, then Dad would have to wait days to eat them, if there were even any left once Mama had her share. If I picked the yellow, overripe ones, then Mama wouldn't have a chance at all to have one.*

*After deliberating for way too long, and cutting into a good portion of my remaining time to complete my shopping, I went with the green. Better to have to wait to enjoy something than to not even have the opportunity to begin with. Dad would be annoyed, I figured, but Mama would be so happy. I liked it when she was happy. Dad was annoyed most of the time, so I supposed this wouldn't be any different. I was used to that.*

*I crossed off the remaining items in record time, even remembering to grab the waffles before meeting Dad. As I was pulling the breakfast out of the frozen case, I heard him from one aisle over, his tired voice unmistakable. He was talking to someone—another voice that I recognized—but I couldn't identify it right away. Slowly,*

*I shut the freezer door and stood completely still, trying to eavesdrop through the row of potato chips between us.*

*"I saw Gloria at pick up yesterday," the woman said over the cries of a baby that I figured had to be hers. The wheels of the cart scraped back and forth against the gritty checkered linoleum floor. I figured this was her way of rocking the child into calm. "Said Eponine's still showing symptoms."*

*"Sometimes, yes." Dad didn't use many words. I wondered if he even liked words at all, unless he was shouting them. He definitely liked to shout his words more than talk them.*

*"I just don't know how you all do it. Gloria especially. The chair of the PTA with a full-time job and a chronically ill child. God bless you all."*

*"I'm not sure we feel very blessed by any of it. Eppie especially."*

*Dad's tone was hard. There was a long pause from the woman, but the baby kept squealing and the cart kept squeaking.*

*"I told Gloria that we added Eponine to the prayer chain at church. Lots of women praying for answers."*

*The newest song playing in the store still didn't have any words, but I had been adding my own throughout my shopping trip to keep me busy as I gathered the items from the list. This particular one I'd composed was about a little girl and a pony named Blaze. It wasn't as good as some of my other lyrics, but I liked the melody. I had tried writing a song once in my bedroom when I couldn't sleep and Mama and Dad argued downstairs about whether it was trash pick up the next day or not. I'd had a hard time with that song. It was easier when the melody was already there. It was like the tune was just sitting there, waiting for the words to bring it to life.*

*The woman continued. "I can't imagine anything much worse than having a sick child. Lord keep you, Mark."*

*"Thank you," Dad replied, but he didn't sound thankful. He sounded frustrated, exhausted. "But there* are *many things worse," he added. The baby had stopped crying as the song changed again. Maybe she hadn't liked that last particular melody much. If only I'd been able to sing my words to her. Maybe then she would have liked it a little better. Maybe then she wouldn't have been so sad. "Eppie might be sick, but she's still with us. She's still here. That's not the case for every parent in our position."*

*"Your family... bless you. Just... just bless you."*

*I could hear the woman wheel away, turning down the aisle as she sniffed, so I panicked, figuring she was heading my direction. I didn't want to see her. And I didn't want to see that crying baby. I felt bad that she had been so upset. I felt bad that the woman had added me to her church's prayer list. I just felt bad about all of it.*

*"I'm all done," I exclaimed, jogging up to the check stand where Dad said I should meet him. My basket swung at my side. Dad was already there, loading his items onto the conveyer, looking like a robot as he did it. Mechanical. Stiff. "I didn't know about the bananas," I admitted as I emptied my contents onto the belt right behind his pile. "I'm sorry, Daddy. I might've gotten the wrong ones."*

*He glanced at them, but not really long enough to even see what I was talking about. His gaze was empty and expressionless. He paused for a while, and then waved his hand at me, like it wasn't a big deal. "It's fine," he murmured. "I meant to tell you not to bother with them, anyway."*

# THIRTEEN

"Ms. Aberdeen," Mr. Moriata, my AP English teacher, called out from the front of the classroom. It was 11:34 on Tuesday, just ten minutes until lunch dismissal, and he was holding a note the size of an index card between his fingers and squinting as he read, his wire-rimmed glasses perched low on his nose. The only thing that kept them from sliding off his face was the round bulb of cartilage at the tip. I supposed weird-shaped noses came in handy for something. "Ms. Aberdeen, you have a visitor in the office."

I'd finished up my practice essay on the psychological themes in *Dead Poets Society,* focusing strictly on Neil and his relationship with his authoritarian father (if you could even call it one). Never before had my pen blazed across the page so furiously that I worried it would go up in smoke. Setting off the fire alarm halfway through class could earn me a crown come Senior Ball, I figured. I'd be a regular hero with that one. My classmates would surely love any excuse to drop their pencils and hightail it to scholastic freedom.

Apparently this specific subject matter was something already stored in my brain, packaged, prepared, and ready to transfer onto paper at a moment's notice. The words to the essay spilled out of me, and four pages and one mild hand cramp later (but still no kindling), I found myself with nothing left to do for the remaining thirty minutes of class aside from stare at the clock on the wall just above Mr. Moriata's poster of a quote that read: *Books, your reward for having an attention span.* I, however, was beginning to think I didn't actually possess one. My mind stuttered from one thought to the next, never seeming to land on anything too significant for all too long. It played a frantic game of leapfrog inside my head.

Well, that wasn't entirely true. I was able to land on one particular item of interest. I'd developed a pretty firm opinion on how it would be to kiss Lincoln, for starters. And then I formulated another opinion on what it would be like to fully make out with him. I was just about to get to the part where my imagination required less garments of clothing, when Mr. Moriata had called out my name. I cursed him quietly under my breath, thanking him for that hormonal buzzkill.

Naturally, I assumed my visitor had to be the boy who'd been starring in my PG-13 fantasies, because I hoped the universe rewarded people in that way. To my dismay, that wasn't the case. I'd definitely never envisioned locking lips with Phil, my actual visitor. Well, except for now, because sometimes when you said things, your brain couldn't help but conjure them up in a physical, tangible way. That was unfortunate in this instance. Phil had halitosis breath and I didn't typically go for guys three times my age. Call me crazy, but I preferred my men a little less long in the tooth.

But I supposed the reason I even knew Phil at all had a little something to do with people literally calling me crazy.

"Philly," I greeted as I swung open the metal door to the administration office. A musky stench immediately filled my nostrils. The room was stale, like no one had cracked its doors since the Italian Renaissance. Or maybe it was the Italian sub that Principal Perry was devouring in the adjoining room. Either way, it made my stomach tumble. "To what do I owe this unexpected pleasure?"

"Eppie." Phil slid in for a hug and I held my breath. "It's been a few weeks, eh?"

I nodded; it had been. I also wondered how Phil managed to become a Canadian in that short span of time.

"I was hoping I could take you off campus for some lunch? Feel like Mongolian?"

It was a stupid question that didn't even warrant an answer because Phil knew exactly my response. I just gave him a toothy grin.

"Thought so," he said. "I already signed you out. I'll have you back before fifth period."

That would be Spanish three. While I wasn't by any means fluent, I'd be fine missing a class or two. Señora Sanchez would give me a pass, I figured. It was all bueno.

"Everything okay?" I asked as we walked out to the school parking lot. I hiked my rucksack higher up by tugging on the strap slung over my shoulder. The air was still weighty and substantially humid. It felt like the sky could split open at any given moment. "Should I be worried by your impromptu lunch appearance?"

Phil was a certified master of emotional disguise. I could tell him that I wanted to move to Antarctica and open up a FroYo franchise and he'd ask me how much capital I was hoping to secure and what flavors I planned to serve. He always heard me out, never giving me anything less than his complete attention. Yes, I knew he was hired at one point to do just that, but those paychecks stopped long ago and he still made a cameo or two every few weeks. Obligation had run its course, but Phil still remained steadfastly committed.

"You should not be worried, no." We'd waded through the rows of cars and trucks, finally approaching his 1980's matte black Datsun parked along the fence line. I opened the door and lowered down, worrying that my butt might actually hit the pavement once I was fully in my chair. This was a low rider for sure. "Look in the backseat." Phil motioned with a flick of his head. "Brown paper bag."

I twisted at the waist. There was a crumpled brown sack with my name on it. E-P-P-I-E. I snatched it from the back and the familiar weight of the bag clued me in instantly as to its contents.

"My fritter! You shouldn't have."

"Really? If that's the case, you can leave it here—"

"I'm only running through the obligatory niceties," I interrupted as I tore an edge off the donut and popped it into my mouth. It was still warm and the sweet cinnamon flavor coated my tongue and pulled up my taste buds. It was divine.

"Don't eat the whole thing; you'll spoil your appetite."

Phil drove out of the parking lot, lowering his aviator shades onto his nose as he turned onto the highway. His hair was too long and too carefree for a man his age, and his whiskers were speckled with flecks of gray in a beard that hinted at a mid-life crisis. If he shaved off his trendy facial hair, he'd look years younger, but my guess was he sported the beard in an effort to appear younger (and optimistically hipper), too. Ah, that sneaky double-edged sword. It sliced him all up with that one, for sure.

Ignoring Phil's suggestion, I inhaled the entire apple fritter as we drove to the restaurant, and I'd already eaten almost half a bowl of Mongolian B-B-Q before I felt my stomach tightening into fullness. Pressing my napkin to my mouth, I let out a quiet belch, alleviating the pain my gut.

"So the reason I brought you here... "

"Wasn't to fatten me up?" The waiter came by to refill our water glasses and I waited as the liquid poured into my cup. Then I took a sip. "I was beginning to think that you were getting me ready for some type of ancient sacrifice. The fattened calf and all."

"First off," Phil began. "They'd take my license away for doing something like that. Secondly, I think lambs are the preferred sacrificial offering. So if I was doing this right, I'd be buying you lots of wool sweaters rather than pumping you full of calories."

Oh, how I'd missed Phil. It was hard to believe that after nearly ten years, I'd gotten to the point of actually feeling an emotional attachment to this man, when at one point in time I couldn't even bear to look at him.

Phil had embodied everything awful in my life. It wasn't entirely his fault, of course, but association was cruel that way. Like a song that wouldn't let you forget the heartbreak accompanied with its memory, Phil's face defined an era that I wanted nothing more than to bury in my past. His smile was the taunting, *You poor girl.* His frown was the, *You would've been better off dead.* His crinkled eyes and his pulled brow were the, *What on earth were you thinking?* Each line on his face, each expression in his gaze, every inflection in his tone was an analysis of my crumbling, fragile state of being.

Of course, I was entirely aware that these were my own thoughts I projected onto him. As I said before, Phil was good at masking. But it didn't stop me from filling in the gaps. It didn't stop me from adding the thoughts I knew had to be there into his expressions and actions. Even though he was forbidden from revealing it, there had to be some judgment there.

Which, in fairness, was exactly how it should've been. That's what he was paid to do, after all.

I didn't sense any analytical assessment today as he offered me a genuine smile over the rim of his water glass.

"You have a birthday coming up, Eppie." Phil twirled his fork in the noodles, spinning them up like a ball of yarn. Then he stabbed a piece of leathery meat that had been frozen just moments earlier. Not necessarily the freshest meal, but that was probably what made it so wonderfully tasty. "A big one."

"That I do." I knew exactly where this was going.

"What are your plans?" He wrapped his thin lips around his fork and pulled all the noodles into his mouth with a slurp. "Anything fun?"

I deliberated. "Let me think." Thumbing my chin, I said, "I've actually got a new sorta-boyfriend and I suppose maybe I'll have shake-the-rafters, rattle-the-windows sex with him since I'll finally be legal and all."

"Eponine," Phil hissed. Maybe I'd only said it for the reaction, because there was absolutely no way that would be happening within the month. I could count the number of boys I'd merely kissed on one hand. I didn't even need a hand at all to number the guys I'd slept with. I figured that integer wasn't about to change any time soon, either.

"Obviously I'm kidding, Phil." His posture relaxed, only slightly. "We'll be quiet."

"I know you say these sorts of things because you are subconsciously looking for the protective paternal reaction, so I assume you're pleased that I just offered it to you free of charge."

I chuckled and scooped up my water glass again.

I wondered if it was possible for someone in Phil's position to ever switch off their analytical mind. Did he go through his days summing up all of his interactions, and then diagnosing these poor unsuspecting folks that made the honest mistake of engaging him in conversation? Shrinks should come with warning labels, I figured. *Hello my name is __________, and I will be sizing up every single thing about you. Nice to make your acquaintance.*

"But in absolute seriousness," he continued. "Have you thought about what you're going to do?"

I settled my glass onto the table and lifted my fork from my lunch to take another bite. The fritter would just have to make room. "About my mom?"

"Yes." He held his firm gaze on me. "About her."

"Of course I've thought about it."

"And?"

Pushing my bowl away from me, I stretched my arms across the table, shrugging. Then I reached out and fiddled with the straw in my glass. Like I was a child, I pressed the pad of my finger over the top of the straw and lifted it from the water by several inches. Then I watched as the liquid trickled out when I removed my finger from its suctioned position. It was only mildly entertaining, and judging by the look on Phil's face, he wasn't even remotely entertained by it.

He grabbed the cup from my grip.

"Eppie, I'd like to know your plan." He scooted the glass to the empty place setting next to him, just out of my reach. "As your doctor—"

"You're not technically my doctor anymore."

"As your friend," Phil corrected. His voice was soft and quiet, especially for a man's. "I want to know what you plan to do."

"So you can tell me I'm making the wrong decision?" I asked, more as an accusation than an actual question. My words were snide, which I knew Phil didn't deserve. I heard my dad's familiar tone embedded in them, spewing from my mouth.

"So I can support you in that decision." The correction was instant, and I felt he meant it. Years ago, once Phil and a few other important doctors finally agreed that mentally I was as stable as should be expected, Phil had told me that he'd always be there. That the end of our professional relationship did not signify the end of our entire relationship. I'm sure he sensed I had deep-seated abandonment issues, and I figured he didn't want to help that issue take further root. Phil always had a hand in my growth, and it was a relief in knowing he planned to carry on in that same way indefinitely.

"I think I want to finally visit her."

His fixed expression didn't waiver. "Have you told your father?"

"No."

"Do you think maybe you should?"

I was thirsty, and slightly resentful that Phil had commandeered my cup. Out of my dry mouth, I managed to speak the words, "I'm not sure I'd be able to find a sober opportunity to share that bit of information with him."

Phil's lips tightened as he inferred, "He's drinking again."

"*Again* would imply that at one point he'd stopped," I explained. "He's on an alcohol consumption continuum. There is no stopping point in that infinite loop."

"Still." Phil swiped the check from the waiter's hand as he arrived at the side of our table to drop it off. I nodded my head toward it and smiled my thank you when he slipped a credit card into the black leather folder. He always paid, and I was always so appreciative. "It's worth telling him, Eppie. Whether he comprehends or even remembers the conversation, it's one worth having. He needs to know that you're finally accepting this reality. This is a big deal."

"I'm not sure."

Phil pushed up from his seat to slip his wallet into his back pocket. Then he brought his hands together and folded his fingers, lowering them onto the ledge of the table as he settled back in. "I think it needs to happen."

I laughed, huffing, "Is that your professional opinion, Philly?"

"Not necessarily. But it's what I would do if I were you. He's trying, Eppie. I know it's a completely messed up position you're in, I do. And he's definitely not the best dad. Not even close. But he's your dad, and keeping the lines of communication open is sort of important."

My stomach tightened and I fought back my frustration, swallowing thickly to keep it buried in my gut. Maybe all the food could keep it there, tucked away. "But *she* was his wife. Maybe she should've thought about keeping those lines open when she had the chance."

"Have you thought about asking him to go with you?"

"No." I was honest, and in truth, I didn't have to ask him to know the answer.

"I don't think you should go by yourself." Phil's concern was overtly sincere, and he spoke with a pleading tone that coated his words. I knew he wanted the best for me, I did. I got that. "I can only imagine how emotional this is going to be, especially after waiting all this time. Would you like me to go with you?"

"I don't think that would go over well," I smirked. Phil scooted my drink across the table toward me, like I'd somehow earned it back, and I caught it with my palm. Lowering my head, I took a long, cooling sip.

He deliberated for a few contemplative moments. The thumbs once tucked into his hands now twirled around one another, twiddling. "What about this new sorta-boyfriend of yours? What about him?"

"Oh, God no!" Nerves rose in me, making my heart pump double-time. The dizzying ring of too much blood thundering into my ears drowned out every other sound within the restaurant. It all became background noise, except for the breathing also now magnified within my own head. Breaths and beats, that's all I was when it came to the mere mention of Lincoln. "I think he might actually like me. The key to keeping it that way is not airing all of my dirty laundry right off the bat. He'd run for the hills. Screaming, most likely."

Phil thumbs must've gotten tired from all the twirling, because one of them had now slowed down to rub circles against his chin instead. "Really?" he asked, his brows so tight they looked as though they could snap, like a brittle twig or even a pencil. They were severe, but not at all angered. Just intense on the most heartfelt level. "I thought the key was merely being yourself."

"No one would stick around if they had that."

"That's not true, Eppie. I've officially been retired for three and a half years now, and yet here I sit across from you."

He had a point, I supposed. But not one I understood. Seemed silly to waste his golden years on a one-sided relationship with a teenage girl who couldn't offer him much more than occasional intellectual dialogue and a sad story he could dissect with his professional friends.

"It's the guilt that keeps you here, I figure," I said, too smug for my own good. "Knowing I'm floundering and at one pivotal point in time you were a sustaining, leveling force. Not seeing how I ultimately turned out—that's the real reason you're still around. It's all about closure."

"Do *not* project with me, okay Eppie?" Low and soft, Phil's voice dropped in tone. He admonished me again as he said, "I do *not* operate based on guilt. I do *not* need there to be a perfect happy ending all wrapped up in a silver bow. I do *not* believe in the term closure." I straightened in my chair, each of his words pulling up my spine. "You haven't turned out one way or another. You're *still* turning out. And this is all part of that process. I'm here because I care about you, believe it or not. It's true I never had a case like yours, yes. But that wasn't because of what happened to you, Eppie. That's not what made your case so different. It's because of who you were. Who you *are*."

Was it possible for your own thudding heart to actually give you a headache? Because that's what happened. The blunt beating right behind my eyes pressed into them so painfully that tears gathered. I'd need both an aspirin and a tissue if it didn't let up. I bit my lip to keep it all pinned back. Then I let go and said, "But I'm who I am because of what happened to me."

"And if you believe that to be true, this visit you have planned has the potential to continue to mold and shape you. I just don't want you to go through it alone, Eppie. That's all."

I listened as I fiddled with the straw in my cup. White dots formed in my vision, the beginnings of a migraine altering my senses. I was used to being nauseous all of the time. Now should be no exception, I figured. If anything, it was comforting to have that level of consistency in my reactions, as weird as that was.

"Honestly, Phil," I began, forcing out the words through the painful mess in my brain. "If I didn't break then, there's no way I'm going to break now."

And at that moment, like he'd had this line prepared from the first day he walked through those hospital doors, he said, "I just want you to keep one thing in mind." His gaze secured onto mine as he continued, "Not all breaks are clean. Sometimes we crumble, sometimes we erode. And those erosions, Eppie—the ones that chip away at our hopes and our dreams and our plans for our futures—those are often a lifetime in the making. It's those we must watch out for, my dear."

# FOURTEEN

"Knock, knock."

I dumped my Coke in my lap. All 24 ounces of it, which was a considerable amount. Enough to soak my jeans and the patchwork quilt on my bed, along with both the top and fitted sheets.

"Eppie?" Lincoln's head popped around the slightly ajar bedroom door. He used his foot to push it all the way open and took in the scene. "What happened?"

"You scared the soda out of me!" I shrieked, ripping the comforter from the bed and wrapping it up into a ball. My arms and legs were sticky with syrup and I used the fabric to dry them off. "How'd you get in?"

Cautiously, Lincoln edged toward me like he wasn't entirely sure if I would throw the wad of cloth at him or not. I guess that would've been a good reaction, had I been going for a little dramatic flare. His hands came up in front of him as he tiptoed closer, not convinced I'd behave myself. "Your dad. Real nice guy."

"Seriously?" I was dumbfounded by what his statement implied: one, that my dad was with it enough to open the door, and two, that he came across as a decent person at that.

"Yeah, we shot the breeze for a bit, then he told me I could find you up here. Apparently, he's a Dodgers fan. Might be a source of future contention between us, but at least he enjoys the sport of baseball. Didn't know that about him."

I stripped the bed sheets and gathered the remaining fabric in my arms, sidestepping Lincoln as I made my way to the laundry room down the hall with my load. "That makes two of us," I said, opening the lid and shoving the bedding into the ceramic basin. The detergent was in a cabinet above the washer, so I had to stand up on my toes and really stretch to get it. Even still, I could barely pull it from the shelf without teetering and losing my footing against the cold tile.

Lincoln laughed, yanking the bottle from my grip. "There are advantages to having a really tall guy around, you know," he said as he closed the cabinet door and unscrewed the detergent cap. He filled it about halfway with the electric blue liquid. I never understood how something with that much color could actually get things clean. It seemed counterproductive to douse your soiled garments with even more brightly pigmented stainy stuff. But whatever, it worked.

The smile Lincoln wore as he began the load of laundry was more than just a smile—there was a whole lot of flirt tucked in there, too.

"I can get things down from those hard to reach places, clean cobwebs, locate missing people in large crowds, and offer a new perspective on the world in general."

"I was following you until that last one." I slammed the washer lid after he drizzled the detergent over the sheets and I turned around to lean against the machine. My arms crisscrossed over my chest because I worried what they might do if they just dangled there freely. They didn't feel all too trustworthy at the moment, to be honest. My arms begged to snake themselves around Lincoln's trim waist. They also hinted at wanting to pull him as close as our bodies would allow, until the space where I ended and he began blurred together.

It was his fault, after all. He'd delivered that too flirty grin.

"Here," he smiled again, effortlessly. "Let me show you what I'm talking about."

Without warning, Lincoln's hands hooked under my armpits, and in one swoop, I was eye level with him, just like that.

And apparently my arms weren't the *only* appendages with their own wishes. I'm sure they were insanely jealous of my legs, which were now wrapped around his middle, crossed at the ankles to brace myself and keep me suspended. Yes, my arms were definitely envious of my legs.

"How do you like the view up here?" he smirked, the air from his words landing on my mouth, almost with the weight of a kiss. Our faces were close, only an inch of separation. Now *both* my arms and legs were jealous of my mouth. A civil war was certain to break out amongst my body parts, I feared.

Lincoln's tongue suddenly ran over his bottom lip. I really wished he hadn't done that because it made my legs weak and if they loosened their grip around him at all, I'd plummet to the ground. And I was currently pretty far off the ground.

He jostled me a little, maneuvering so he could bring his hands under my thighs to support me. Oh crap, my sticky, soda drenched thighs. And he was grabbing them. How unsexy could this get?

"You like it?" he asked again.

"The air must be thinner," I blurted, struggling for breath, sanity, and all the other things that disappeared when a guy had their hands so close to the inseam of your shorts.

Despite all those losses, I pulled in a deep breath and I didn't smell the soda that covered me, but instead was filled with that minty, musky scent that clung to Lincoln's skin. Was it weird that I was overcome with the desire to lick it from him? Didn't lizards or something smell with their tongues? Did that make it less strange that I had the urge to suddenly do it, too?

*No, Eppie, attempting to relate to an amphibian did not lessen the strangeness.*

Thank goodness Lincoln started talking and pulled me out of my head. "In fact, I do think it's thinner up here, and I think that partly explains my frequent need for an inhaler."

Holy heck, was he cute. I mean, *really* cute. Not at all awkward like I'd thought before. Maybe my short-girl perspective from earlier had been distorting my view of him the way those fisheye lenses did, because now that we were directly face to face, I could see his features in such a new way, and let me say, he was freaking adorable. Downright sexy even, since I could see the pulse in that thick vein along his neck. Maybe it was beating so quickly as a result from the strain of having to hold me like this, but I chose to believe it was from something else. That was a huge turn on.

"I like you, Lincoln."

He didn't falter a bit. "I really like *you*, Eppie."

I sighed a contented, longing sigh. Who did that? I mean, if you were a southern belle maybe you could get away with literally swooning. But I wasn't. I wasn't a southern belle, nor a lizard, so none of my reactions were fitting in the least.

I was just a girl with too much trouble in my life and in my head.

"I have a lot of dirty laundry."

"It's just a couple sheets and a comforter." He began sliding me down the length of his body. If I joked that the change in altitude had messed with my brain earlier, I was a delirious mess from this latest act, dizzy with sensations that felt every single amount of friction created across every square inch of my body. When I landed on the floor, my knees forgot to lock and they left me dangling, completely unhinged.

Lincoln's hand at my back steadied me and I looked up at him, grateful.

Once on solid ground, he didn't revert to looking awkward at all. Maybe because now I had a true glimpse of his hotness as a reference point. And my body also had its own reference point of just how incredible *his* body was. No, awkward was definitely no longer a fitting descriptor when it came to Lincoln.

I gathered my air and collected myself to the best of my abilities in order to elaborate on the laundry comment while I silently contemplated his immense hotness. "Not *literal* laundry. Figurative. I'm sort of a mess."

"I know."

I wasn't sure if I should've been insulted or relieved by that.

"You know."

"You're sorta messy. Something happened to you when you were young, and I suspect that might've influenced your decision to pick up a stray, wounded creature."

"But I like Herb," I defended. I did. That dog was with me every waking moment when I was home. I enjoyed his unlikely companionship, and I thought he was pretty fond of me, too. Could've been the treats I snuck him that influenced that fondness, but I didn't mind. We had a mutual adoration for one another, whatever the reason.

"I wasn't referring to Herb."

Lincoln's finger reached out and swept across my jaw, just the tip of his nail gliding along my skin. My breath shook out of me in unsteady panting sounds and my toes and fingertips tingled. With his head cocked slightly, his eyes slanted, he took my chin between his thumb and index finger and tilted it up with the most gentle guiding, directing my eyes to angle toward his. "What on earth do you see in this sorry, wounded creature, Eppie?"

"I don't see any of your wounds."

Lincoln had said we all had more that we were hiding. Though I supposed it would make sense for him to be included in that all-encompassing statement, the truth was that Lincoln just seemed so together. If he had wounds, they'd healed and scarred over and I sure couldn't detect them at first, or even second, glance.

"You don't see my wounds, hmm? Well, I don't see your dirty laundry."

"Are we just blind then?" I laughed. Lincoln joined in, and his face lit up with that customary smile.

"I'm not blind, Eppie. I can just see just fine. And what I see standing here is a girl that I'm really quite fond of. One that I actually haven't been able to stop thinking about since I first saw her carrying a limp, bloodied dog into a veterinarian's office weeks ago."

"That visual doesn't make me out to be very attractive."

"Not sure what's more attractive than someone helping something so utterly helpless. It's like compassion in the purest form. That—to me—is incredibly hot."

"That's funny."

"I'm not kidding around, Eppie. I really like you. I've liked plenty of girls before, so I'm completely aware of these feelings inside me and what they indicate." Lincoln searched me out with his eyes. I didn't hide from them. I didn't even want to. "And I'd really like to kiss you, too. I've also had this feeling before, and it's the *everything in me is begging to kiss her* type of sensation," he chuckled and it was the best sound in the whole world. I'd record that sound and play it over and over again in my heart. "So far, there's only one known cure that I'm aware of."

The room was spinning just like that washing machine. I figured it didn't stop at just the room, and I assumed the entire house had been swept up in a *Wizard of Oz*-like tornado. Everything became a blurred mess around me.

I didn't figure we were in Kansas anymore.

"Can I kiss you, Eppie?"

I nodded my yes, several quick nods in a row, not quite sure how it was possible for my body to answer without getting permission from my mind first, but somehow it did. Bodies and minds must not always be connected. Or maybe my mind had lost the most recent battle in my warring body parts. Oh man, I was certainly out of my wits and felt no control over my limbs or body, either. It was all haywire.

Then, just as tenderly as he'd reached out, Lincoln lowered down to me again. I pressed in, my hips against his thigh. He stooped over, bending at the knees, bringing his face in line with mine, so our mouths were right there and ready for each other's. With both hands cupped softly along my jaw, he crept closer, diminishing the gap.

This was the part where I usually closed my eyes. When I'd kissed other guys in the past, I always had my eyelids sealed tightly shut, almost as a means to imagine they were someone else, I supposed. Sure, I'd had crushes before, but nothing that elicited the feelings in me that Lincoln did. I'd wanted to kiss those guys, but each time the build up never matched the end result. All the nervous visions and the waiting and the anticipation, it was all of the hype before the great let down. The hope of a passionate connection with someone always turned into a sloppy, clumsy mashing of too limp lips and too eager tongues. Nothing ever lived up to my daydreams, so I'd close my eyes to at least try to daydream someone, or something else, into being while the disappointment played out.

I didn't want to close my eyes with Lincoln. I needed them open, just to be sure of him.

And so we were right there—right in that place where personal space was no longer a real thing. We'd barreled through it, and it dissipated like vapor. Being like this—so near to someone's own furiously beating heart—caused panic to wedge in my throat. I figured I trusted Lincoln, but I wasn't sure how much I trusted emotion in general anymore. It had lied to me too many times before. The heart was often a deceiver.

"It's okay, Eppie," he whispered across my lips.

I nodded again, knowing it was. Hoping it was.

Then his mouth was on mine.

So softly, almost not even there at all. I wasn't sure if I should press in to feel more of him on my lips, but in the time I vacillated, Lincoln's warm hands on my face urged me closer. I gave up on trying to determine what would happen next and just let my body and my mind relax into the moment. Surrendering, my eyes slipped shut, not to block Lincoln out, but to focus on him so much more. Because it wasn't all about looks and attraction like it had been with the other guys. It wasn't superficial like that. It was so much deeper in a beneath my skin sort of way.

It was the buzzing in my fingertips that flared up when one hand slipped down to tangle with mine. It was the stutter of my heart as he slowly—almost methodically—tilted his head to approach the kiss from a different angle. It was the dizzied swirl in my brain when he let out the quietest of groans from the back of his throat. And it was the numb, weightless feeling in my bones when he took his other hand and splayed it across the small of my back, begging my body toward his.

Just as cautiously as he'd approached the kiss, he pulled back with a gentleness that almost made it hard to tell when it was actually over. Even now with our eyes open and locked and then flitting across one another's lips and skin and mouths and eyes again, it was still just as intense. The emotion clung to us and breathed out from us. The moment wasn't over. If anything, it had only begun.

"That was..." Lincoln spoke, swiping his thumb across his bottom lip.

"That was..." I echoed. Perfect. Innocent. Intense. Magical.

"Phenomenal." He slouched over and brushed his nose to mine. "In my opinion, it was absolutely phenomenal, Eppie. Just as I thought it would be."

He stood back up fully and swung his arms around me, pulling my head to his chest as he curled his shoulders over to cocoon me in the space there. And then I realized the most important advantage to being tall. One he'd failed to mention.

"Your heart..." I said, pressing my head in closer to his body. "It's right here." I pushed my palm to his white t-shirt, feeling the steady beats thrumming on my skin as I heard them pulsing into my ear, a unison of sensation. This was the best part by far, to hear and feel his heartbeat so close to me.

"It is," he smiled down at me. He grasped on to my hand with his own and threaded our fingers together. Squeezing and tapping them to his chest lightly, he said, "And yours is right here with it, too."

# FIFTEEN

"Beer?"

I could hear the popping suction of the refrigerator door as it pulled open in the kitchen, followed by the clinking of bottles when the door rattled back into place. I imagined penguins bowling in it and that the clinking sound was a strike, because that's what it sounded like to me. Someone had once told me not to "let all the penguins out" when I'd left the door open for too long, trying to decide on something to eat. I knew that was a weird visual, so I tried to stop thinking it and instead focused on normal thoughts like answering the question asked of me. Did I want a beer?

"Nah," I called out through the narrow, beige hallway separating us. There was a brass light fixture on the ceiling, its bulb darkened and gray, burnt out for who knows how long. "I'm good."

The small duplex had an actual mantel, and it was well decorated, which impressed me significantly. Bachelor pads typically repurposed traditional architecture like this into something more bachelor-y. Like converting bathtubs into oversized ice chests, or swapping out a kitchen table for a much more functional pool or foosball table. But this mantel was proudly fulfilling its intended purpose with over a half-dozen framed images perched on its wooden ledge.

I picked up one photograph and brought it closer to my eyes.

There were three guys, all decked out in ROTC gear on what looked like a freshly groomed football field, green and trimmed for an upcoming game. In the upper left corner of the picture, Old Glory was captured mid-flap as her Stars and Stripes twisted together in a frozen billow. The boys were smiling enormously with their high and tight cuts framing their innocent, youthful faces. It felt like an ad for America—all it needed was a hotdog and a bald eagle.

The wheels to Dan's chair squealed to a halt against the hardwood a few feet behind me.

"Who's this with you?" I pointed to the boy in the middle as I rotated the image for Dan to view. But he didn't look up, and I doubted he needed to. After all, it was his photograph.

The amber-colored bottle in his grip hissed as he popped the cap of it off. After a long guzzle, he swallowed, then cleared his throat.

"That was Charles."

It didn't take a detective to notice his choice of tense.

"You guys went to school together?" I studied the image. Though the two flanking Charles bore the obvious resemblance to Dan and Lincoln, they clearly weren't the same boys the picture depicted anymore.

There was so much hope captured in their eyes here. So much wonder. The worldliness that was so evident the moment you locked eyes with Dan hadn't existed when this shot was snapped. That must've been born at a later time in his life. If this picture was any indicator, it hadn't always been in him. "You all look so different."

"Yeah, I was a little taller then."

"That's not what I meant—"

"Calm down, Eppie. I'm only kidding. Trying to make a joke," he smiled, genuinely. "Coping mechanism. We all have them."

"Don't I know it," I sighed.

Dan gripped on to his right wheel and gave one forceful push forward, swiveling up to me and finally glancing toward the frame. "That was my senior year of high school. We three musketeers had high hopes at the point of blasting the terrorists into the next century. We planned to single-handedly save the Western World with our Uzis and our tanks and our indoctrinated patriotic mantras. It was a grandiose plan of heroically naive proportions."

I caught the slight exasperated laugh at the end of Dan's explanation.

"But didn't that happen?" I joked, as much as the moment would allow, I supposed. "Correct me if I'm wrong, but I remember you recently bragging about effectively securing the freedoms of all generations to come." I replaced the frame back to its home above the fireplace and turned to him. There was a couch close by so I dropped down to sit on the arm. The fabric was velvety and I ran my fingers over the edge as I spoke.

"Well, let's think about that for a minute. Lincoln's been stuck in this godforsaken town, I'm stuck without the use of my legs, and Charles is stuck six feet under." Dan threw back another gulp of his beer and laughed again, but this time it was maniacal and uncontrolled. It caused me to hold my breath. "You take a wild guess as to our success."

"Dan," I sighed, letting out a breath I hadn't realized I was holding.

"Before you say something that resembles 'I'm sorry,' please think for a moment, okay?" There wasn't much left in his bottle, but he took another pull from it. My dad would do that—drain every last drop from an already depleted bottle or can. Like he didn't want to waste any bit of that liquid courage. But maybe it wasn't courage they were gaining from it. Maybe it was something else entirely. "Because I've heard 'I'm sorry,' at least half a million damn times. And words like that lose their meaning when they're used up and abused."

"But what if I really am sorry?" I offered, because what I felt was exactly that. Maybe others had worn out the meaning in the word, but I hadn't yet. I still had plenty of apologies to give.

"What would you have to be sorry about? It's our own damned fault for thinking we could change something so much bigger than us." Dan dropped his now empty bottle to the glass coffee table. It spun like a top on its circular bottom before wobbling to a stop. He clamped his hands together in his lap and shook his head, defeat in his shoulders and in his tone. "Life is not meant to be a peaceful experience, I don't think. Don't know how we can be so arrogant as to believe that's something we could ever even achieve. When we're not warring with one another, we're warring within ourselves. When we no longer have enemies, we become our own. It's all a goddamned mess."

"I'm sorry." I meant it. I was.

"Don't be."

"But I am. I'm sorry that your experiences did that to you. Made you lose any hope that maybe we actually are meant to be happy in this life."

Dan threw back his head, groaning. "Listen, Eppie. I've heard about you. I know your own life isn't all unicorns and flowers."

"You're right," I nodded, shrugging in mock surrender. "It's actually pegasuses and balloons. Slight difference."

That got a well-placed laugh out of Dan, which made me a little proud.

"But just because you've heard my story," I continued, "doesn't mean you actually know it."

Reaching down into his chair, Dan retrieved another cold beer placed next to his hip, busted the cap, and brought it up to his lips. "And just because you think you can see mine," he said, right before he took a drink. "It doesn't mean you actually know it, either."

..............

"Honey, I'm home!" The front door slammed as Lincoln's voice trilled into the duplex.

"In here, sweet stuff!" Dan called out, a too high lilt to his voice. He did a really terrible job of impersonating a girl. Someone should give him some tips on that, I figured. Sam probably wouldn't be the best one for that task.

I could hear the rustling of grocery bags on the counter, followed by an almost melodic slam of cupboard doors as the bags' contents were placed onto the shelves. After just a few moments, Lincoln appeared in the hallway, still clad in his construction gear: a thin, white shirt and baggy, faded jeans that bunched up at the bottom as fabric accordions near his steel-toe boots. Effortlessly, without even having to push up at all, he unscrewed the light fixture and replaced the dead bulb with a brand new one; those energy efficient kinds that spiraled tightly like a mattress coil. Flipping the switch on the sidewall next to him, the hallway burst into brightness like the literal sun was trapped inside that bulb. This was the kind of light that required polarized lenses, and I had to squint against the glare.

"Wow. That's nearly radioactive," Lincoln said, shielding his brow with his forearm. "Might need to wear protective glasses and clothing when utilizing this hallway, but for now, it's all fixed."

"Thanks, man." Dan nodded his appreciation. "How was work?"

"Decent. Had a furry little mutt there to keep me company the whole time. He's currently snoozing in the camper. Didn't have the heart to wake him." Lincoln shot a smile my direction. It had been over a week since our kiss in the laundry room, yet the feeling he left me with then hadn't worn off at all. Every time those lips of his moved—whether to speak, yawn, honestly, even to sneeze—I was reminded of the power they had over my sanity. "Something I've been meaning to talk to you about actually, Eppie. Herb's really slacking. Like, he's absolutely useless with a hammer and you should see him wield a nail gun. Sprays those things everywhere in Terminator-like fashion. He's an utter occupational hazard. The boys are starting to complain."

"Maybe I should consult with the vet about that," I teased.

"In all seriousness, he probably is due to have someone take another look at that back leg." He slid down next to me in the empty space of the love seat, the outsides of our thighs pressing together as we sloped to the middle. We'd gotten past the weird triangular gap from weeks back, and now our appendages were allowed to do these sorts of things. His arm stretched out over the back and his hand curled around my shoulder, another allowed occurrence. "I've gotta work late all week at the site, but I can probably take him in next weekend."

"Nah, I have a minimum day on Thursday for AP testing prep. I can schedule an appointment."

Lincoln's hand squeezed against my skin. "So. I got everything for dinner," he spoke as he nodded his head back toward the kitchen. "What time are we planning to eat?"

We'd had this night in the works for a while now. Since our first official double date ended in a sad game of comparative tragedies, I figured this one could only go better. No way but up, right? Dan and Sam had been hanging out together daily, and while I wished that had been the case for Lincoln and me as well, homework and house building thwarted our attempts at scheduling any quality time. One thing we had done was exchange at least a dozen texts per day, as well as spent hours on the phone each night. I didn't figure Jimmy Fallon put Lincoln to sleep anymore since on more than one occasion, a long pause in our conversation would lead to the echo of deep, peaceful breathing on the other end. I put him to bed now. I liked that.

"I told Sam to come by at six after her shift at the food bank."

I looked toward the clock hanging on the pale yellow wall. That meant fifteen minutes.

"I'll get the water boiling."

"I'll help you with that," Lincoln smirked, coming up behind me as I rose to stand. His hand lighted on my waist as he gently pressed me forward. I had enough basic culinary skills to know that boiling water was sort of a one-man job, but I didn't complain.

"I'll just stay here and look pretty," Dan called over his shoulder. As I walked down the hall to the kitchen, I heard the television click on, and the occupancy of the family room increased a thousand fold as the roar of a stadium filled with elated fans blasted through the speakers. "Shit!" Dan yelled, clapping his hands together loudly. "Martin just hit a grand slam!"

I expected Lincoln to go racing out of the room, giddy with equal excitement, but instead he just echoed back, "That's awesome, man."

With question in my eyes, I looked up at him, almost concerned. "Aren't you excited about that?"

"Not really. I'm much more excited about me possibly getting back on first base with you." Spinning me around, Lincoln pinned me up against the kitchen wall, his hands bracketed on either side of my shoulders, trapping me in. He dropped down, his mouth hovering there, and popped his eyebrows up as he grinned.

Then his lips pressed to mine and all that replaying and daydreaming and fantasizing about our last kiss collided in my brain and tore through my nervous system. I was suddenly one gigantic exposed nerve. That couldn't be healthy.

"You are such a dork," I spoke as he pulled back for air.

"I know," he smiled against my lips. He came in for more, this time sliding his fingers into my hair at my neck. He cupped the base of my head, and then he pulled me up closer to him. I had to stand like a ballerina en pointe, but the way he coiled one hand tightly around my waist and the other at my neck nearly lifted me off my feet. Every surface on me pressed to him: my chest, my hips, the length of my legs. I was weightless as his mouth moved back onto mine, and just when his tongue attempted to tease apart my lips, Lincoln all but dropped me to the floor.

"Quit making out in my kitchen," Dan asserted as he loudly entered the room, his voice reaching us first. "You're going to contaminate the food. Totally unsanitary."

"Get back to your game." Lincoln ran his hands up and down my arms and kissed the top of my head quickly before releasing me to walk to the fridge. He pulled out all the fixings for our Caesar salad and dropped them onto the tile counter.

"The fact that you're choosing a girl over baseball pains me, Linc. *Pains* me." Apparently Dan was only in need of another beer because after retrieving one he made his way back to the family room, leaving us to our cooking or making out or whatever it was we planned to do. "You're a sell out!"

Ignoring his last jab, Lincoln just grinned and lit the stove and then placed a large metal pot that practically resembled a caldron onto it. There was one of those fancy waterspouts attached to the wall right behind the range, and he turned it on to fill up the pot.

"For a bachelor's pad, this is impressively state of the art," I acknowledged. And it was; there were so many random additions to this house that a typical duplex wouldn't normally have.

"Oh." Lincoln shut off the water and then bent down to find the salt in a lower cabinet just to the left. He scouted around a bit before locating it, and then he tossed a dash of it into the water over his shoulder as he flashed me a goofy grin. He really was a dork and that made me smile so big. "I had that installed for him. Being in construction has its perks. Usually someone always owes you a favor, so you can work out some pretty sweet deals."

"You did that for him?"

Lincoln's shoulders lifted a little. He was being humble, I could tell, but it wasn't necessary. "It's not a big deal, really. But what *is* a big deal is having to fill a pot to the brim all the way over there... " his finger flicked to the sink at the other end of the kitchen, "...and then carry it all the way to here if you happen to be in a wheelchair. Not super easy to maneuver with a ten gallon pot in your lap."

And that right there made me feel a little like I might actually be falling for this guy.

"You're a really good friend, Lincoln."

"I'm not. I'm just a relatively good kitchen designer." Humble people's shoulders must get really tired, because they sure did a lot of dismissive shrugging. "Plus, I love the guy. He'd do the same for me. Probably more."

I hadn't realized I was still smiling, but my cheeks began to hurt—tremble almost—and my lips were dry. Apparently everything about Lincoln produced a silly, wide-eyed grin on my face. "You think so?" I asked as I located the spaghetti noodles and a jar of red sauce that promised to be just like homemade. I placed them on the counter next to the stove and spun around to face him. Our eyes met instantly.

"Considering he nearly gave his life for another friend of ours, I'm pretty positive on that one."

"So dying for someone is the true test of love, yeah?" I wasn't saying it as a challenge, but more for clarification. I honestly wanted to know his opinion on this one.

Thinking for a moment, Lincoln looked down at me intently. His gaze softened and it felt like that first day again. That time when we were in my kitchen and he was sizing me up, reading me. Back when I wasn't sure if I wanted him to take a further look. Right now, I wanted him to stare so hard that he would be able to summarize everything about me in just one glance. I wanted to be discovered by him. I didn't want to have to do any of the necessary explaining myself.

Several moments of quiet passed and he paused, hesitating before he spoke. After a long breath released as a sigh he said, "Maybe not." He looked away, breaking our connected gaze and returning to the now simmering pot of water. "Maybe not, Eppie. Maybe *living* for someone is actually the truest test."

# SIXTEEN

*"These are absolutely horrible!" Mama chucked a burnt banana nut muffin across the counter and doubled over in laughter when it collided with the toaster. I laughed too, a little nervous at first, but when I realized she seriously thought it was funny, I allowed myself to let it out. "Oh my God, Eppie. How did we manage to ruin these?"*

*"I think the bananas were bad," I giggled, covering my mouth with my small hand. I spit the mushed up crumbs into my palm.*

*"Probably true," she said through her uncontrollable cackling. She hadn't laughed like this in so long. I really liked the sound of it. I'd forgotten it. "They sat on the counter for weeks. Maybe even a month!"*

*I couldn't even swallow the rest of the muffin, so I walked to the trash and spit out the remaining pieces into the garbage before sitting back down on my barstool. Those muffins tasted so bad, I wasn't sure I'd ever get the taste out of my mouth. We really messed that one up.*

*Dad was gone on another work trip and Mama and I thought it would be a good idea to make breakfast in our pj's and then lounge around the house watching Disney movies all day. It had been another sick week for me, and she never liked to push me too hard on those first days when I started feeling better. But I'd managed to keep my food down for the last 24 hours, though the banana muffins were questionable. We probably should've started off with something much more bland. Or at least more edible.*

*"You have any energy today?" Mama came around the breakfast bar and ran her fingers through my bangs. I had been trying to grow them out for the last month, but I wasn't very patient with things like that. Last night I took scissors to them and now I looked so stupid. Luckily, Mama didn't make me feel that way as her manicured nails combed through them gently. She made me feel pretty. "Feel like getting out of the house?"*

*"Yes!" I jumped down from the stool. Boy, did I. Being sick wasn't any fun, obviously. But not being able to get out was the hardest part. Luckily, this time I was able to stay at home and didn't have to go to the hospital. Last time I was really sick like this, they kept me there for almost two weeks while the doctors ran tests and I regained my strength. I would see all of these other kids without hair or in casts or on crutches and I wanted so badly to be them. Not because I necessarily wanted cancer or broken bones, but because I wanted a diagnosis. I figured knowing you had cancer had to be better than not knowing at all. At least then you'd be able to treat it, right?*

*So this last week I actually prayed for cancer. And then I prayed for polio. And then the flesh-eating bacteria I'd seen earlier in the news. I prayed for anything that I could find a word for, because so far there were no words when it came to me. Any illness or disease that affected your body—that was what I wanted. Especially since the doctors were moving away from those options and had started focusing on my mind. The body seemed easier to fix.*

*“Let’s do something amazing today, Eppie!” Mom clasped her hands together and held them to her chest. She looked like she could explode, but at the same time she looked like she was hugging herself. “Let’s get all dressed up and go out to brunch and then get our nails and hair done down at that fancy salon on Briar Street. Let’s be spectacular!”*

*That seemed like so much fun and Mama’s choice in words was so beautiful. We had never done anything like that together before and she made it sound so exciting.*

*“What do you feel like eating? We need something extraordinary to erase that terrible muffin memory.” She squeezed my shoulders and smiled so wide I thought her face would crack. “Anything. You name it.”*

*My answer didn’t take long. “I want an Eppie Fritter.”*

*Mama’s bright eyes squinted at the edges, crinkling them. “A what?”*

*“An Eppie Fritter. I think it’s a kind of donut or something. I saw them making them on the cooking channel this week when I was supposed to be resting. They looked really good.”*

*Her eyes rolled up into her head as she nodded and smiled even harder. “You mean an* Apple *Fritter,” she laughed. “Though an Eppie Fritter would be grand, wouldn’t it?”*

*I probably should've felt embarrassed for that mistake, but Mama didn't make me feel that way. Especially when she added, "Let's ask Miss Ruby if she can make a special change to her menu." Her face was full of life and she bounced on her heels as she spoke. "I think an Eppie Fritter is exactly what everyone in this town needs."*

# SEVENTEEN

"Why didn't you tell me Senior Ball was this weekend?" Lincoln flipped from his stomach onto his back, like a spatula scooped him up and rolled him over. It made me crave pancakes. Those would be really good right about now.

I peered over the edge of my bed and glanced at his body stretched out on my floor, still thinking of breakfast food. Early evening light sliced through the windows and left diagonal lines across the room, casting a warm hue on every surface, including Lincoln. He tossed a foam basketball I'd gotten years ago at some carnival up in the air, catching it and then throwing it skyward again. "That doesn't leave you much time to pick out a dress."

I closed my Chemistry textbook with a satisfying thud. "We're not going to the dance, Lincoln." We'd been dating for over a month now, but the thought of asking Lincoln to accompany me to a dance at a school that he never even attended made my stomach do painful flip-flops. That just wasn't going to happen.

"Are you embarrassed by me?"

That was laugh-worthy. "Um, no. Not at all."

"Do you have another date already?"

"Definitely not," I snorted.

"Are you worried that I will overshadow you with my impressive foxtrot and hypnotizing hip moves with my first-place-ribbon-winning samba?"

"Yes, that's exactly it. You got me."

Lincoln slid up and hooked his arms loosely around his knees. "'Cause see, the thing is that Sam and Dan are going, and Dan is so far out of high school. I don't know." His shoulders jumped up to his ears in a boyish shrug. This was a gesture of insecurity and Lincoln didn't wear it well. "I just sorta thought you'd want to go, too."

"I'm not sure I do. I mean, I don't know if a dance is something I want to do with you."

"You don't want to dance with me?" Lincoln's expression fell. "I want to dance with you."

"It's not that I don't want to dance with you. It's just I don't know if I want to *go* to a dance with you."

"I'm not understanding how those two things are different."

I thought for a moment about how to string my words together to have them make sense. "I don't really do extracurricular stuff."

"Like sports?" He was now rolling the ball back and forth on the carpet in front of him. My eyes looped around as the orange ball twisted under his hand. What he was doing now with that toy ball could even be considered more sport than anything I'd ever been a part of.

"No. I mean…sorta. It's just…I stayed home a lot when I was younger."

"Like, you were homeschooled?"

"No." I was doing a terrible job explaining myself. "Like, I just wasn't a super healthy kid. I was sick. A lot. And so I could never sign up for anything because I couldn't commit to a full season. Undoubtedly, I would end up sitting half of it out or spend the other half in the hospital."

"Wow." A lock of Lincoln's unruly chestnut-colored hair fell across his brow and he swept it back in place with the back of his band. "So we're not talking just the sniffles, are we?"

"No. We're not." I swallowed thickly and ran my sweaty palms over my comforter beneath me. I was certain I sounded like a freak. "So I've never been to anything outside of school, really. Including dances."

"And you don't want to change that now?"

Man, his honey eyes were mesmerizing. We weren't even talking about anything remotely suggestive, but that gaze he so freely gave me made all of my insides into mush. Oatmeal. Jeez, more breakfast food. I should probably eat something.

He smiled again. "I mean, since you're healthy and all. Cutting a rug with me isn't on your bucket list?"

"I don't know, Lincoln. I mean, yeah, I'd love to dance with you, but Senior Ball? It just seems like a lot of unnecessary money and shopping and obligatory awkwardness. I think I just might not be a high school dance type of girl. Plus, the responsible thing would be to save our money for Herb's surgery. We're getting so close."

"Well." He was up on his feet now, and he walked the two steps it took to reach the bed before dropping down on it next to me. "Then we definitely don't have to go. I agree, dances are excessively expensive." My heart stuttered at the notion that he knew this from firsthand experience. Of course Lincoln had been to proms and balls and dances before. Of course he had, because that was the normal thing for high schoolers to do. Of course, he was normal. "But I still want to dance with you."

He was swiftly up on his feet, though bowed a little, his palm up and hand outstretched. "Eppie," he smiled. "May I have this dance?"

"What?" I couldn't say this felt normal at all. We were in my room on a Friday evening, Lincoln in a blue flannel shirt and jeans and me in a gray hoodie and yoga pants.

"Dance with me, Eppie," he said, tugging me off the bed and up against his chest all in one choreographed move. "Don't make me beg."

"There's no music."

"Then we'll make some." One by one, he coiled each long finger into mine and then dropped his mouth into my hair, which he did a lot, like he was searching out my ear in my mess of curls, wanting to get his words as close as possible. "I happen to know a beautiful girl who has a magical voice."

Was he asking me to dance? Or was he asking me to sing for him? Or was it both, in which case, it felt like a pretty tall order. One I was sure I couldn't fulfill.

"This is so weird," I murmured into his chest as he began swaying gently side to side. And then I heard it. His heart pressed to my ear, thumping so erratically and off-beat that there was no way I could sing. The unsure rhythm would throw everything off kilter, like a broken metronome. "I can't do both. I can't be this close to you and sing, Lincoln."

"Because?"

"Because all I can focus on is your heartbeat, and it's all over the place." I leaned my head back to look up at him. "And so is mine. I can't sing like this."

"Then show me how you *can* sing."

I slunk out from his arms and flopped down on the bed again. With my right hand, I patted the mattress to have him join me, not ready to give up our physical closeness just yet. "What do you want to hear?" I'd never sung for someone before, other than the night at the construction site, but I wouldn't really even call that singing. It was only a few lines and a few notes. And it was spontaneous. This was practically a personal concert.

"What do you love to sing?"

"I don't love to sing."

Lincoln's forehead tightened, confusion settling in his dark brow. His mouth dropped open just a bit. "How can you not love to sing when even the angels must be jealous of your voice?"

I had no idea how to receive that compliment. I had no idea how to respond to anything Lincoln ever seemed to say or do. I had *absolutely* no idea what to do with this unreal boy in front of me. No idea whatsoever.

"I've never had a reason to sing other than to drown everything else out," I offered readily, but hesitantly at the same time, as strange as that was. My heart hurt to admit it with words more than it did to just secretly hold on to that truth within myself. "I never sang for pleasure. I always sang to cover up pain."

"What would you sing then? When you were covering up?" The edge of Lincoln's nail ran mindlessly along the inside of my forearm. When he got to my wrist, my fingers curled into my palm, almost reflexively. His finger trailed back down the soft flesh slowly, toward my elbow, and now my toes were tingling, another involuntary reaction to his tender strokes. This was weird. I'd become a kind of marionette, his instruction guiding my movements.

I cleared my throat.

"You know Lovely Oblivion?" I knew they were before our time, but I figured classics like theirs withstood that test. Lincoln nodded. "You heard of *Falling Stardust*?"

Again, he bobbed his head.

"Five in the morning and I'm lying awake," I started, my voice catching on to the melody halfway into the song, the part I knew the best. With my eyes closed, I crooned the words out from me in short lines and verses. "Breathing your memory on my skin.

Knowing when tomorrow begins, our once-forever will fade like the black of a life we were meant to share together."

I paused, then peeked from one slitted eye. Lincoln was staring directly at me.

My heart beat furiously out of time.

I inhaled quickly, picking back up to the chorus. "I can't fall for you anymore, 'cause I fell when I should have soared, and you couldn't catch me on the way down. My burden was a broken gift, and one that you couldn't lift. Some loves are best left to chance. But some lives are worth a second glance."

Lincoln cut me off.

"I don't plan to catch you the next time you fall, Eppie." His palm molded onto my face and his body slithered forward on the mattress. His forehead dropped to mine, but his eyes flickered ever so briefly toward the window. I tried desperately not to notice that. "I'm not even going to let you fall this time."

We'd never talked about it, but apparently he knew. Everyone knew. That was what happened when you grew up in a town like this. We all had a clear view of one another's clotheslines, strung out with our dirty laundry.

But knowing never led to reactions like Lincoln's. Knowing led to judgment and fear or avoidance and pity. Lincoln didn't show me any of that. All he showed me was who he was, and how maybe, just maybe, who *I* was might not be such a scary thing after all.

"No more falling, Eppie." His mouth, warm and soft, lowered to my temple. I could feel his full lips melt onto my skin as he pressed them there, kissing me.

But I was falling again.

I was falling hard, and this time, all I wanted to do was keep falling.

All I wanted was to keep falling into Lincoln.

# EIGHTEEN

**Lincoln:** You are cordially invited to the Ross residence tonight for an evening of pretentious conversation and foods so rich your bowels will need to join a philanthropic team heading to the absolute poorest of South American slums just to counteract its effects.

**Me:** I'm not sure how to reply to that invitation...

**Lincoln:** Oh, and I'll be there.

**Me:** Well, why didn't you say so? ;)

**Lincoln:** But so will my two older brothers—Rick and Tommy—and the two other people that created the three of us.

**Me:** That math has me confused.

**Lincoln:** Yeah, me too.

**Me:** Thanks for the invite. Sounds fun. I'm excited to FINALLY meet your family!

My fingers hovered over the touchscreen as I awaited Lincoln's reply, but this one took a few minutes longer to show up. All of his others were instant, like he was in the room with me and we were simply conversing back and forth. I glanced down at Herb in my lap and stroked my fingers through his thick fur as he let out a contented groan. Then my phone lit up again, buzzing in my palm.

**Lincoln:** My family is... Well, they're not much like me. And to be honest, they don't really like me much, either.

That seemed absolutely absurd. Every single person that came in contact with Lincoln appeared to love him. Adore him, even. How his own family wouldn't follow suit was beyond me.

**Me:** Well that's just plain crazy.

**Lincoln:** Crazy enough to be true.

**Me:** I look forward to meeting this bunch of crazies. Bring 'em on!

**Lincoln:** Don't say I didn't give you fair warning. They're completely embarrassed by me, and I just hope they don't transfer that same humiliation onto you. One out-of-line comment from them and we're outta there.

**Me:** Well, they should be embarrassed of themselves if they're embarrassed by you. Nothing about you is embarrassing.

**Lincoln:** Not even the sleepwalking in my Superman skivvies?

I chuckled and Herb looked up at me, his brown, sleepy eyes blinking. "Sorry," I whispered as my fingers punched the keys. I patted him gently on the head.

**Me:** I didn't know that about you, but even that doesn't seem all too embarrassing.

**Lincoln:** Not even when I watered the neighbor's petunias in said skivvies while sleepwalking? (Side-note: not sure it was actually water.)

**Me:** Well, maybe that—

The phone vibrated against my finger suddenly.

**Lincoln:** I'll pick you up at 4:30. Like you, bye!

**Me:** ...

**Lincoln:** Damn. That didn't really translate well, did it?

I stared at the phone, my heart tapping just a little bit faster.

**Lincoln:** Most people sign off with a very common four letter word, yeah? Well, since we're not at that point in our relationship yet, I felt like I should still say something meaningful. "Bye" didn't feel like enough. Though "I like you" isn't quite enough, either.

My heart was now beating much more than just a little bit faster.

**Me:** LOL. I'll see you in a few hours.

I waited, and then typed one last message.

**Me:** And I more-than-like, less-than-love you, too.

**Lincoln:** :)

...............

Lincoln's lips parted, the words he had ready to push through them getting lost on their way out. He shoved a bouquet of purple flowers toward me, and their petals of violet ruffles were all bunched together. I could smell them from where I stood on the other side of the threshold and it felt like spring just blossomed in the entryway. I scooped the flowers out of his grip and buried my nose in them, inhaling deeply.

"Wait," I said, eyeing him over the bright leaves, "these aren't the ones from your neighbor's garden, are they?"

"No," Lincoln smiled. His eyes dropped down to his shoes where he toed at the unwelcoming welcome mat. "They're from an actual store. You're safe."

"Good." I grabbed on to his hand and quickly pulled him through the house and into the kitchen. "Up there." Pointing a finger toward the cabinet above the fridge, I motioned for him to open it. "There should be a vase that's just perfect for these."

I was doing as he had suggested and taking advantage of his tallness, though I really wanted to take advantage of him altogether. He looked absolutely adorable in a button-down white shirt with a skinny black tie knotted around his neck. His jeans weren't his typical faded construction ones, but these were more fitted and darker in color, almost a true indigo. Lincoln sure did clean up quite well.

The bouquet fit perfectly into the glass vase, so I walked to the sink to fill it up with water.

"You look beautiful, Eppie." He came up behind me and put his hands on my waist as I pressed into the counter. "I've never seen you in a dress."

I spun around within his grip. "I don't wear dresses much."

"I don't wear ties much," he said as he twisted uncomfortably at his collar. His neck craned back and forth in a strained, robotic manner. "Evidently, something about spending time with my family makes us feel like we have to become something we're not, huh?"

"I don't know, maybe it's just..."

"It's okay." He looked down at me with the sweetest grin on his face. "I want to impress them, too, Eppie. I always have."

Lincoln's parents didn't live too far from my house. They were just on the outskirts of town, where the rolling fields picked up and tract homes left off and expanses of golden wheat and flowering cherry orchards lined every gravel country road. The only buildings that stood out here were the plantation-like homes with their massive white columns that stretched two stories tall, almost as though reaching to the sky.

Lincoln's house was one of those.

"Don't be nervous." He squeezed just above my knee as he killed the engine to the bus. We were parked in the U-shaped driveway, hedged in by green bushes as tall as the vehicle, and just a few yards from the door. "I wish I could say they're going to absolutely adore you, but my parents aren't quite like that. So you'll just have to settle with knowing that I do, okay?"

It was a slip up, to say he adored me. It had to be one, because Lincoln didn't even acknowledge the words as he jumped out of the camper and skipped over to my side to open the door for me. He bent at the waist in a bow and held one hand up to help me out of the vehicle, the other angling toward the mansion behind him. "Your evening awaits, my lady."

We were up on the porch in no time. How we got there I wasn't sure, but I was pretty certain I'd floated because being with Lincoln tonight made me unrealistically light and airy. He dropped three loud knocks on the solid wood door with a balled up fist, apparently not as airy feeling as me.

I could hear light footsteps skittering on the ground on the other side, and with a click of the lock as it turned over, the door swung open on its hinges. A man in a tuxedo stood in front of us, a tight grin on his lips. Somewhere in my head there was a faint, *Ta-da!* followed by the fashion police's sirens wailing as they came to haul me off because I was definitely underdressed.

"Lincoln," the penguin suited man said as he reached a white-gloved hand into the gap between them. "How nice to have you back at the estate."

This wasn't his dad, I didn't think. I knew he said things were off between them, but this formal introduction was nearly laughable. It was something out of a high society movie, rich with culture and ostentatiousness.

"Bentley." Lincoln nodded, and then pulled me closer and swung a lazy arm over my shoulder. "Nice to see you again. This is Eppie, my girlfriend."

Good gracious, I was on fire. Though I knew I was undoubtedly his girlfriend, hearing that definition fall from Lincoln's lips was the best sound I'd ever heard. I closed my eyes briefly just to block out one extra sense and focus on the pure ring as it funneled into my ears. I wanted to memorize it in my being and keep it there forever. *I was Lincoln's girlfriend.* Though he'd promised savory foods on tonight's menu, nothing would be sweeter than that introduction.

"Nice to make your acquaintance, Eponine." I stumbled slightly on his formal words and my footing as I edged toward Bentley to shake his hand. He didn't seem to notice my clumsy falter. "The family is out back."

Through the massive marbled foyer I could glimpse the opening into a living room. Windows climbed to the vaulted ceiling, and just beyond, a family of four was playing some sport involving wooden sticks and balls. Croquet, probably, though I'd never seen it played in real life. Between the pleated khaki pants and the meticulously starched polos, I was staring directly into a Ralph Lauren add, torn from the pages of a high fashion magazine.

And it was stunning. Truly. The smiles they wore and the laughter that echoed into the house made my stomach instantly warm. This was absolutely lovely.

"This way," Lincoln spoke as he pulled me through the house toward the back, getting me closer to the catalogue-like family display. The beginnings of the sun about to set filtered a haze into the room. Dust danced in the golden light and sparkled around him. I almost wanted to reach out and scoop it up into my hands. "This is your last chance to bolt."

"I'm not going to bolt."

His mother, a woman with tumbling blonde hair and rosy cheeks, giggled into a man's shoulder a few feet away. Their backs were to us, but I could see the joy radiating out of them like they were somehow in cahoots with that setting sun and the shimmery dust. They were positively glowing.

"This is amazing. Totally mesmerizing."

"We'll revisit that opinion of yours again two hours from now."

I wasn't sure my opinion would change, but I nodded and stepped through the French doors and onto the brick patio. As though we'd been formally announced over an intercom, Lincoln's parents swiveled around to meet our gaze while his two older brothers argued raucously over a missed shot, not acknowledging our presence in the backyard.

"Junior," a dark-haired man, tanned and just a few inches shorter than Lincoln, addressed. He slipped a hand out toward his son. Lincoln grabbed on and delivered the firmest handshake I'd ever seen. Clearly, he was trying to pulverize his father's hand.

"Eponine." Reaching two arms out toward me, Lincoln Senior (I assumed that had to be his name) folded me into his chest. The cologne in the fabric of his blue shirt stung my nose, though it had to be the most expensive brand out there. Yet something about it was just so unnatural. Definitely not the way a man would ever smell on his own. *Definitely* not how Lincoln ever smelled. "Welcome. I'm Lincoln, and this is my wife, Margot." Lincoln's mother grinned over his shoulder. She was a classic beauty—one that deserved to be on the silver screen with her flawless looks and radiant demeanor.

"Nice to meet you." My words shook out of me, vibrating with the nerves I tried to keep down but failed. I'd never been introduced to a guy's parents before. "Thank you for inviting me over. You have a lovely home."

Lincoln's fingers were low on my back.

"Richard, Thomas!" Mr. Ross called out. His mouth was megaphoned with two much-too-womanly hands. "Come say hello to your brother and his friend."

The young men dropped their game and jogged over to the patio where we'd gathered. One was significantly shorter than Lincoln, just a few inches taller than me, and he had thick dark hair that landed over his brow and was parted in a sharp line on the side. The other had light hair and eyes, taking more after their mother, and he stood almost eye-level with Lincoln as they hugged and roughed-up one another's hair the way boys often did.

"Hey, brother," the taller of the two chimed. He shrugged out of their half-embrace, then turned to me. "I'm Rick. Nice to see our littlest bro has finally brought someone home to meet the 'rents."

I didn't know how to answer that other than to blush. I guessed blushing was answer enough.

"I'm Tommy," the dark-haired one interrupted. His teeth were so white. He had to be a dentist. It was almost one of those *don't-look-directly-at-them* moments. His smile was very nearly an eclipse. "And I'm in agreement. This is a first for Lanky." Though he had to practically jump to do it, Tommy swatted the side of Lincoln's head playfully. "Presentable clothes and a presentable girl? Not too shabby."

The brothers rotated away from us to head back to their game while Lincoln's parents scooped sparkling flutes from a tray balanced on Bentley's hand, which had materialized out of nowhere it seemed. It almost looked like the glasses were filled with that glittery dust from inside the house, just in liquid form.

"Lanky?" I mouthed through a giggle to Lincoln when all eyes were turned from us.

"Don't ask," he groaned. He ushered me with his hand toward a bistro table and chairs just to the side of the artificial grass turf. I hopped up to sit on one of the tall stools. "Is this still as amazing as you originally pegged it?"

"It really is."

Bentley came up to our table next and offered the tray. Crystal glasses etched with geometric lines tossed rainbows across anything within a two-foot radius. I waved my hand to him, thanking him, but declining. "I'm fine for now. Thank you, though."

Lincoln lifted a flute and then rested it on the tabletop once Bentley slipped back into the house. He twirled the stem and reflections of color streaked across his neck and face. I'd never seen him drink before, so I figured it was just a polite gesture—one that went along with the overly dressy attire, and one that tolerated being called childhood nicknames by older brothers that truly didn't act much older at all. This was keeping up appearances at its finest.

"They put on a really good show, believe me."

"I know how that goes," I said. "But your family's show is so much more sophisticated than mine."

Lincoln's father walked toward us, about to guide us inside for the commencement of dinner, I assumed. It seemed fitting for there to be a formal invitation to gather around the table. Before he began speaking, though, Lincoln groaned under his breath, nearly silent, but audible enough for me to hear, "Oh, Eppie. I wouldn't be so sure about that."

# NINETEEN

I'd almost had enough. Part of me wanted to dramatically slam my napkin to the table, push up from my seat, and make a beeline toward the front door, Lincoln in tow.

But I continued to wait on Lincoln's cues, just like I had been for the past hour. He wasn't ready, I could tell. So I waited.

It was an hour filled with stories of prestigious articles in the top educational publications and medical heroics in poverty-stricken countries and galas held at the country club to raise funds and awareness for local children recently diagnosed with untreatable cancers. All good things on their own. All incredibly admirable things when discussed in isolation. But when they were paraded in front of you, one after the other, accompanied by excessive applauding and self-congratulatory toasting, it became a production.

So I completely understood what Lincoln meant when he'd said it was all a show, and it was one they didn't even give him the opportunity to play a part in.

"Lincoln gave me a walk-through of the most recent house he's been building," I said as I pushed the strips of filet mignon around my plate with my fork. Lincoln had also told the truth when he'd said the food would be overwhelmingly rich. My gut ached just looking at the remnants of my meal in front of me. "It's gorgeous. He's very talented with that tool belt. I was beyond impressed." I smiled, reaching my hand under the table to squeeze just above Lincoln's knee. His frame tensed, and I could see the evident waiver in his composure.

Above the rim of his wine glass—almost drained to the bottom with merely a splash of red wine left within it—Mr. Ross said, "I take it you're quite easily impressed, then."

This is where Lincoln's mother would jab her husband, silencing him with an admonishing look or furrowed brow. That's what most people would do, right? So I wasn't at all prepared for the chuckle that passed through Margot's lips. I was even less ready for the agreeing nod that she delivered as she rubbed her husband's back in slow circles.

"If you really want to see something impressive," he continued, swaying his glass in front of him as his upper body followed. "We should spend some time watching Richard's latest documentary on his recent travels to Malawi." He turned sharply in his seat to face his eldest son. "How many nods did that get at the Crest Film Festival?"

With more smugness than I'd ever seen on any one person alone, Rick shrugged apathetically and said, "Four. Unless you count Desmond Pointelle's literary lovefest in the Sun Tribune as an actual nomination, which obviously no one ever would."

I had no idea what any part of that sentence meant, but clearly the rest of the table was fluent in the language of pretentiousness, and they erupted in laughter so loud that, for a moment, I worried the crystal in Lincoln's father's hand might actually shatter into pieces.

I couldn't dismiss their attempt to shove Lincoln completely aside any longer.

"Those sorts of things don't actually impress me much," I began, my hand still planted firmly on Lincoln's thigh. The tablecloth brushed against my skin. "I'm much more taken by someone who not only builds homes for a living, but helps make his own home a comfortable living space for his roommates and friends."

"Oh, lord." Margot's hand flew to her forehead and an exaggerated eye roll accompanied her sudden movement. "Please don't tell me you're referring to Daniel Stewartson."

"That boy would have been better off coming home in a pine box if you ask me," Lincoln's father huffed. He tilted his glass to his lips and paused there for a moment, contemplating how to come across as an even bigger ass, I could only assume. "His current situation has to be a constant reminder of what a failure he was on that horrific mission."

Bile rose in my throat. The look on Lincoln's face matched the acid that stung the back of my tongue.

"I thought I told you never to talk about anything having to do with Daniel or the war in this house ever again," Lincoln seethed. It was the first sentence he'd uttered in the last hour, and his voice was gravelly and strained like he hadn't used his vocal chords in months. Like it hurt to finally speak.

"Oh please, Lanky," Tommy chimed in from his position opposite us at the long table. "Like you have any stake in it at all. You couldn't even get yourself recruited into the damn army to begin with. Seriously, how hard do you actually have to work to have them deny you? Don't they take just about anyone with a U.S. citizenship?"

My stomach burned within me and the overly potent dinner worked its way up my throat.

"Now, now, Thomas," Margot cautioned. A little piece of me eased back into my seat, grateful and hopeful for some motherly wisdom. Finally. "It was Lincoln's asthma that kept him from joining the military."

"Asthma," Rick shrugged. He held one hand out at his side, the other one just a little bit lower on the other, like a balance. He alternated their positions, back and forth. "Panic attacks. Same difference, right?"

Mr. Ross groaned. "Honestly, Junior. Those attacks were the absolute best thing that could have ever happened to you. Though Stewartson might be a tragic hero in some people's eyes, you'd likely never even have made it home at all. And what would that do to your mother?" He cast a thoughtful look Margot's direction and squeezed her shoulder delicately with those creepy lady hands of his. "To lose a son? The worst possible fate. The worst."

I couldn't read Lincoln's expression. It transitioned too quickly, a blur of emotion on his face. It went from angry, to wounded, to spiteful, to apathetic all in one glance.

"But I suppose your own parents knew a little about the scare of that reality, didn't they, Eponine?"

I'd introduced myself as Eppie—I knew I had—yet they'd continuously addressed me as Eponine throughout the course of the entire night. This obviously wasn't their first introduction to me. How had I missed that? How hadn't I known?

My heart raced within my ribcage. Sweat gathered on my upper lip. I bit down hard on the inside of my cheek, which hurt quite a bit, and blood sprinkled into my mouth.

"I'm sure your mother was terrified that night when she thought she'd almost lost you." His eyes burned into mine. Where Lincoln's were a warm, golden brown, his father's were so dark the irises could hardly be detected within their blackened hue. If a devil were to exist, this had to be his twin, no question about it. "Though I do wonder if she was even able to decipher her own emotions, really. I imagine the amount of medication they'd placed her on would lead to some sort of convolution of realities, wouldn't it?"

The gasp that slipped out gave up any ounce of power I might've had. I was caught off-guard, but I figured that was the plan all along. Words should have readied themselves, a defense should have formed, but all I could do was fight back the sting of tears that pressed into my eyes and scratched through my raw throat. I didn't even have the chance to get into fighting mode; I'd instantly gone into survival instead.

He didn't stop talking. "But maybe when you're that ill, you don't have to face those truths head on." Lincoln Senior's glass was empty, yet he still held it between his fingers. Lifting it to his face, he gazed my direction. Like the mirrors in a funhouse, his image was distorted and twisted, a mangled display of taught lips and sharp, ridged eyebrows. To look directly at him muddled my already confused brain, so I broke our stare-down and held my eyes on Lincoln, hoping for some transfer of courage to occur.

But Lincoln looked just as distressed as I was. He couldn't offer me anything.

"Is that how it worked, Eponine?" Lincoln's father continued, cocking his head exaggeratedly to the side. "When you lose your mind, do you get the luxury of forgetting that your very own daughter tried to take her life?" he asked. He leaned his body over the table. "I suppose after all these years it doesn't truly matter anymore. But if that was the case..." The points of his elbows dug into the surface like two sharp daggers. He paused, drawing out each word as though it were its own sentence, continuing, "If that was the case, doesn't that just... make...you...*sick*?"

In a movement that occurred so suddenly I could hardly pinpoint what was even happening, Lincoln's fingers grasped on to my hand and he pulled me from the table, racing toward the foyer in the longest, loudest strides. The early evening air blasted against my cheeks when the door flew open, and as we raced down the driveway to the bus, the wind whipping at my skin felt like thousands of little needles driving into my tender flesh. I wanted to believe that was the real reason I was crying, but I knew the pain wasn't physical. I shoved the heel of my hand to my eyes and twisted them back and forth like a screw, hoping to keep the tears in place, but they wouldn't obey.

We were in the VW and on the road in a rush, and Lincoln's silence hung in the air like that familiar thick weight of humidity before a storm. It made my skin clammy and my breathing shallow as I tried to fight through the thoughts that crashed noisily in my head. I wanted to shake everything out of it—to erase the past two hours and the spiteful words spoken around that dinner table. Mostly, I wanted to erase them from Lincoln's memory. I wanted to go back to a point in time, just earlier this afternoon, when he'd never heard those phrases and truths. I wanted to go back to when he was blissfully ignorant and possibly in more-than-like, less-than-love with me.

Though he didn't speak, his heaving chest and frustrated air that rhythmically left and returned to his body communicated, independent of his wordlessness. His movements were maniacal, and when he suddenly screeched to a halt, swinging the camper onto the dirt shoulder with clouds of dust billowing around the vehicle as though smoke from a raging fire, my heart stopped just as abruptly as the engine.

Throwing the door open, Lincoln burst from his seat and ran out into the waist high fields. Grain crunched underneath his feet like popping glass. I hesitated for just a moment, eyeing him through the dirty windshield, and then I was out there with him, racing up behind. His back was to me; his broad shoulders shook under his white fitted shirt. Like undoing a tourniquet, Lincoln ripped the tie from his neck and threw it to the ground. Then he doubled over at the waist with his palms to his knees, dragging in air sharply in painful, sucking sounds.

I panicked, not knowing what to do. "Your inhaler!" I finally shouted. I figured I could race back to the camper and grab the one I knew he kept in his glove box. I could do that for him. I could make this better.

"I don't need my damn inhaler, Eppie," he almost growled. Still not facing me, Lincoln fought out the words through desperate gasps of air. His entire frame trembled. "It's not an asthma attack."

I couldn't speak, and I wondered if that was my reaction, like how Lincoln's was to stop breathing. I had no words, he had no air. So there we stood, mostly silent except for the grating gasp of Lincoln attempting to get his lungs under control.

I'd rather us be screaming at one another, truthfully.

That once-magical sunlight was slipping away into the horizon beyond us, dropping quickly out of the sky. But it didn't feel golden and warm anymore. It burned like an inferno, sweltering and suffocating. I fought against its heat, but sweat coated my skin and fever rushed through my body in nauseating tumbles.

"Lincoln," I spoke. I reached a hand out to him, needing to touch him, but then tugged it back into myself and crossed my arms instead, unsure. He still wasn't facing me. It was like he couldn't look at me. It was like he couldn't be near me. It was like I'd ruined everything before we even had a chance to start.

Swallowing felt similar to razorblades slicing through my gullet, but I managed one and tried to speak again. "Lincoln, I'm so sorry," I actually cried. "God. I'm so sorry I humiliated you back there."

Tears shouldn't be audible. They should slip silently down your face without making themselves known in any other form. They already gave away so much just through their presence alone. But when they coupled with your voice and added hiccups and gasps into your speech, it was more than crying.

They should have a word for that, when your whole body cried.

Maybe they did. Maybe it was hysteria.

Maybe I was hysterical.

It was as though all sound was sucked out of the world as we stood in the field. No birds crowing, no cars driving by. The only thing I could hear in our pause was my failed effort to keep my tears silent. Even Lincoln's breathing had regulated slightly. It was almost completely still.

And then the grit of dirt under his shoe echoed against the rubber tread as he turned slowly around.

His eyes did more than just look at me. He'd used them before to read me, but now it was as though he needed me to read him. Tears welled up in them, and the lines already streaking down his face in salty rivulets tore my heart open and then shredded it right in front of me. His eyelashes were slick and stuck together and he swiped a finger across his nose as he sniffed back his emotion. When his mouth opened, I expected the words to blast out of him, charged from that scene back at his parents' house and the getaway in his bus. But they didn't. They were silent, barely audible. He took two small steps toward me. My chest tightened and my hands shook.

"Is that what you think?" he whispered. "That you humiliated me?"

Tucking my quivering bottom lip into my mouth, I bit down and nodded.

"You can't be serious." These were angry words, but still, he didn't shout them.

He had both hands on my shoulders. For a moment, the tense look in his eyes made me think he was about to shake me. About to shake me out of my senses, about to shake some sense into me. But that was projecting again. Like Phil so often reminded me, I had the horrible habit of doing that.

Lincoln didn't do those things.

Pulling me into his chest, he buried me in his arms and clung to me so hard that my lungs gasped for air as my body crushed against his. His pulse matched the rhythm of mine completely and I couldn't decipher whose was whose; they'd morphed into one. He raked his fingers over my back, into my hair, down my neck, his movements frantic, anxious. I gripped onto his waist and wound my arms so tightly around him that I felt like they could wrap around twice. If I just held him there, if I never let go, then he wouldn't be able to leave. He wouldn't be able to leave me if I didn't let him.

Then Lincoln's lips were on my skin, just as frantic as his fingers had been. They pressed onto my forehead, my cheek, the corners of my eyes, kissing away my tears, over and over. But the more he did so, the more they spilled, and I also felt the ones falling from his eyes as they skimmed down my cheeks when he dropped kiss after kiss onto my skin. Even our tears kissed one another.

"I'm so sorry," he started saying in between presses of his mouth to my face. "I'm so sorry, Eppie."

I couldn't understand this. I couldn't understand why he would apologize when I was the one who brought all of this about.

He cried out the words, as softly as the water that continued rolling down his cheeks. "I'm so sorry I brought you there. I knew better." Another kiss into my hair. "I said you wouldn't fall, but instead I just watched as I let them push you completely over the edge." He gripped my jaw with his hands and pulled my eyes up to his. If I hadn't been crying before, this would've sealed that fate. The pained tightness in Lincoln's voice and the deep hurt held in his eyes was more than I could take. I shook my gaze from his, but he forced my eyes back up. "Look at me," he demanded, though his volume remained quiet. "Look at me, Eppie."

"They think we're all crazy, Lincoln."

His eyes narrowed. "I don't care what they think." He grabbed my face again because I'd let it fall back away from him. "They're also the ones who think Dan would be better off dead. I'm sorry, but I don't get my mental stability assessments from them."

I slunk further into his arms. My body was giving up at the same time as my mind. Everything was shutting down. Or maybe it was finally starting up. It was a weird in-between.

"But they're right. About her. About me." I felt each piece of who I really was slipping out in my words. I felt the truth beating in my chest and pumping through me. "She was ill, Lincoln. It's been nearly ten years. I've never even once visited her." I couldn't believe I was telling him this. I'd never told anyone this. "They say she's crazy because she actually *was* crazy."

"And you think they're not?" Lincoln's chin tucked back sharply into his neck. His tone was accusatory and sudden. "You think *they're* not crazy?"

I gave him a blank stare.

"Maybe not clinically, but it's crazy to belittle someone you just met. No sane person does that."

I stroked at his jaw, swiping away a damp tear with the pad of my thumb. I held it there, not wanting it to coat his skin anymore, but needing to feel his raw emotion again on my own flesh somehow. I rubbed my thumb and index finger together until it was blotted away. “It’s also crazy to belittle someone you’ve known your entire life. Your own flesh and blood.”

Lincoln closed his eyes and shook his head. “They’ve always been that way, Eppie. They’re the first to throw stones. The first to point out faults. I’ve dealt with it my whole life. And I should’ve known they would do it to you. I’m not like them, and they hate that. They don’t love me like they love their political ideologies and their upper class mentalities. They just don’t love who I am and what I represent. Or maybe what I don’t represent. They never have.” It surprised me that the tears had stopped, because if anything, this felt like the time for crying. But maybe all of Lincoln’s tears had already been used up over this. Maybe he didn’t have any left. It made me grateful to have kept just one of them for myself—to tangibly feel what he felt in that vulnerable moment. “They don’t love me, so of course they could never accept someone I love.”

There was no mistake in his words here. Lincoln knew what he was saying, and I was in tune with every syllable.

“I’m just so sorry that I thought things would be different.” The grain waved around us, brushing against my bare legs. Crickets chirped and dusk had completely fallen. The sky was a watercolor painting of purples and blues that splashed over us in a canopy of pastels. I shivered in Lincoln’s arms, so he pulled me in closer. “I was hopeful, though, you know?” His voice caught. “I was hopeful that they would see what I see in you, Eppie. That they would recognize how different you are from them. That you would be their epic revelation or some sort of realization that all of their beliefs about what truly mattered were wrong. That somehow, meeting someone like you would make them human again. Some kind of beautiful metamorphosis."

I laughed against his chest. "That's a lot of pressure to put on me, don't you think?"

"No, I think it's actually more pressure to put on them. To ask them to suddenly change into something they never even were to begin with. I should've known they'd never be capable of such a dramatically positive transformation."

I shivered again and Lincoln took notice.

"Come on," he said. "Let's get out of here."

I nodded. There was more dark than light around us now, and the cold crept in with the sun's exit.

"Where do you want to go?"

"Home."

It was strange that the first day I'd met Lincoln, I'd told him I was still searching for home. But I didn't think I was searching anymore. It turned out that what happened within those four walls didn't make it any less of a home. I wasn't sure home was always meant to be a happy place. I think it was just the place where life was lived out.

Because life wasn't always happy. I gave Dan a hard time about that—about letting his experiences shape his hopes and his happiness. But I think that's exactly what they did. I didn't know how I could have ever thought otherwise.

So I wanted to go home, even though my home wasn't all that different from the home Lincoln was raised in. We all had our own brand of crazy. But for the first time in my life, I preferred the crazy I grew up with.

"I'll take you back to your place. I just want to stop by the duplex and grab one thing first."

"What's that?"

"My guitar," he said as we trampled through the tall grasses. "I think this time we're going to need more than just your voice to drown out this latest dose of pain."

# TWENTY

*"There's nothing wrong with her!"*

*I watched the blinds on my window. How could they possibly shake when no one was even touching them?*

*"Dammit, Mark!" Mama screamed. The window didn't shake when she yelled. I looked, but it didn't even rattle. Her scream was less screamy than Dad's. "You're not the one who takes her to all of the appointments! You're not the one who holds her hair back when she's up at two in the morning! You're not the one who has to tell her she can't go on the field trip to the tide pools because she's too weak and it isn't safe! You're not the one who is there for her,* I *am!"*

*My blanket slipped from my shoulders. I knew I was too old for a blanket. Most eight-year-olds didn't need one anymore. And I probably didn't need it. But I still wanted it, and luckily, Mama rescued it from the garage sale box last summer before Dad had the chance to set it out on the driveway.*

*"I think I'm too old for a blankie, Mama," I'd said, hoping she'd disagree.*

*She did just that. "Oh, Eppie. It's not a blankie." She swung it over my shoulders and knotted it loosely at the neck, then admired me with her head tilted. "It's a gorgeous knit shawl, lined with the finest satin. All the rage for fall, I hear."*

*I'd pulled it tighter to my small frame.*

*"Thank you."*

*"Of course, dah-ling." Her grin was genuine and wide. "Anything for fashion," she'd winked.*

*Mama and Dad continued screaming downstairs. I hugged the blanket around me again, wrapping under it like it was clothing.*

*"I'm going out." I heard Dad's keys jingle from their hook on the wall. "I can't do this with you any more tonight."*

*"I think you have a problem, Mark." Mama's voice was much louder than earlier. I didn't like the sound of it when it was this loud. It was like her volume was turned all the way up. "You're drinking more and more lately, and I don't think it's healthy."*

*The silence that followed hurt my ears more than their actual screaming. I wondered what they were doing in that silence. I wondered what their faces looked like when they yelled at each other like that, but I wondered even more when it was quiet.*

*"Oh, I'm sorry," Dad's voice boomed suddenly, but he didn't sound sorry at all. "You think* I'm *the one with a problem now, do you? You think* I'm *the one that's not healthy?"*

*"Mark." She said Dad's name like she was begging for something, like how you would say the word please. "Mark! Mark, don't do this."*

*"I'm not* doing *anything, Gloria!" The front door squealed open. The hinges had been squeaky for so long. Dad kept forgetting to fix that. Maybe now he would remember. "I'm not doing a damn thing, and that's the whole goddamn problem!"*

*I cringed and my tummy twisted sharply. I didn't like that word. It sounded so ugly and scary in the tone of Dad's voice. It sounded mean, and I didn't like that he was being this mean to Mama.*

*I plugged my ears and started to hum.*

# TWENTY-ONE

"I want you to meet someone." I slammed the door to the vehicle behind me as I lowered into the seat. The leather was hot on my skin, and even though it was just the beginnings of spring, it was unseasonably warm. "His place is just a few streets over. Off Crescent."

Phil glanced across the console, his eyes covered in those awful aviator sunglasses. I should tell him they weren't doing his aged face any favors. That's what a true friend would do. "Is this the maybe-boyfriend of yours that you're having lots of underage sex with?"

"Yes to the first, no to the second."

"That's a relief. Just had to check."

I dropped my messenger bag to the floorboards and relaxed into the seat.

"So tell me about him," Phil said, eyes forward. "Gimme a five sentence synopsis of this guy."

"Five sentences?" I thought for a moment. How could you summarize someone who stole both your heart and your senses in one short paragraph? "He's tall and works construction."

"That's one."

"He's prone to panic attacks that his family historically covered up as asthma attacks."

"Two."

I thought for a moment, realizing I hadn't really described Lincoln much with those two wasted phrases.

"When I'm around him, everything wrong in the world flips around to being right."

Phil slipped his glasses down and eyed me above their gold rims. "Three. Now we're getting somewhere."

"He's loyal to his heart and his friends, and likes to rescue both dogs and people from distress."

"Four." Phil nodded. "And very interesting. A modern-day knight in shining armor of sorts."

I waited a moment as I worked to unscramble the many words fit to earn the prestigious title as Lincoln descriptors. Then I had it. "He knows about my mom and he knows I'm messy and have loads of baggage but I think he might actually be falling in love with me, despite all those things."

Wrinkles creased Phil's forehead. His lips pursed tightly and his teeth moved behind them like he was literally chewing on his thoughts. "Very good, but I think you have that last one all wrong, dear. I think he's likely falling in love with you *because* of those things."

"Who falls in love with baggage?"

"Oh, Eppie." Phil took the glasses off and tossed them onto the dashboard. Good call. "You don't ever fall in love with the current version of someone, because I hate to burst your pretty little bubble, but that doesn't exist. We're the summation of our histories, so if this guy is truly falling in love with you, he's falling for your past as much as he's falling for your present."

Somewhere along the way, I figured Phil stopped adhering to his psychological textbooks and began formulating his own non-professional opinions. I liked these ideologies much more than some of the others he'd offered me over the years.

We pulled up to Lincoln's house five minutes later, and he was already waiting for us on the porch. Both Herb and Dan were with him, and Dan waved with his hand, Herb with his tail, as Lincoln bounded down the tiered walkway toward Phil's Datsun.

I got out of the front seat to give up my chair, but Lincoln grabbed on to the lever at the base to fold it over and slide into the back, letting me keep shotgun. Like Phil pointed out, he really was a gentleman.

"Lincoln." Phil's hand shot over the chair between them and Lincoln shook it, a casual, friendly shake. "Nice to meet you, buddy."

"Likewise," Lincoln smiled. "Eppie's told me a lot about you."

Giving me a fake, wary glance, Phil narrowed his eyes. "All *good* things, I assume?"

"Oh, Phil," I teased. "You know what happens when you assume."

"Yes. Someone makes an overdone, trite joke about the spelling of a commonly used verb."

A laugh burst out of Lincoln from the backseat. "I like this guy already."

Phil glanced to the review mirror to safely make eye contact. "Feeling's mutual, son."

I caught Lincoln off guard. I'd told him we were going out with Phil, and he probably figured we'd be heading off to an early dinner or a cup of coffee down at Roast House. When we edged up to the newly completed two-story home Lincoln spent the last six months working on, confusion draped across his face.

"We're here!" I sang as I jumped out of the car. I waited for him to stagger out, my hand hooked over the door. I wasn't sure how the speed of his movements was at all affected by the fact that he didn't understand why we were here, but it was. He was like a turtle walking through glue as he climbed out of that backseat.

"And what are we doing here?"

Phil put those stupid glasses back onto his face and shaded his eyes with a flat hand to his forehead. "Eppie tells me you work construction."

Still, Lincoln looked about as confused as they come.

"I used to do a little building myself when I was right around your age. Before I headed off to college to get a degree that would later lead me into a life of picking apart pieces of other people's lives, only to slowly build them back up. So, sorta still in the building industry, but not quite."

"O-*kay*." My goodness, Lincoln's words were just as slow as his pace today.

"I wanted Phil to see what you do, Lincoln." I threaded my fingers through his and wrapped my other hand around his elbow. "I want you to show him around."

"It's really not all that impressive." The recycled words that his father spoke just the other night made me cringe. I hated that he latched on to that lie so freely.

"Shut up, it is!" I slugged him, but Lincoln wasn't at all prepared and he doubled over when my fist connected with his gut.

"I'd love to see it." Phil was great. I appreciated that he wasn't even playing along. He truly did want to view every square foot of the house that stood in front of us, no humoring necessary. "Let's take a look."

Hesitantly, Lincoln walked us up to the home and punched a few numbers into the lockbox. He gave me an uncertain look as he pulled the key from it and shoved it into the groove as the metal gripped and the lock turned over. The door swung open silently and the smell of fresh, probably still-wet paint met us. I inhaled deeply and took in the beautiful architecture and natural light that flooded through the windows. It was absolutely gorgeous, the most beautiful home I'd ever seen. And Lincoln had built it. Way to go, big time.

"A tour?" Phil suggested, his hand splayed out in front of us.

"Sure." With a nod, Lincoln complied. I could see a flicker of excitement that I hoped was also mixed with pride flash through his eyes. "Let's start with the office first. I did most of the finish work in that room. Come on, just down that hallway."

..............

"Oh my God, Eppie, you should've seen it! Her dress was classically atrocious in a 1980's after school special sort of way," Sam said, her voice loud enough for the couple in the next booth over to hear her every word. Even still, Lincoln, Dan, Phil, and myself all leaned closer over the table as she spoke, enthralled. She tossed another French fry into her mouth and chomped down. "Rhinestones, sequins, taffeta *and* some sort of reflective, iridescent crap. She was practically a disco ball wrapped up in a big bow. Totally hideous prom queen material right there."

"I thought she was ravishing," Dan mocked. Not missing a beat, Sam's elbow rammed into his side. "But nowhere close to the near-goddessness of you, Samantha."

"Samantha?" I choked on my Diet Coke, liquid sputtering between my lips.

"I'm trying it out," she shrugged indifferently as she twirled a strand of magenta hair around her finger. "Aren't these the years of self-discovery? Shouldn't we be finding ourselves and all that proverbial coming of age jargon?" Sam cast her eyes over to Phil. He was wedged in between Lincoln and the window, and as uncomfortable as both the seating arrangement and the juvenile conversation should've made him, he didn't appear uncomfortable in the least. "Am I right, Dr. Phil?"

"It's not Dr. Phil. Just Phil," he corrected through a smile. "And I don't necessarily think self-discovery is limited to the teenage years. Learning about one's self is a linear, forward moving thing." He'd already lost Lincoln completely to his dinner, and Dan was a close second as he pushed his mac and cheese around with his fork. But both Sam and I held on to his words and paid attention, ignoring the lukewarm meals that lingered in front of us. "I don't know about you, but I just found out that I'm a huge fan of the Spamwich." Phil held up a half-eaten meaty thing pressed between two pieces of mildly burnt toast. Cheese oozed out of the corner and he swiped a finger at it and licked it off. Everything about it was utterly disgusting. "Took me nearly forty-nine years, but who knew? It's a real gem."

"Not to be outdone by its bigger, juicier, heart-attack-inducing older brother, the Spamburger." Lincoln waved his dinner high in the air as grease dripped from the patty. I swear I saw it actually congeal before hitting the ceramic plate underneath. "And I think if you're playing around with the idea of changing up your moniker, *Spam*antha should *definitely* be in the running."

"Good one," Sam nodded sarcastically. She continued with the head bobbing as she said, "If you're taking suggestions, Lincoln Logs should be at the top of your list."

"Let me see if I've got this straight." Dan ran a hand through his sun-bleached hair. Though every ounce of me was head over heels for Lincoln, I could appreciate a good-looking human being when I saw one. Dan was definitely that. He deserved a lot of appreciating. "Dr. Phil, Spamantha, Lincoln Logs, EpiPen, and Lieutenant Dan." He turned in his chair toward Sam and grabbed her shoulder, squeezing it. "Are you alright with this, babe? You're not having flashbacks from your freak-show days, are you now?"

Sam flattened the back of her hand to her forehead. She feigned exasperation quite well. "I am. I really am."

"I don't see any freak-show here." Phil took another bite of his cheesy, spammy, sandwichy concoction.

I couldn't help but laugh at that. "I think that might be what happens when you spend too much time at the circus, Philly. Can't see the forest for the trees sort of thing. If you hung out with normal people more often, then our glaring freak-showdom would be just a bit more obvious."

"If you hung out with these so-called 'normal' people you speak of, Eppie... " I knew that tone. It was the, *'I'm going to singlehandedly put you in your place with this one statement alone'* type of tenor. He continued, " ...you'd realize that it's much more welcoming in the self-proclaimed 'freak' crowd."

"Ahhh." Sam reached across the table and clasped Phil's hand. Her hot pink lips spread into a coy grin. "We love you, too, Philly."

"I do hate to break up this lovely party," Lincoln interrupted. He'd been relatively quiet since the tour at the house, but I figured that was because he'd spent over a solid hour talking about beams and posts and drywall and molding. His vocal chords were due for a well-deserved rest. "But I gotta get back home. Have a guy coming over at seven to take a look at our extra room."

"Nice," Dan said. "Just as long as he doesn't piss all over the bathroom floor like the last guy. Slacker Steve had the aim of a potty training three-year-old."

Lincoln's bottom lip hooked into his mouth and he bit down. "Umm," he stammered, eyes squinting. "That might not have actually been Slacker Steve's fault. That might have been Sleep-Walking Lincoln's doing."

"Well, Dumb-Ass Dan might've actually been the one who burned the hole in the leather sofa three months ago. Cigarettes and charades don't mix. And when coupled with literal mixed drinks, it's a combination what can only go up in smoke."

"You know what else doesn't mix?" Sam huffed, truly annoyed. "Taffeta and prom queens. Should. Not. Go. Together."

Dan gave Sam an incredulous glance. "If I'm reading you right, I'd actually venture a guess that you're a bit annoyed by the outcomes of this painfully insignificant popularity contest."

"I just don't get how someone with absolutely no style sense could win!"

"Maybe she's a nice person," Lincoln offered with a shrug.

"She's not! She's awful. Truly. Told Mr. MacMillian that his mustache looked like a sunbaked turd from a dachshund. She's horrific!"

"I think it should be considered an honor just to be nominated, right?" Dan suggested sympathetically. His fingers that stroked Sam's back would have been taken by any other person as a sincere gesture, but Sam wasn't having any of it. She shrugged him off with cold, jerky motions.

"An honor to realize that people like you, but they just don't like you quite enough?"

This completely caught me off-guard. Sam wasn't usually one to seek the approval of others, the least of which being her peers. I couldn't understand why she was so bothered by this. It made me truly grateful that Lincoln and I had opted out of prom altogether. Sounded all kinds of awful.

"*I* like you enough, babe." Dan pressed his nose into Sam's fuchsia hair and kissed her cheek. "I like you *more* than enough."

For a moment I'd forgotten that we had a near senior citizen at our table. Phil just seemed to so easily mesh into whatever setting he was placed in. I wondered if that was a learned skill, or something you were born with. I always felt like that noticeable, sore thumb. But not with these guys. With them we were all bruised and broken, like a fist that had been in a bar fight or pummeling incident with a brick wall. None of us stood out any more than the other, and even ol' Phil was a welcome finger on our decrepit hand.

"I'm going to offer some advice, if I may?" he finally spoke up.

Was this going to be clinical? Was it going to be practical? Friendly? A word of caution? Had Philly been sitting in his corner—relatively silent for the most part, other than his Spam-love declaration—only to size us up and pass out diagnoses around the table?

"You need to be enough all on your own." He thrust an index finger toward Sam. His eyes were tight, but so warm and earnest, like he truly wanted her to understand what he was saying. "Don't let others decide if you're enough or not. Their approval is not the measuring stick of your worth. Not your friends'. Not your family's." He passed a deliberate gaze to each one of us, but this wasn't diagnosing. This wasn't admonishing. This was true, life-tested, heartfelt guidance. This was a dose of love if ever I'd felt it. "You are enough. You're enough, understand?"

"Understood," Lincoln said.

Dan nodded along with him. "Understood."

Phil wiped his mouth briskly with a checkered napkin and returned it to his lap. Stretching out against the back of the booth, he shrugged, "Just my two cents. Take it for what it's worth."

But what it was worth, I was certain, was something that couldn't be measured at all.

# TWENTY-TWO

**Lincoln:** I have a surprise for you ;)

I glanced down at my phone. The vet said he'd be right back, but his right back apparently wasn't the same length as my right back. I'd been waiting for over twenty minutes with no sign of his return any time soon. Even Herb had given up his patient waiting and instead curled into a fluffy golden ball at my feet, completely surrendering hope.

**Me:** I'm not sure I like surprises.

I wasn't sure. The things they did to the heart bordered on unhealthy. Pulses shouldn't spike that quickly. I was positive that's what led to a heart attack—when you were scared out of your wits from an unanticipated surprise. I knew my heart couldn't handle those sorts of things.

The heart was a muscle, but I'd never exercised mine much—if at all—in the past. Love hadn't taught it the ropes just yet. But since meeting Lincoln, it was like my heart had been enrolled into boot camp. The rigors he put it through were enough to strain it, strengthen it, and make it into something completely new. It was like he'd finally shocked it back to life.

Lincoln was the defibrillator to my tired, worn out heart. A surprise could very well be the death of me, which would be a shame after all the work he'd put into making it beat again.

**Lincoln:** How can you not like surprises? Everyone loves surprises.

**Me:** Not me. I don't like being scared.

**Lincoln:** What if I promise you it's not a scary surprise?

Herb rolled over on the linoleum, groaning as he slid onto his back.

I punched the keys on my phone, my interest piqued.

**Me:** Elaborate.

**Lincoln:** Then it wouldn't be a surprise now, would it?

**Me:** See, this is where the scary comes in. My brain is running through millions of possibilities A-Z. There's an incredible potential for scare in that sample set.

**Lincoln:** Just trust me.

There went that darn heart again.

I did trust Lincoln, so much.

**Me:** I trust you. But I'm still scared of surprises.

**Lincoln:** Sounds like a control issue to me ;)

He was right, and I stared down at that text for so long the words blurred together through the sting of water that came from holding your eyes open too long. Quickly, I blinked and typed out a reply.

**Me:** Well, I obviously have some issues.

**Lincoln:** Sorry. I didn't mean anything by that. Just trust that you're going to love this surprise. It involves me, so naturally <3

Right then, someone knocked lightly on the door, the way they do at a doctor's office just to make sure you're decent before they spring into the room and ask you all kinds of detailed questions about your medical history like it's a completely normal thing to hold conversations when wearing dresses made of paper and nothing else. It made me want to laugh just a little at this vet's assumption of Herb's right to privacy. Good thing he wasn't getting into all kinds of mischief with the jars of treats or playing around on the scale at the back of the room.

"Herb?" A silver-haired man, probably in his late fifties, asked as he peeked around the door.

I didn't wait for Herb to bark his reply and instead answered, "Yes."

"So." He hugged a manila folder to his chest. He cocked his head to the side, studying me, studying the dog. Then he said that saddest thing I'd heard in nearly ten years. "Herb's not well."

"I know," I nodded as I waved a hand to his bent leg. It had healed—sort of—and wasn't as crooked and jagged as before, but it still didn't serve much of a purpose other than an aesthetic one. "In all fairness, I'm not sure how functional it was to begin with, but I'm led to believe he had four working limbs before I found him."

"No, Ms. Aberdeen. It's not that."

There was a computer screen hooked on what resembled a long, metal arm, and the vet swiveled it out and toward me as he punched a few buttons on the keyboard. The machine hummed to life.

"These are his x-rays." He double-clicked on a file and two mostly black images maximized on the screen, hazy white bones and body parts illustrated across the frame. "This is his leg." With an index finger, he pointed to Herb's hindquarters. I could see two distinct fractures, little hairs of bone broken apart and then hastily rejoined in a crude ball of dense mass. Evidently, Herb's healing hadn't been all that pretty.

"Do you see these?" In a scooping motion, the vet drew an imaginary loop around the upper portion of the screen. "These are Herb's lungs."

I nodded. I could see them.

"And these white circles." Narrowing his circle, he pointed to dozens of patches that riddled nearly every square inch of Herb's lungs. "These are tumors."

Well crap.

Suddenly Herb felt too far away, so I slunk off the cold metal chair and onto the floor. I pulled him up next to me, and he lifted his head and then dropped it softly onto my lap. His pink tongue darted out of his mouth and lapped at my fingers as they drug through the thick fur on his neck, and he hummed in delight.

"The interesting thing, though," the vet continued. He closed out the program with the current x-rays, and then pulled up an entirely new set from a different folder. It still resembled the same dog-like outline, but without the jagged lines of Herb's right leg. "I knew

I'd seen a very similar x-ray before." Peering up at the screen, I could still make out the tumors in the lungs. There were far fewer, but still enough to make those lungs look like a game of PacMan. "This was Ralph's x-ray three months ago."

"Ralph?"

Herb's ears twitched, perking up into these pointy, alert triangles on top of his head. He looked like a completely different dog, and I felt like crying instantly.

"Yes, Ralph." The vet lowered himself into a chair, making him much closer to eye level with us. I read this as a really bad sign. When people adjusted their posture before speaking, it usually meant the words were going to come out differently, too. "This dog used to belong to a family that brings their animals here to be treated."

My heart clenched.

"They brought him in several months ago and I diagnosed him with cancer. I gave them several options for treatment, but they declined, which was their choice." He leaned forward, his elbows resting on his kneecaps.

"So he has a family?" Hope took root in my stomach or wherever it was that hope resided internally. It was overwhelming to learn that Herb was really Ralph and that Ralph had not only a mangled leg, but terminal cancer, as well. But it was a relief to know that he had someone else out there that once loved and cared for him. Someone that might be able to actually take care of him now, so much better than Lincoln and I had been trying to do.

"He *had* a family." The vet stroked his chin. He was doing that weird thing were you half-smiled, but also half-looked like you were about to cry. I think that was what empathy looked like in physical form. "I just spoke with them on the phone, which was what took me so long. They said that Ralph 'ran away' several months ago." The air quotes hooked around his words made me cringe, knowing the truth in that statement. "But I let them know that we had located him—"

"So they're coming to get him."

"No, Ms. Aberdeen." The man shook his head slowly, but his eyes stayed with mine. "They're coming in to put him down."

I gasped. Yanking at Herb's fur with my hands, I drug him all the way into my lap. Something in me wanted to cover his ears, but I knew how ridiculous it would be for me to do that. I just rocked him gently back and forth.

"I'm so sorry, Ms. Aberdeen."

"But we have the money," I blurted, trying to think quickly. "Maybe, if his leg is okay enough, then we can use that for treatments instead?" My words were a hurried rush, their cadence all over the place with sharp staccato syllables and loud, panicked breaths.

"I wish we could do that, I truly do. But this isn't our call anymore." I caught that he'd tacked himself on in that sentence. Maybe it was only for my benefit, to make me feel less alone in this decision I wasn't even allowed to make, or maybe he truly did have other hopes for Herb/Ralph and his future. I couldn't tell. "They'll be here in fifteen minutes, at which point I'll have to ask you to go." He stood upright. "I'll leave you two alone to say your goodbyes."

Tears, hot and reckless, streamed down my cheeks. The door clicked shut after the vet's exit and it was quiet, but my ears rang and my heart thudded and I realized just the awful extent to which I hated surprises. I truly despised them. My heart could absolutely not handle them. This was it attacking me from the inside out.

"Oh, Herb," I cried, pressing my cheek to the top of his head. My tears clung to his hair and stuck against my skin. "This sucks. This just completely sucks."

He groaned contentedly, blissfully unaware. At least I hoped so. I knew that sometimes being ignorant was the best thing possible.

"How can I say a forever goodbye to you?" I sobbed as we rocked together. "How can I give you over when I know what they plan to do to you?" I knew he couldn't answer, but I still had to speak it. "I couldn't take care of you as well as most people could've, but I tried my best, and that has to count for something."

Minutes went by and I filled them with ramblings and apologies, and then the door opened again, no knock this time.

"They're here." His tone and his expression brought on the rally of tears again. "I'm so sorry, Ms. Aberdeen. I truly am."

Giving one last hug, I pulled Herb as tightly to my chest as our bodies would allow and squeezed him there, blanketing him. Then I slipped out from under his furry weight, rose to stand, and walked to the door.

"I tried my best," I muttered again, but I didn't know who I was trying to reassure with those final words.

Then I walked out the door.

I didn't look back.

# TWENTY-THREE

*"How's that?"*

*The nurse fluffed my pillow once more and then slid it behind my back. Each time I moved, my ribs felt like they were breaking all over again.*

*"A little better. Thank you." It wasn't any better, but she was nice and I didn't want to hurt her feelings. I'd done too much of that lately.*

*She smiled. I liked her smile a lot. It was a pretty smile. It reminded me of Mom's. "Is there anything I can get you, sweetie? More of that raspberry Jell-O you like?"*

*I nodded. "What about my mama?" I said quietly. My voice hurt to use. Everything hurt to use. "When can I see her?"*

*The smile dropped from the nurse's face. "I'll have to check on that for you, sweetie."*

*"Another nurse was already checking, too." And a janitor that came to clean the bathroom during the night shift. And the nice boy who brought lunch just an hour ago. I'd asked every person that entered through the door to find her whereabouts, but it was taking them all a really long time.*

*"I'll be back with your Jell-O in a jiffy."*

*She shuffled out of the room and then everything was quiet again. There was some beeping from a machine hooked up to me, but even that I couldn't really hear anymore, especially when I hummed quietly to myself. Humming got rid of all those background sounds, like always. Plus, I was used to the noises of the hospital. In a way, it felt like a home away from home.*

*I closed my eyes to sleep and a little while later there was a soft knock on my door. Maybe it was Mama. Maybe she didn't want to wake me by barging in. Mama was thoughtful that way.*

*"Eppie?" I didn't recognize the voice, but it wasn't hers. It was a man's, but it wasn't my dad's, either. "Can I come in?"*

*I tried to scoot up in my bed to get a better look, but my body wouldn't allow it. I supposed I would just let him in. I was safe at the hospital. At least that's what they kept saying, 'You're safe here.' But I felt safe at home, too. Safer than here.*

*The man slowly pushed the door open and stepped inside. He was a grown up, probably ten or so years older than my parents. His shirt was baggy and green and yellow plaid, and he wore khaki cargo pants that looked like the pockets were stuffed full, weighing them down. Pulling his sunglasses from his face, he tucked them into the collar of his shirt and smiled.*

*Everyone was sure smiling at me a lot.*

*"I'd like to talk with you for a moment, if that's okay with you."*

*A nurse followed in behind him. She skirted the edge of my bed and walked over to the IV that hung above me like a liquid-filled balloon. With a syringe in her hand, she pressed it into the port and then patted her palm lightly on my shoulder. Surprise, surprise. She was smiling, too.*

*"Eppie, I'd like to ask you a few questions, if you're up for it." His movements were delicate, not like he was a woman or anything, but like he was trying not to startle me. I didn't figure I startled easily, though.*

*"Are you a doctor?" I asked.*

*The nurse was still at my bedside, scribbling something onto a chart.*

*"I'm a friend."*

*I shook my head. Ouch. Even that made my whole body ache. "How can you be a friend if I've never met you?" That was a very funny thing for him to say.*

*"You have a point. I'm not a friend just yet, you're right. But I hope to be one. And I'm not a doctor in the sense that you're used to them. I don't work on healing the body the way they do. I work more with the mind." This guy sounded like a hippie to me. He kind of looked like one, too. "My name is Phil."*

*"Is there something wrong with my brain, Phil?" For the past six months, the doctors in this hospital had told my parents this might be the case. I figured this man was here to finally make that official.*

*"Not with yours, no." Phil pulled the chair he was sitting in closer to my bed. The metal legs scraped on the linoleum. "Eppie, I'd like to talk to you about your mother."*

*Even though it was so painful to do it, I sat up as straight as I could, alert and at attention. "Do you know when I get to see her?"*

*"Eppie." I didn't like that he kept saying my name. "Eppie, there's something going on in your mother's mind that isn't healthy."*

*I blinked fast and shook my head. "You mean something in* my *mind," I corrected. He was right, he wasn't a doctor. I guessed that was why he didn't have all the information. "They've been saying that for a while now. I've had lots of tests done."*

*"No, Eppie. There is nothing wrong with your mind." I couldn't understand what he meant. He leaned back slightly in his chair and crossed his ankles. Then he sighed, hissing through his teeth. "Your mother has a condition called Munchausen by Proxy."*

*That was a very funny word. I hadn't realized Mama had even been sick. That made me feel bad that she'd had to take care of me so much when I was sick, and apparently she was sick, too. Dad should have helped out with that more.*

*"Do you know what that is, Eppie?"*

*"No."*

*Phil nodded. "It is where a caregiver—often a parent—makes a child sick." He looked me in the eye. "On purpose."*

*"Mama didn't make me sick." Phil didn't seem to understand any of this. He was a very confused man. And he didn't dress very well. There was just a lot about him that didn't go together. "Mama was the one who was trying to get the doctors to make me healthy."*

*"This is very hard to grasp, I'm sure." Phil looked like maybe he was a nice person, but I didn't like the words that came out of his mouth at all. They weren't nice in the least. "It's a form of medical child abuse."*

*"Mama didn't hurt me," I said quickly, defending her. I didn't like the mean things he was saying about her. I didn't like the lies he told. "She took care of me."*

*I could tell that he was trying to form his words carefully, because he waited a lot longer to speak this time, like he was writing them out in his head first. "There are people whose brains don't work quite the way yours and mine do, Eppie."*

*Mama's brain was just fine. She was so smart and so funny and so wonderful. There was nothing wrong with her brain.*

*"In your mother's mind, it was important for her to gain attention by constantly having someone to care for. The attention of doctors, of her peers, of your father."*

*I couldn't swallow. I couldn't speak.*

*"Your mother has been making you sick, Eppie. For years. But she can't make you sick anymore. That's over."*

*Panic spiked in my heart. "Where is she?"*

*"She's in custody for now, Eppie." Phil had a mustache that he kept biting with his lower teeth, almost like he was combing it with them. It was a weird thing to do. I didn't like it. I wanted to shave it off of his face. "But she's going to get help. Trust me. She's going to get better. There are people who can help her get better."*

*I couldn't believe any part of anything he said. It didn't make sense. Mama was always there for me. She always talked to the doctors, always told the other moms at school how worried she was, always held me at night when I didn't feel good. She was the best mother anyone could ask for.*

*Phil made her sound like a monster.*

*I paused, looking him straight in the eye. I wanted his eyes to be scary and mean, but they were the opposite. They looked so nice and trustworthy. That made my stomach roll. "How do you even know that any of this is true?"*

*"Because she told us."*

*Bile seeped into my mouth and I choked it back. Phil could see that, and he pulled the nearby trashcan to my side quickly.*

*But I didn't throw up. I held it all in.*

*"She told you she made me sick?"*

*"Eppie." Phil settled the wastebasket back onto the ground and it rattled quietly into place. "Some very bad things happened to your mother when she was a little girl. They are not excuses for what she's done to you, but they are explanations."*

*"So she knew what she was doing?" I didn't want to cry in front of Phil. That would be embarrassing. I didn't even know him. But I couldn't help myself. The tears spilled from my eyes and skimmed down my chubby cheeks freely. I figured I would probably never see him again, so I didn't waste time feeling embarrassed about the tears that soaked my face.*

*"This disorder is so complex and complicated. There are many underlying parts to it, but yes, ultimately your mother was completely aware of what she was doing. She was intentionally making you—and keeping you—ill."*

*It was weird that for as often as I'd been sick in the past few years, I'd never felt as horrible as I did right now. This was the worst. This was so much worse than all of the stomachaches and the hospital visits and the tests and procedures combined.*

*"My father. Where is he?"*

*"He's talking with some people about what happened. But he'll be back soon." Phil crossed him arms over his chest, the same way his ankles were crossed. His head tilted to the side. "Would you like me to wait with you until he comes back?"*

*I looked at him. "Yes."*

*"Not a problem. I'm happy to wait with you, Eppie."*

*I was surprised I didn't have someone already waiting with me in the room. Last time I was admitted, there was a girl who was fifteen and couldn't be left alone. Something about her being on "watch." Her wrists had been bandaged tightly with white cloths and she stayed in a separate wing of the hospital, away from everyone else.*

*But no one was here to watch me. Unless that's what they'd sent Phil to do.*

*"I wasn't trying to kill myself," I explained, needing him to know.*

*"I know."*

*I didn't believe him, that he believed me. Why would he believe me? I was just a kid.*

*"We don't have to talk about that right now, Eppie."*

*"But I need you to believe me," I pleaded. The tears hadn't stopped, and this only made them come down faster.*

*"I do believe you. And I will continue to believe anything you care to share with me. But for now, you really need to rest."*

*That's what they'd all said. I needed my rest. I couldn't figure what I was supposed to be resting up for.*

*I tried to close my eyes, but all I could hear was Mama's sweet voice in my head. Her whispers of* I love you *as she cradled me to sleep. Her angelic, beautiful singing as a soft lullaby. Every thought that ran through my head was in her voice, covered with her tone. I tried to think on my own, but it was all her. Everything was her because she was my mom, and that's how it should be.*

*"Having trouble settling in?" Phil asked after long moments of quiet between us. I could hear a newspaper crinkle as he turned the page. The clock read twenty minutes since our last conversation.*

*"Yes."*

*I knew he would think it was weird, but I did the only thing I knew to do. I started to hum, just a few bars at first, but Phil quickly joined in.*

*We hummed together and his voice was nice and strong. "I love that song. One of my favorites," he said during a break in the melody. He placed the newspaper onto the bedside table and folded his arms behind his neck, angling his face to the ceiling, closing his eyes.*

*Then he started humming again.*

*He hummed me all the way to sleep.*

# TWENTY-FOUR

When I walked out of the veterinarian's office, I studied each vehicle in the parking lot, trying to determine what kind of car a dog murderer would drive. I didn't know what I expected, truthfully. It wasn't like there would be a bumper sticker reading, "I kill puppies for sport," slapped on its backside. But I needed to find something. Something that would clue me in to just how on earth someone could hurt a perfectly lovable, helpless creature.

I didn't find anything, of course. There were just a bunch of steel facades parked in rectangular spaces.

When Lincoln's tires rolled in front of my field of vision along the curb where I sat, I didn't immediately get up from my post. I remained planted as the gurgling engine shut off, and I tracked his heavy black boots as they scraped across the pavement. His knees popped when he lowered, and he nudged his shoulder into mine as soon as he sat down. It threw me a bit off balance, but I'd been feeling like that already. This was just an added push.

"How long have you been out here?"

"I don't know," I shrugged. "Ten minutes?"

"Then there's probably still time," he surmised, his voice gaining speed. It was laced with an optimism I knew we didn't have the right to hold. "I can go in there and talk to his owners and tell them we've got the money and then maybe—"

"Stop." I pushed a hand to his arm. My eyes pinched closed and I breathed in painfully. "Just stop. Please."

He did.

"He's not our responsibility anymore, Lincoln." I hung my head down, almost between my knees like you did when you were about to pass out, and tears dotted the pavement in damp circles as they dripped from my eyes. I smudged at the stains with the tip of my shoe but they stuck there, these little wet reminders mocking me. "He's not ours."

"So just because he belongs to someone else, that means we aren't allowed to do anything for him?" Lincoln's voice was uncharacteristically loud. "That we just stop fighting for him?"

"I don't know, Lincoln. It just that... He's their dog and... I just... I don't know."

To not even have any clue if Herb was alive or not in this very moment was too much. I couldn't allow myself to think about it. To think about anything.

So I created a void in my head and my mind and took up residence in that empty, thoughtless space. It was like a big vastness of blank. I didn't allow myself to feel because feeling was something. I didn't allow myself to process because processing was doing. I just became blank. It wasn't altogether too different from my whole ritualistic humming thing, just significantly quieter.

We sat in blankness for nearly an hour.

Every car that exited the parking lot could have been them. I studied their drivers, trying to see if I could pick out Herb's owners, but each one was unreadable. Or maybe I was just horribly terrible at reading people. History would favor that second option.

After a while, the noises from the road started swishing past us in uneven intervals. A car here. The low rumble of a big-rig there. Their sporadic movements indicated it was quitting time, and the growl in my stomach echoed that, too. I was hungry, but to eat right now felt selfish for some strange reason. To do anything that had to do with living felt selfish. Dying obviously didn't feel appropriate, but living felt like too much.

And I could tell Lincoln was angry, which left me with no appetite. Angry with me or the situation, I didn't know. When he finally spoke, I sensed it was more with me, which was a very painful, unwelcome epiphany.

"So what if Phil had given up on you just like we gave up on Herb?"

I shook myself out of my blankness. "What?"

"What if you didn't have a Phil? What would've happened to you, Eppie?" Lincoln fidgeted with the brim of his worn hat, rolling it between his hands and pulling it low over his eyes. "From the little you've shared with me about your past, it sounds like you were just as helpless as that dog, but you had someone willing to rescue you."

"It's not that I was unwilling to rescue Herb, Lincoln." I couldn't bring myself to be upset with him, though fighting would be so much more satisfying than whatever it was we were actually doing. "It's that he belongs to someone else. He has a family."

"But *you* belonged to someone else, too." His eyes nailed into mine. His face was tired and his lips were chapped from sitting in the wind for so long, the air sucking the moisture from them. He licked along his mouth, then swung his gaze back out toward the street. "All I'm saying is sometimes the ones who have the right to you aren't necessarily the ones who *know* what's right for you."

Lincoln's toes tapped on the sidewalk as he hugged his knees to his chest and he rocked every so slightly side-to-side. Staring at him was all I could do, and had he been looking back at me, I'm sure my scrutiny would have come across as intense, but he wasn't looking at me, so I doubted he noticed. I didn't think he was looking at anything at all, actually. He was in his own version of blank over there, it appeared.

"Who has the right to you, Lincoln?" I interrupted after a bit.

Twitching, he shook off the strands of hair along his ears and tucked them up under his hat.

"Lincoln?"

"I don't know that anyone does anymore."

That was even sadder than the vet telling me Herb wasn't at all well. I had no idea what to do with that amount of sadness from the happy boy with the constantly-there smile.

He swallowed. "I think I want it to be you, though."

There were times when your soul anticipated an answer before your brain did. When it recognized the words before they were spoken, like maybe somehow it caught that in-between moment and read it like déjà vu, deciphering what was about to happen next. A premonition of words. So even if your mind was shocked to hear them, your heart was at ease because they knew they were coming all along.

Maybe that was called hope. Or maybe just wishful thinking. Whatever the case, my soul needed Lincoln to say that, and as senseless as it sounded when it entered my ears and into my head, it already made complete sense in my heart. And that's all I really cared about.

"I want it to be me, too."

His hand slipped out from where it crisscrossed around his legs and he dropped it onto my hand so his palm pressed to the back of it, like our hands were spooning. Then he slid his fingers in between each of the spaces of mine and gave them a squeeze.

"Good, because I think you've already earned that right."

I squeezed back. "I'm just not too altogether sure I'm a very good rescuer, Lincoln. Look what happened with Herb." Maybe it was too soon to say that, but I didn't care.

"I think the true problem lies in the fact that you're a crappy listener," he corrected, laughing quietly. I adored the sound of that laugh. It was infectious joy bundled up and delivered in the most amazing sound possible. It was one of those sounds that you couldn't help but imitate, just to see if it felt as good doing it as it did hearing it. I tried hard not to giggle along with him as he said, "It's a little rude to so quickly dismiss the sage advice of the man who tried to tell you that *you alone are enough.*"

"Maybe," I said. "But if that's true—that each one of us is enough all on our own—then you really don't need me at all now, do you?"

Lincoln lifted his head to look at me, wonder in his eyes. "I'm not one who settles for enough, Eppie." That quirky smile was there again, making me forget what he could even look like without it clinging to his lips. "You should be aware, I'm all about exceeding life's expectations to the highest degree." Suddenly, he swung his arm around my shoulders and leaned into me. "Also, I figure your enough plus my enough has got to equal all sorts of incredible."

He brought his face close to mine, so close that I couldn't actually see what his lips were doing, but the way his eyes crinkled made me aware of just how large that smile was.

"That math confuses me," I teased, just like I had during our texts about his family a while back.

"Not me." His lips dropped to mine, swift and determined. After a kiss cut way too short, he said,

"That's pretty much the one thing in this life that I'm actually not confused about at all."

..............

I was terrible at guessing games.

"Surprise, our dog is dead?"

"Wrong. Well, not really wrong, I suppose, but not it."

"Hmm... Surprise, you bought me a puppy?"

"Let's be clear," Lincoln began. "This surprise has nothing to do with once pets or future pets. Guess again."

He was feigning impatience a little too well for my liking. He spun back and forth on the desk chair in his bedroom, the bedroom I'd never been in before, until this night. As should be expected, that reality made me nervous, to be in his room alone with him. Sure, we'd been alone in my room on multiple occasions, but that was *my* room. I knew that space intimately. But this space? Being here with him was infinitely more intimate.

Lincoln had been spinning in full rotations for a while, but after I'd admitted how I was getting some sort of transfer of motion sickness just by watching him, he'd slowed his full-on spinning down to just small swivels.

"Surprise, your name's not really Lincoln and you're actually a government spy trying to extract highly sensitive information from the townspeople of Masonridge about an impending alien attack?"

That statement deserved a full spin. Once he'd made it all 360 degrees around, even his eyes were rolling. "Why is it that something along the lines of *'your name isn't really such and such and you work for such and such government agency'* is always the go-to? I mean seriously, anytime anyone in any movie or novel or even a comic book uncovers some sort of hidden truth, it's all about concealed identities and plots against humanity." He was still shaking his head. "Sadly, I am just Lincoln and the only plot I've been hatching is the one in which I round second with you on that bed that you're perched upon right now."

The nausea continued, but not from the spinning. That unabashed admission set free the entire world's population of monarch butterflies in my belly.

"I'll give you one more guess."

I was still too stuck in his last phrase to decipher anything in the present one he uttered.

"Damn, Eppie." He launched from his chair and grabbed ahold of my wrist, dragging me out the bedroom door and through the hallway. "You're truly terrible at this."

We were suddenly standing in front of a closed oak door, the one that belonged to the room where their newest roommate supposedly lived. Lincoln was shaking his head at me—still smiling, of course—and lifted our interlocked hands to the door and knocked on it three times with all of our knuckles together.

When the door swung open, Lincoln, Dan, and Sam all sang out, "Surprise!" in an atrociously out of key chorus.

"I'm confused."

"And what else is new, sister?" Sam laughed. She plopped down onto a bed that was clothed in Hello Kitty.

"Wait a minute... "

"Yep! Meet the newest roomie!"

"What happened to the pool house?" I asked, still a bit stunned.

"Evidently the storage of filters and chlorine tablets ranks higher than the storage of flesh and blood. I got the boot. Guess eighteen is the magical age in which parental love ceases to endure."

Lincoln huffed out a laugh as though he were a sputtering horse. "I think you're a few years off in that calculation."

But Sam just spoke over his words, hardly hearing, much less acknowledging him. "No skin off my back. The boys had this open room and now all is well."

"So you live here... With your boyfriend... In this house... With my boyfriend."

"Oh Eps, isn't it just perfect? To have all the people you adore under one roof? It's remarkably convenient, am I right?" She tossed a glance to everyone in the room and we all smiled and nodded our hesitant agreement. At least mine was hesitant. Dan's look was genuine enough. "We entertained the idea of asking Ol' Philly to slum it on the pull-out couch in order to really consolidate all of your loved ones, but that felt creepy since he's a grown man and all. Plus, something about asking a shrink to sleep on a couch felt all kinds of silly."

"He's not truly a shrink anymore," I defended, for no other reason than to change the subject. Sure, I should be overjoyed at the fact that the three people closest to me were under one roof, but all that stood out was the fact that I slept under a completely different one. It felt stupid to be self-pitying so pathetically like this, but I couldn't help it from taking place.

"Whatever." She waved me off. "Seriously, how awesome *is* this?"

"Very awesome," I nodded. Lincoln looked down at me. He knew me well enough to detect the lack of awesome in my tone. "Congratulations, Sam. Truly."

Her smile was so huge and she was so happy that I had to feel some of that for her. Maybe it was the dead dog or the fact that in one afternoon they'd transformed this house into the happy home that I hadn't been able to do with my own home for the past ten years, but I didn't feel one hundred percent great about this. Maybe only fifty, which didn't feel very great at all.

"Come on." Lincoln's head nudged toward the door. He knew I needed an escape.

I followed him out, and once back in his room, I honestly didn't feel much better.

"You were right."

I looked up at him, all the way up since we were both standing. "About what?"

"The fact that you hate surprises. You wouldn't've been able to conceal the amount of distaste on your face even if it were covered with a Nacho Libre mask.

And we have one of those. Dan went through a weird obsessive Mexican wrestling phase. I could demonstrate if you like."

"I didn't hate that surprise."

"Yes," he pressed. "You did."

"No. It's just that... I don't know." I sighed loudly. "Sam gets to be with you all the time now. She gets to wake up and you're there, and when she goes to sleep you're just down the hall in the other room."

"Just to be clear in case there were some outrageously mixed non-existent signals, but I'm not at all interested in Sam. Like, the opposite actually. If there is an opposite for having feelings for someone, then I have those for Sam. Don't get me wrong, she's an eclectic gal with a big heart, but I'm oppositely attracted to her."

"You're repelled by her."

"Well jeez, that doesn't sound very nice, but if that helps, then yes. She repels me." Lincoln's fingers were in my hair. How had he become so good at doing that? Knowing how to offer his touch at just the right and appropriate time in the right and appropriate way? "Sam and I are magnetic forces flipped completely apart."

"I appreciate your overboard assurance, but that's not what I mean. It's just that I'm completely jealous. Jealous of the fact that she's here. Living life with you. On a daily basis."

"Were you jealous of Dan, too? Because he's been my roommate for much longer than the thirteen hours Sam has." His head flicked up to the corner of the ceiling, leading my eyes to follow. "And see that hairy little spider over there? He's inhabited that same spot for nearly a week. Hasn't moved a muscle. You should have insane amounts of jealously over that slothful arachnid. He's seen me naked."

When I laughed into my shoulder, Lincoln pulled my chin up with his fingers, forcing my eyes to his.

"Honestly, Eppie, no one has ever cared this much about being close to me. I sorta don't know what to do with it," he admitted. "And though I'm completely flattered that you are envious of the physical closeness these roommates and bugs share with me, you've forgotten one thing."

"What's that?"

His words were doors, each one of them opening up another part of him, inviting me in.

"That your heart already lives here." He picked up my hand and pressed my palm flatly against his chest, directly over his heart. "And you can't get any closer than that."

# TWENTY-FIVE

I got used to the idea of Sam living with Dan who also lived with Lincoln pretty quickly. It turned out it actually was very convenient to have all three of them residing within the same 1,500 square feet. Our dinners were spent together, most of our free afternoons, too, and even the viewing of a few baseball games were all enjoyed within the comfort of one home.

The part that wasn't so comfortable was the noises and sounds that echoed throughout that shared living space. Sometimes they'd come from Sam's room, other times from Dan's. And on really late nights when neither of them actually made it to their own bedrooms, it pounded against the common wall between Lincoln's room and the family room like the freight train that traveled the tracks at the edge of town.

Sam was like that, I knew. And realistically, I supposed they'd been dating long enough to warrant that kind of stuff. I mean, it wasn't like I expected them to wait until they were married for it. Seriously, I didn't even know how to verbalize what it was they were doing without blushing.

Sex. There. They were having sex.

I couldn't figure out why I was so embarrassed to actually acknowledge that truth. I think maybe it was that I was embarrassed to acknowledge that Lincoln and I *weren't* having it.

It wasn't that I didn't want to. Of course I did. At least I figured that's what I wanted. I'd never slept with anyone, but these impulses and feelings that tingled through me had to mean that I wanted him that way. I mean, ultimately, that had to have been what my body wanted, right?

And I figured Lincoln wanted that, too. But on more than one occasion he'd cut things short, saying it was late or that he was tired, though nothing about what we were doing made me any kind of tired. He effectively woke up every square inch of my being. He lit me up like a fuse—a fuse that never burned quite long enough to actually detonate. It was all sizzling, no fireworks.

Tonight was one of those non-sex nights for us. Sam and Dan were at it again, and even though it would be audibly obvious to anyone in the neighborhood just what they were doing, Lincoln didn't acknowledge it at all as he sat at his computer, typing something onto the keyboard with clumsy index fingers. He was a hunt and peck-er, plunking out key after key. I'd been reading *Catcher in the Rye*, or at least attempting to, but I worried that all I would retain were fragments of story, filled in with inappropriately placed, *"Yeah, just like that"* and *"That feels so good"* add-ons. It was like sexual Mad-Libs in my brain.

After twenty or so minutes, giggles and grunts resonated down the hall, followed by Sam's door shutting with a thud.

Lincoln looked up from his computer screen, the quiet finally surrounding us.

"Well, I'm sure glad that's finally over," he said. "I almost felt like I should've paid some kind of admission fee for just listening to it."

I breathed my own cautious sigh of relief. "So I'm not the only one who lost all ability to focus?"

"Eppie, I think that focus during something that graphically loud is an impossible feat."

"It sorta makes me uncomfortable to actually hear them do that."

"Yeah." He stroked his hand through his russet hair and leaned back in the office chair, a half-smile on his face. "Me too."

That put me at ease, that we were kindredly awkward-feeling together.

"Methinks I need a drink," he admitted, hands pushing on his knees. "Will root beer suffice?"

"Sounds good," I nodded, and he scooted out of the room, a playful hop, skip, and jump added to his movements, as would be the expected pattern of walking for someone who just spoke like a leprechaun.

My back was killing me from sitting hunched over on the bed for so long, poring over my homework, so I stole his much more comfy leather chair at his desk and sank into its puffy material, already warmed by his body. I was just about to pick my book back up when my eyes locked in on the computer screen.

More accurately, they locked in on the webpage Lincoln had been browsing.

Even more accurately, they locked in on the title.

*Eight-Year-Old Leaps from Bedroom Window,*
*Deranged Mother Heads to the Slammer,*
*Then Loony Bin*

My jaw came perfectly unhinged.

"My mistake. We only have cream soda." Lincoln appeared in the doorway, two frosted, amber bottles in his grip. Like someone had pulled the plug on his face, all of his features went slack, loose and formless. His gaze landed on the screen. Then his hands with the bottles fell to his side, dropping next to his jean-clad thighs, clanging there.

"Why wouldn't you just ask me?" I whispered, not truly meaning to whisper at all, but my voice had no power to it, no push.

"Eppie."

Somehow, I found my volume dial and sent it out louder this time, "Why wouldn't you just *ask* me?"

He delicately placed the two drinks onto the pine dresser along the wall like the glass in them would shatter unless he acted gingerly like this. I assumed it was to buy time. When he looked down at the floor, back up at the popcorn ceiling, and then down at his untied tennis shoes once more, that was also to buy time, I figured.

I wasn't buying any time.

In a flustered rush, I yanked my messenger bag from the carpeted floor and tried to shove my paperback into it. Once, twice. Somehow it took three tries before I got it successfully tucked away. Nothing worked the way it should. My lower lip quivered and I bit into it, trying to scold it into submission, but in reality just hurting it so bad that it trembled even more from the unwarranted pain. My eyelids fluttered and tears clung to my eyelashes. Even my knees buckled when I pushed back hard from the desk and threw the strap of my bag over my shoulder.

Though he was standing in the doorway—the ultimate barricade—I shoved forcefully past. "I would have told you if you just asked me, Lincoln."

He whirled around. "Eppie. Stop."

Footsteps matching my quick heart rate, I didn't turn around to verify that he was chasing my movements out of the house, because I clearly knew he would follow me, that I wouldn't be able to shake him. There were so many steps to the sidewalk, and they were all slick with the rainwater that pummeled from the sky so I stumbled down every single one like I'd just learned to walk. Or maybe more like I was drunk. Or maybe just like I'd been heartbroken by a boy I'd been giving my hope to.

"Eppie!"

In any other time I would've thought this was inherently romantic, having someone call out your name in the pouring rain, running after you the way they do in movies.

The thing that movies failed to mention was the fact that when someone ran toward a person, that other person was usually running away.

"Eppie!"

Leaving him in the rain, under a cloud of deep gray and in a consuming fog, I ran away from everything I recently knew to be good in my life.

The crazy thing was, it sure felt a lot like jumping.

# TWENTY-SIX

**Lincoln:** Are there ways to hate someone, yet still peaceably communicate with them?

The glow from my phone illuminated the room instantly, spreading shards of light into each corner the way a flashlight does during a game of shadow-puppets. My lamp looked like a crane and the slats on the back of my chair resembled jail bars as they duplicated onto the wall in a blackened outline.

I rubbed my eyes to bring the room and the numbers from the alarm clock into focus. 2:34 a.m.

**Me:** I don't hate you, Lincoln.

It took two tries to get that message punched out correctly. My fingers hadn't woken up just yet.

**Lincoln:** I was referring to my own state of self-loathing, actually. I'm wondering if there is a way to run through this internal dialogue in any other manner than the one that constantly says, "Just shut up, you nimrod. You have no right to words, anyway."

**Me:** You have a right to words, Lincoln.

**Lincoln:** But you didn't want to hear the ones I hoped to speak.

I rolled onto my back and held the phone up above me, a slow smile pulling at my lips. My biceps trembled when they were suspended like this, but I ignored them for the moment and continued my text.

**Me:** Because I've heard them before. Lincoln, I've heard it ALL before. Believe me. I just didn't want to ever hear those words coming from your mouth.

**Lincoln:** Will you please let me explain myself? Then, if you despise everything I have to say, you can revoke my right to speech.

**Me:** If only I wielded so much power, to possess control over your first amendment right ;)

I had to flip onto my stomach; my shaky, weak arms just couldn't take anymore.

**Lincoln:** You possess control over my right to the pursuit of happiness, and that's just as bad.

**Me:** So I've effectively made you a sad mute?

Delirium had settled in, tainting my words with an even sillier banter than we were accustomed to. But it felt good. So much better than yelling at him in the street in the pouring down rain. I'd always thought a scene like that would be so satisfying, thrilling even. But it was nothing if not absolutely horrible. Fighting with Lincoln was horrible, no way around it.

Another text.

**Lincoln:** Precisely. I'm a sad mute. Just like that mime at the circus with the painted white face and permanently drawn frown. Sam is, in fact, suffering from flashbacks. It's a bad situation we're all in over here, Eppie. Please rescue us from this quiet, clowny hell we're in.

I giggled at that, even though I was still trying desperately hard to cling to any ounce of frustration I could muster up toward Lincoln. I sucked at mustering.

**Me:** Okay. Then talk.

**Lincoln:** Open your window.

My phone dropped onto my pillow.

I scooped it back up quickly.

**Me:** What?

*Tap, tap, tap.*

The quilted comforter was off in a flurry. And then I panicked. I'd only been wearing an oversized t-shirt I'd won at a triple-A baseball game I went to with Philly a few years back. Remarkably, I'd caught it when they'd fired it into the stands out of one of those big guns that sometimes shot out burritos, sometimes balled up apparel. It had the horrifically inappropriate phrase, *"Come on down to Leesle's Automotive. We like 4-play,"* on it, featuring a pixelated graphic of a truck, motorcycle, van, and car, one in each quadrant. It was awful, so I ripped it over my head and raced to my closet to clothe myself in something less... well, just something not that shirt.

*Tap, tap, tap.*

Oh crap, what if he could somehow see in? The room was so dark that I stumbled my way around, worrying that if I flicked on a light, I'd be silhouetted just like those furniture shadow-puppets. I did not need my meager breasts showcased in that way. They didn't need to be showcased at all.

Picking a pair of navy yoga pants and my dad's old Cornell college sweatshirt out of the hamper, I slipped into them quickly and then drew back the aluminum blinds covering my window.

Sure enough, like a bird or some stray cat, Lincoln was perched on the other side. On my roof. Lincoln was sitting on my roof.

He twisted at the waist, holding up his phone and waving it to me.

I retrieved mine from my bed.

**Lincoln:** What's taking so long in there?

**Me:** Wardrobe malfunction.

He smiled as he received my text.

**Lincoln:** I would've been happy to help out with your malfunctioning wardrobe.

I shook my head and he shrugged like he was nothing but absolutely innocent, and then I pulled on the lever to the window, unlocking it so I could slide it open. The track was dirty, filled with grit and probably the remains of a colony of dead flies, too, making the frame catch on it a little, but the screen had never been replaced so Lincoln was able to reach back and help pull it all the way open.

"Hi," he said, just air between us now and no glass.

"Hi," I said back.

He settled in on the shake shingles again, patting the spot next to him with his palm.

"I think I'm better off staying in here," I admitted. "And I'm trying to decide if I should be worried by the fact that your actions are slightly stalkerish, sitting on my roof in the dead of night and all."

"I think what you should be more concerned with is that fact that I've waved to, smiled at, and exchanged pleasantries with at least three of your neighbors while up here, and not a single one of them has alerted the authorities."

"They must be used to crazy people hanging out on rooftops, then."

"Eppie." He said my name like it hurt him. "I want you to know that I didn't read any of those articles."

I think he gave up the hope of me joining him out there, so he swiveled to face me completely. His confidence had to come from his work in construction because he didn't look like a person that was at all unsure or unsteady up at these heights, even though I knew there was fear rooted deep in him. But in truth, he was so unnaturally tall that maybe this didn't even feel high up enough to be considered fear-worthy. Maybe it just felt like standing on tiptoe. Maybe he feared greater heights.

"I didn't read them," he said once more.

"But you wanted to."

"No," he corrected quickly, shaking his head fast. "I mean, I don't know. It's just that my parents obviously knew your story already, and I guess I wanted to know why the version of you they supposedly knew was so different from the version of you I think I know."

It would've been easier if he had just gone ahead and read the articles. Less explaining. Less reliving. Then it would be a clean break and he'd realize most people where better off without extra drama in their lives and that he fell into that most category. I was the outlier in this.

"Maybe the two versions aren't so different," I said.

"They *have* to be different, Eppie." He was almost leaning into my window, his hands hooked on to the wooden sill. "Eight-year-olds aren't in the business of attempted suicide."

"And mothers shouldn't be in the business of child abuse."

His shoulders sagged, a marionette whose strings had been dropped. "I'm coming in."

Before I could stop him, all six-foot-five of Lincoln was climbing through my window, one lanky leg at a time.

"There." He brushed off his pants and stood immediately in front of me, feet resolutely planted. "Give me your headline."

His hair was wet, long strips made darker by the rain that clung to them in beads. He shook the errant strands from his brow the way a dog shakes off after a bath, and looked down at me with sincerity in his eyes. Puppy dog eyes. Fitting.

"My headline?"

"Give me the one true headline about what happened to you, Eppie," he said. "A simple Internet search comes up with approximately 341 articles on you and your family, but that doesn't necessarily make any one of them true. There are an infinite number of pages relating to Sasquatch, but we all know he doesn't even exist." He paused, then smirked. "Well, we mostly know he doesn't exist. Like 97% know. I'm allowing for the improbable reality of unicorns, leprechauns, trolls, and saber tooth tigers in that 3% margin, too."

"I think saber tooth tigers actually did exist. I've seen *Ice Age*."

"Okay, so more like a 2% window." Lincoln laughed and, for a moment, I worried that my dad might hear and realize I had a boy in my room at 2:30 in the morning, but then I figured I had the advantage of Dad's fresh drunkenness on my side, since he'd probably only gotten home a short while ago, anyway.

As his laugh trailed off, Lincoln said, "But I'm 100% sure the girl in those news stories isn't the girl standing in front of me right now. I'm certain, journalistically speaking, they got it all wrong. So I want yours. Gimme your best headline, Eppie. Help me understand."

This was hard. So much harder than any of my school assignments. Harder than any of my college application essays. I wasn't sure I could do this, sum up my life in two sentences.

I breathed in slowly through my nostrils. Then I puffed out the exhausted air through my mouth. The least I could do was try.

"Eight-Year-Old Girl Seeks Help for Incurably Crazy Mother, Father's Guilt-Ridden Stupor Leaves Her to Suffer Alone."

Well, that was awful.

"I knew it."

"Knew what?" I asked.

"That you weren't trying to kill yourself."

"Of course I wasn't trying to kill myself." How that had always been the explanation, I could never figure out. "I was eight. They made it sound like I was so sick and my mom was so horrible and I just wanted to end it all." Once the words started, they wouldn't stop. Apparently I did have more than two sentences worth in me. "Jumping from a second story window is not likely to result in death, no matter what they say. I was trying to get help for her, Lincoln."

"I know." He didn't know, but I supposed that's what you said when you wanted someone to keep talking. How you validated them and encouraged them to continue.

"They were yelling downstairs like always." It wasn't like the memories suddenly came flooding back, because they'd always been hanging there. In fact, they were just waiting their patient turn on the tip of my tongue. With permission finally granted, they flew out of my mouth so quickly, I didn't really even have to formulate them or prepare their delivery. They just dropped out. "Dad was angry, not drunk at that point, but mad. Mad at himself, mad at her. Mad that he'd suspected it all along, but never did anything about it. She'd been making me sick, but I didn't know that at the time. He'd known, or at least he figured that might be the case." There was absolutely no judgment in Lincoln's eyes. He did a really good job of holding a flat expression, another thing I wanted to learn from him. How to both feel and how to hide that feeling. "Dad kept saying, '*We need to get you help,*' over and over, like he was on repeat. But no one was leaving to get that help." My voice was steady, calm. "I kept thinking, *'Why aren't they getting her help, then?'* If she needed it so badly, why were they still downstairs arguing and screaming? I knew I couldn't go down there. Anytime they fought and I showed up in the middle of it, it didn't end well for me," I said. "So I just sat here, staring out my window. I figured it wasn't far to fall. That I could climb out and get someone like a policeman or doctor and they would come back and help my mom. That *I* could be the one to help her this time."

Though his jaw was set and his eyes were still rounded, they gathered with water and it made me instantly feel bad. This was why I didn't want to share this with him. This sort of reaction was exactly what I'd hoped to avoid.

"They gave me too much credit, you know?" I said. "Like they made me out to be so much older and more worldly than I could've possibly been at that age. I think maybe it helped strengthen their case, to make it seem like all of the years of her mistreating me finally drove me to the edge. That she was a villain I was trying to escape from, in every possible sense of the word." I shoved the heel of my hand to my nose and sniffed. "The age of reason. That's what they all clung to. That I'd magically reached a time in my life where I could understand the things that adults had only been privy to before." Lincoln's hand reached out and softly touched my elbow, just one slight tap. "But the only thing I could understand was my heart. And in my heart, she was my mom and she needed help, and after all her years of helping me, it was finally *my* turn to help *her*. But all I ended up doing was sending her to jail, then to the hospital. Now she's gone. Where's the help in that?"

Lincoln leaned over and kissed my forehead, then he pulled me into his arms. I felt his chest puff up with air, so tight it could burst, and then deflate slowly against my own.

"But you did exactly that, Eppie. You got her help the only way you knew how."

I huffed. "I'm not sure if you missed the newsflash, but she was incurably ill in most people's opinions, Lincoln. I honestly think being in that facility just made her more crazy. Plenty of people live out their crazy within the comforts of their own homes just fine."

"But that's only in cases where it doesn't directly harm those around them."

"Yeah," I agreed, if not reluctantly. "I guess so, if we're only talking physical harm."

Lincoln looked down at me for a moment. His teeth pierced his bottom lip briefly in a way that led me to believe they were blocking some thought from coming out. Some enameled barricade. Whatever they were trying to do, they failed, because he ended up saying. "Awkward Teenager Prone to Panic Attacks Falls Incurably in Love with Tragic Girl Prone to Amazingness."

"You're not awkward, Lincoln," I shot out fast, blushing at the same time. "And I'm not at all amazing."

"My ego is wondering why you choose to focus on those two bookends, when the real news is that I'm incurably in love with you, Eppie." His full lips kissed the corner of my mouth lightly. "Incurably."

Then his lips kissed my chin.

Then my cheek and the corners of my eyes and then the tip of my nose and top of my forehead. Finally, like they'd been blind and were searching everything out through touch alone, they fell on my mouth.

I hadn't been in love before, and I assumed neither had Lincoln, because this sort of kiss was a once in a lifetime, only for your first love, type of kiss. The kind on reserve for that moment when it truly needed to come out of hiding and prove its worth. It was the kind of kiss that stopped the continuum of time and the earth's rotation and light and sound and movement and breath.

It was the kiss that existed in its own realm, deserving of its own category of being. The kiss to end all kisses.

And I recognized the value in it. I knew this was something that would never happen again, at least not in this way and in this mindset and form. This moment was as unique as the boy in front of me, and as unique as the love he offered me.

So I grabbed on to it—onto him—and fell wholeheartedly in love with Lincoln right there, like this was some combustion of all that feeling I'd stored up for him since the first day with the rotating hamster wheel and the dirty baseball cap and Namaste and peanut butter sandwiches.

Every moment between us—each interaction, every word spoken—stacked one on top of the other until they filled up every hole in my heart, plugging it, repairing it.

Love was not a feeling anymore. It wasn't a four letter word. It wasn't even a word at all.

Love was a tall, gangly boy with floppy brown hair and an asymmetrical smile whose heart beat against my cheek and whose words made me insane, but for all the right reasons.

Lincoln was all of that, and all of that was love.

I wondered if I was that for him, too. If I'd become a definition of a word so powerful people died for it. I couldn't imagine anyone ever ascribing that sort of importance to me. It seemed blasphemous, almost.

"I'm so much in love with you, Eppie."

I pulled away to tell him, "I'm so much in love with you, too," not wanting to waste a moment between his declaration and my reciprocation. Wanting the moment to be one continuous thing.

And then we were kissing again, this one different from the last.

His hands were gripped on my hips, both of his thumbs teasing up the hem of my sweatshirt, touching my bare skin, but not touching it in unison, so it made me focus all of my attention on one side first where one finger rested, and then the other. There was no rhythm to it; it was all frantic energy leaving Lincoln in the tips of his fingers.

I was sucking on his bottom lip, feeling weird at the amount of sucking I was doing. Like he'd look back and all he would remember was me mauling his lip as though it were a pacifier. So I stopped sucking, mostly because I didn't want him to remember it that way. But I doubted boys did that—I doubted they had analogies for kissing maneuvers. And I doubted they had running commentaries forming in their heads as they kissed because seriously, who did that?

I needed to just shut up and go with it.

So I did. I went with it.

And going with it looked a lot like letting Lincoln take the lead. Those fingers on my hips moved up, brushing against my ribs, feeling each one. Was he counting them? How many ribs was I supposed to have, anyway?

I breathed into his mouth.

*Breathe, just breathe.*

I could do that. After all, I'd been doing it my whole life. But not like this. Never before had I needed to continue breathing while doing something so detrimental to my normally regulated, consistent breathing routine. People hyperventilated as a result of the types of breaths this kiss made me breathe.

"Are you okay?" Lincoln pulled his mouth from mine. His chest heaved erratically.

"Mostly."

"And which parts aren't mostly okay?"

I couldn't collect all of that data quickly enough. "I don't know... It's dizzying, all of this."

"The kissing, or the knowledge that I'm in love with you?"

"Yes. That."

Lincoln pulled my face up to his with his hands on my jaw. Then he smiled against my mouth. For all the times that I'd seen that smile and what it had done to my heart—that was nothing compared to feeling it on my lips like this, curled against my skin.

Lincoln smiling on my face was going to be the death of me. That was just the reality of how things were going to end up.

And then I started worrying about Lincoln smiling on other parts of my body and what that might do. Or frowning. Even worse. What if at the point in which he saw me without my shirt on, he frowned? If his smile felt this good, his frown would ruin me forever. I didn't think I'd ever be able to handle anything but a smile from that face, and even the smiles I couldn't actually handle.

Things were not going very well in my brain.

Lincoln drew back.

"I'm sensing the parts that were mostly okay have now transitioned to being mostly un-okay."

"No," I blurted. "No. It's all still in the okay category." I needed my mouth against his. "Nothing un-okay."

Holding me down by the shoulders, Lincoln halted my incoming kiss.

"You don't need to be worried about me trying anything tonight, Eppie. This is as far as it will go, alright?" His head dipped to catch my eyes.

I sort of hated that his statement made me feel relieved, because it wasn't like I didn't want to take things further. Relief shouldn't be an appropriate response to this. An appropriate response should be to tear each other's clothes off and have passionate, no holds barred sex, right? I was three days shy of adulthood and Lincoln was already one year in.

And that's what I figured came next, after the "I love you."

"I know you're not ready, and believe it or not, but I'm not, either."

Even more relief settled in.

"You're not? I mean... I don't know... I want to, I do. And I love you. And Sam and Dan are having sex and I'm not even sure if it's love for them, and it seems like if it is for us, then we should be further along than they are and—"

"Stop." His finger touched my lips. "I'm going to withhold your first amendment right for a second, okay?"

I nodded, his hand still at my mouth.

"I love you, Eppie. And I love kissing you, and one day, if we *do* decide to have sex, I'm sure I'll love that, too, no question about it." His eyes. Jeez, those eyes. I could hardly handle them. "But believe it or not, there is a whole lot of in between that I want to do with you first."

I ran through the bases quickly in my head, trying to recall what each one stood for.

"And I'm not talking about just everything physical, okay?" he said, reading me. "I'm talking about showing you I love you in every way I can, in every method available to me."

Knees. Nope, I didn't have them anymore.

I held on to Lincoln's lean waist in an effort to stay upright.

"I'm going to show you I love you in what we do, and I'm going to show you I love you in what we don't do, too."

Not only did I not have knees, I didn't have bones either. I was mush.

"Everything—absolutely everything—will be my *I love you*, Eppie."

He bent forward to press a kiss on my lips, and I sure felt his love in that.

And I felt it on his hand and in his smile and on the breath that fell against my skin.

"So tell me," he whispered into my hair, holding me pressed tightly against him. "Are there any un-okay parts left that I need to take care of?"

I shook my head.

"No, Lincoln." Slinging my arms around his neck, I pulled him down to me this time. "For once, everything in me feels remarkably okay. Better than okay."

"Me too, Eppie." With one more slow, sweet and downright phenomenal kiss, he muttered the words against my mouth, "I'm finally okay, too."

# TWENTY-SEVEN

*Dad said he'd be home in time.*

*He'd promised.*

*I looked at the clock once more and tried to ignore the fact that the minute hand had done a full rotation since the last time I'd glanced its direction.*

*He was going to make it. There was no way he'd forget.*

*I smoothed down the ruffle on the bottom of my dress with my hands and the sweat that stuck to my palms dampened the lace fabric. Marcie from school had taught me how to French braid this week during P.E. when we were supposed to be doing the sit-up challenge, and I'd attempted to twist my hair into something somewhat resembling a braid this morning. My ears wore the earrings I'd stolen from Mama's jewelry box. They were the pearl ones, and though they were heavy on my ears, they looked so pretty. I felt like a mermaid who'd found the winning oyster.*

*Thirty more minutes passed. My stomach rumbled.*

*Just then, the phone in the kitchen rang. I raced to pick it up.*

*"Dad?" I practically shouted into the receiver, my breathing quick and fast.*

*"Happy Birthday to You! Happy Birthday to You! Happy Birthday, Dear Ep-pie, Happy Birthday to You."*

*My heart sank. "Oh… Hi, Phil."*

*"Happiest birthday, Eppie!" It was nice of Phil to remember, but his voice was higher than the one I'd hoped to hear, and his wish wasn't from the person I'd wanted it to be from. "Am I interrupting your breakfast with your dad? I know you two had big plans."*

*I swallowed the lump in my throat, wondering how it got there when I hadn't even eaten anything to choke on.*

*"No. He's not here just yet. He'll be here soon, though, I'm sure. He promised."*

*There was silence that followed. It was a thinking silence, I figured. Phil did a lot of those. Lots of pauses before talking.*

*"Well, I have something I'd like to drop by, if it's okay."*

*I wanted to tell him that he'd have to leave it on the doorstep, that I'd be gone with Dad by the time he drove over here, but instead I just said, "That's fine."*

*Twenty minutes later, when Phil's Datsun pulled into the driveway, Dad still wasn't home.*

*"Eppie." Phil smiled at me so wide when I opened the door. His mustache looked like it would break into a million little hairs. "You look beautiful, my dear."*

*I wanted it to mean something, but it didn't mean enough. Phil wasn't my dad. I just shrugged at him.*

*He held out a brown paper bag. "Brought you a little something."*

*Giving him a questioning look, one that involved my furrowed eyebrows, I grabbed the sack from his hands.*

*"Apple fritters?" I asked after taking one out. I waved it in the air, almost annoyed.*

*"Eppie fritters." His smile was going to crack that face of his.*

*"They're not called Eppie fritters." My voice probably sounded mean, and in truth, I felt a little mean.*

*"Sure are. You must not have been to Golden Barn recently. They changed their menu."*

*He was right, I hadn't, but I also knew that not all adults told the truth. I didn't figure Phil was telling the truth right now.*

*"They did not."*

*"Eppie." Phil pulled the bag from my hands and took out a donut. He bit down on one and talked with crumbles of food still in his mouth. "If I was going to lie to you, it wouldn't be about something as insignificant as a donut."*

*"They're not insignificant!" I shouted. I stole the bag from him again, this time quite angry.*

*He smiled even more, if that were possible. "Exactly my point. Such a delight, these donuts are. And now they have a delightful name to match."*

*"How did you know I thought that's what they were called?"*

*Phil swallowed. "Your mother told me."*

*My heart jumped within my chest. This time I choked on actual food. "When did you see my mother?"*

*"A few days ago. I visited her at Serena Vista."*

*"How is she? Can I see her?" I knew I shouldn't want to know the answers to these things, but I couldn't help the questions from flying out of my mouth. "I mean, am I even allowed to see her?"*

*"Eppie." Phil sighed, and he did another annoying thinking pause. "I'll have to check on that for you. I'm not sure what the guidelines are. There is a level of safety involved here, considering what she was charged with. You're still a minor, and these decisions need to be made by someone a little higher up."*

*I gave him a puzzled look. "What's a minor?" I hadn't heard that term before.*

*"Someone under eighteen. Someone not an adult just yet."*

*I did the quick math in my head.*

*Nine more birthdays from today and I wouldn't be a minor anymore.*

*Nine more birthdays until I got to make my own decisions.*

*Nine more birthdays and I could finally see my mother.*

*In nine more birthdays, my world would be right again.*

# TWENTY-EIGHT

His newspaper was high above his eyes, just the grayed tufts of hair spiking out the top. Each time he would lift his mug to his mouth, I could hear the methodical slushing of liquid into it, a swallow, a throat clear, and then the settle of the ceramic back onto the tiled counter. I'd been working up the voice to speak. At some point he'd have to refill his mug, get up from behind his paper post. Then I'd pour out my plans to him. I'd tell him what I was going to do.

There was an endless supply of coffee in that cup, it appeared.

"Dad?"

The newspaper's upper half folded back in on itself and Dad's flat eyes met mine.

"Eppie."

Go time.

"Dad, I'm going to visit her today."

The cup was empty. Dad tried to drain more contents from it, but got nothing. He folded the paper into four quadrants, slowly, and lowered it in front of him like an origami placemat. Then he put the cup on it, directly in the center. Fingered at the handle. Twisted the mug side to side.

He waited too long to speak. I was going to have to say it again. He was going to make me say it again.

And then suddenly, "Why, Eppie?"

"Today's my birthday."

Dad moved to the sink and placed his coffee cup in the basin. He turned around, and then he hooked his hands on to the counter's ledge, ankles crossed in a contemplative stance.

I didn't look any different, that I was sure. Maybe a little zombie-like, since I'd been awake for the past twenty-four hours, unable to sleep. But I was certain I still resembled the same person. When you were little, people always asked if you felt any older on the day of your birthday. It was a silly thing to ask, but adults asked kids silly questions all the time. But right now, with Dad looking at me like this, it was as though I looked like an entirely different person on this day. He gave me the look reserved for a complete stranger. I glanced down at my arms, my legs, feeling like I was still the same, but not quite the same.

"Why now, Eppie? Why suddenly today?" One hand darted up in the air, slicing. "Why not yesterday? Or last week? Why not last year?"

"I wasn't eighteen," I half whispered, unsure.

The sound that gurgled out of his throat couldn't be likened to laughing. But that's what it tried to be, a laugh. Mockery echoing out of his thick vocal chords.

"That has absolutely nothing to do with anything."

"Of course it does." I was feeling defiant. I was feeling crumpled. How could the two coexist?

He shook his head fast. "Eppie, you could've gone years ago. All you had to do was ask." His steel eyes softened. I didn't appear to be as much of a stranger anymore. I was now an acquaintance, so it seemed. "I would've taken you."

No, no that wouldn't work. "I couldn't ask you to do that."

Dad's hands and head dropped at once. "Where do you think I go everyday?"

Anywhere serving beer, I thought. Anywhere with a liquor license. "To the bars."

"Before the bars."

I never concerned myself with Dad's comings and goings. Sure, I supposed he had a routine, but it didn't pertain to me. I had my own routine to stick to. Sleep, school, homework, and the recent addition of Lincoln thrown into the mix. "Don't know."

It surprised me that I couldn't feel the breath from his sigh reach me all the way across the room. It was that deep, that exhausted.

"I'm there everyday, Eppie." His words were bland and his delivery tired. "I don't always get out of the car. Most of the time I just sit, staring through the windshield. But she knows I'm there. I'm sure of it."

I quickly reassembled my expression. Flipped my mouth and brows back up, widened my eyes from the slitted glare they'd adopted.

"Why didn't you tell me?" I asked, wondering why my throat was strangling my words this way, viciously turning on itself. Why did even my own body revolt against this news? "Why didn't you tell me you've visited her?"

My dad and I didn't share much. But that much I thought we had shared: the fact that in nearly ten years, neither of us had visited a woman who used to mean everything to us. Who *should have* meant everything to us.

There were no bonds between my father and me now. They were all severed with that newest truth alone.

And now I was alone in this.

I stood up quickly from the barstool.

"Eppie." He wished for his coffee cup, I could tell. Hands not knowing what to do, words not knowing how to form. The pacing from the sink to the counter, to the breakfast bar and back to the sink was a glaring red flag. He was a broken man. Maybe he thought he'd be able to collect the pieces of himself somehow, moving about frantically like this. How had I not seen that on the day she'd left, he'd been torn in two? Though what he just told me had finally severed any thin union between us, he'd been severed long ago. Cut completely in half. By her.

"Eppie." He used my name once more, my nickname, not my given name, the one he'd always preferred. "What she did to you was inexcusable. Wrong. Absolutely just wrong." A calm washed over his voice and his movements, some soothing balm to his senses. I couldn't figure out where it came from. He wasn't historically a calm man. "It was abuse, no way around it. She abused you, Eppie. Your own mother," he said. "And I couldn't protect you. Or maybe I just didn't protect you. I don't know. I should've seen it all sooner."

The blame game was ugly, especially when it consisted of just one player. I didn't like watching my father play it out with his current self and his former self—the one who could've done something to alter our outcome. We'd all lost in that game. Every single one of us.

"The first time I went, it was to get answers. Like if I prayed hard enough, the skies would somehow rain down truth on me. How could she do this to us? To our family? What was going on in her mind that made any of this okay? Like maybe if I'd given her more attention, she wouldn't have sought it out in such a horrific way." We exchanged expressions, blank and void, so I supposed there was really nothing to exchange at all, but it felt like something. "I didn't get answers. I just ended up with more questions. Then it was like this big thing I had to solve. This great mystery to unfold. I had to put the pieces together. Then maybe it would make sense. Then maybe I would understand. Maybe in understanding, we'd all be able to heal."

Dad's Adam's apple spasmed. His eyebrows drew together, close enough to look like a solid, dark unibrow.

"I'll never be able to solve your mother, Eppie," he said, worn down like he was admitting defeat. "I can't solve her. And I think the real problem is that she couldn't solve herself."

I sat back onto the stool.

Eight years of memories, followed by nearly ten years of void. It was like that void had washed over the memories, bleaching them. That's what the time without my mother was. It wasn't healing. It wasn't a steady slipping of thoughts and remembrances. It wasn't even forgetting. It was just bleach, oxidizing, changing the form of my original life into something else, something different, but not getting rid of it altogether. Not getting rid of her. I couldn't get the stain of her out of my life. Time just burned out the bad, but the fibers still existed there. She existed in those fibers.

"I'm still going."

"Right." Dad's thumb smoothed his chin. "I figured as much."

I wasn't sure he had the right to assume anything about me, but I let him keep it.

"I have to, Dad. For me. For my own answers. I have to finally accept this reality." His posture and tone left no need for justification. Still, I felt like I should attempt to offer it, maybe more for my sake than for his. "Your answers are different than the ones I need. I need to do this for myself." At some point in life, every teenager uttered this phrase to his or her parents, I was certain of that. No longer was the umbilical tether enough, you ultimately had to separate and forge your own path. I was ready for that inevitable forge. "I've been waiting so many years to do this, Dad. I *have* to do it."

I never really took my father for a smart man, even though he'd attended a prestigious college and once held a lucrative job. Whatever intelligence he'd had was laced with alcohol and rage, dumbing down his thoughts and his voice as it slurred his wisdom. But I was good in school. I received straight A's and praise from each one of my teachers, grade after grade. I'd always figured my education proved my brain's worth, proved *my* worth.

But evidently Dad was still smart, or at least tragically wise.

Right now, when he looked across the room to me, his eyes pressed into mine. Then he said, "There is a difference between waiting upon something and putting something off, Eppie." Then he paused, feeling so much like Phil before saying, "Don't let your heart confuse the two, and only let your head make those types of decisions."

Turning around, he flipped the faucet on. Water streamed into his empty cup. I watched him rinse it out, once, twice, and then a third time. Finally satisfied, he shut off the water, swiped over the mug with a towel, and set both items on the counter. Then, over his shoulder, just as he was about to leave the room, he muttered, "Happy eighteenth birthday, Eppie."

# TWENTY-NINE

Adults often forgot what it was like to grow through childhood and into adulthood. They forgot that adolescence was a process of circumstances and emotions, chained together over time, the linking of epiphanies whose only requirement was to be experienced firsthand. Life was a firsthand sort of thing.

But some adults didn't realize that sometimes you needed to create opportunities for the sake of allowing that childhood to take place, giving that rite of passage the safe space it needed to unfurl. That's where parental responsibility and guidance came in.

My Dad hadn't created opportunity or taken responsibility in my life, but I didn't hold that against him. I doubted he even knew how. Nevertheless, I never got my slow and steady, handheld transition. Childhood fast-forwarded to adulthood all in one flash. All in one leap.

Now was the time to create my own opportunity.

"You sure about this, Eppie?"

"Yes."

"Okay."

Lincoln rolled his turn signal, the yellow arrow on the dash pulsing. Whether intentional or not, his left leg bounced in the same staccato intervals. Thank goodness it was the left. The right would have resulted in such a stop-and-go, jerky motion that we might as well have been participants in a round of bumper cars. But his right side was controlled. That was a good sign. I needed at least half of Lincoln to be in control, because all of me felt out of it.

"Okay," he said once more after sliding the camper into an empty parking space, next to a two-door beige sedan and a tree whose blossoms were trickling off like rainwater in the low, warm breeze.

Windows stood immediately in front of us, a whole spread of them. Four down times six across, equaling twenty-four. I paused, counting their number. "Did you happen to see how many windows were on the east side of the building?"

"No, I didn't." His voice was quiet, calming. Usually when people didn't understand what was going on at all, they had a higher cadence to their dialogue. Their sentences ended with trills that rose upward, like fingers reaching for the answer. Lincoln's intonation was steady, no reaching. Lincoln was persistently steady, apart from the occasional fit of panic.

"My guess is twelve."

"This building's a rectangle. That would make sense," I surmised.

He nodded. His eyetooth snagged the corner of his mouth and bit down just a little into his lip. Maybe that's why his smile was always so crooked, from chewing his lip in this way.

"So twelve and twelve and twenty-four and twenty-four is seventy-two." I did the math out loud. "Unless there are stairwells on the east and west sides. I'm going to knock off about six from each of those to account for the stairwells. Emergency exits are code, yeah?"

"Yes. Six sounds like an appropriate amount to deduct." Lincoln was kind, much too kind.

I kept going. "That leaves sixty windows in all."

"Correct. Sixty windows." His hand flicked over to the driver's side door and he cracked the window with his fingers on the crank. It was hot. Muggy. Sweat pooled in my armpits and on my lip and behind my knees so quickly.

"What's our town's population?"

Lincoln swiped his forehead, then refit his cap back in place. "Hmm. Don't know. Twelve hundred, I think?"

"Twelve hundred."

I looked in front of me at the small compartment in the dash that no longer had a door to it. There were a lot of things in Lincoln's glove box. An inhaler, a map that had been folded haphazardly into a very unmap-like shape, a deck of playing cards with a half-naked gypsy lady illustrated on the torn box, and a handful of napkins embossed with a big, arching M. I snatched one of those and the capless blue pen that sat in the cup holder attached to my door.

"If twelve hundred equals one hundred percent," I said, chicken scratching the tissue. "Then sixty equals what?"

My fourth grade math memory was failing me fast.

"Five percent."

Yes. Right. "Five percent."

"Eppie—"

"Five percent of Masonridge is effectively crazy, Lincoln," I gaped, careening over his words. Then I started laughing, hysterically. It scared even myself, and those noises originated in me, so they shouldn't be startling, but they were. Unnervingly so. "Can you believe it? That's an absurdity!"

"Eppie, what's going on?" Lincoln's body sagged deep in his seat. His arm dropped onto the console between us. But it didn't give me goose bumps this time. It almost resembled someone tossing out a life preserver. I wasn't sure I wanted to grab on.

"I'm baffled by those statistics, and I don't even know if that's a high amount or a low amount!" The laughing shut off, but in sound only. My body still shook from the force trapped within me, like it was tapping on me from the inside out, needing release. "Baffling!"

His eyes were shrouded with worry, and I knew I put that worry there. "If this is too much, we can just go home. Rent a movie. Eat cake. Celebrate *you*."

"God, Lincoln!" His name came out in place of one of the shuddering laughs. "How can I celebrate someone I'm not even sure I know?"

He took his life preserver offering away, hugging his hand into his chest, folding his arms there.

And I started to sink.

"I know you." Stone-faced, stone-walled. "And you know you. You don't need your mother to tell you who you are, Eppie. You don't have to listen to her voices anymore. I don't listen to my mother's. I don't listen at all when it comes to her."

My mouth popped open, then clamped shut. I did that two more times, then realized I probably looked like a fish. "The problem is that her voices aren't all that awful, Lincoln. When I hear her, I hear love."

"I'm not sure that was real love."

"That's what it felt like. That's all I ever knew of her. For as long as it's been, I still can't reconcile the two different people she seemed to be. There's who she was to me, and who everyone else keeps trying to tell me she was," I said. "What if I don't know how to love any differently than what she taught me? What if all I have to offer is this faulty version of the love I thought she had for me?"

The typical Lincoln smile had been replaced by one so much less him. It was a crappy stand in. I didn't believe anything about it. He must've caught on, because it slipped from his face, melted almost, and then only a flicker of a grin could be seen in his eyes. Anyone else would've missed it, but I knew what to look for. That crinkle in the corner, the too-many-lines-for-his-age creasing together like the folds of a paper fan. I think I loved this hidden smile almost as much as his trademark one. It was a smile only seen by me.

"Eppie," he said. His fingers reached out to sweep my cheek for no other reason than to just touch my skin. There wasn't a hair that needed moving or a tear that required drying. Just touch, that's what this was. "Your love isn't her love. Your life isn't her life. There's nothing faulty about your love."

But I felt faulty. I did. "You want to know something funny?"

"Hmm?"

"Me jumping out of a window landed her behind one of those windows." With a straight finger, I pointed to the shiny glass wall decorating Serena Vista. Which one was hers? What box belonged to my mom?

"Something else put her behind that window, Eppie. Not you," Lincoln assured. "Sure, some people had no choice in the outcomes that landed them here. Maybe their brains didn't give them any other option. Maybe their situations didn't let them or their chemicals weren't in their favor. But I'm not sure your mom was in that category, Eppie. She had options."

I knew that, I did. I *thought* I did, at least.

I glanced back at the windows. "There're just so many of them." The pattern was almost dizzying to take in, so many reflections, so much glass. "I wonder if they at least got to choose their view." I knew it wasn't like renting an apartment or selecting your dorm room, but there had to be *some* comforts provided to the residents here. There had to be some benefit to being shut out from society indefinitely. Some benefit other than the loose promise of healing.

"I think some of us—the lucky ones—get to choose our view in life." He rolled up the window, getting ready. "Others don't. And then there are those who just aren't so good at the choosing."

I looked over at Lincoln, at his much too dirty hat and his too long hair and his out of proportion legs. But there were other things not right about his size—the size of his heart. It was too big for his body. Way too big. It spilled out of him in his words and his voice and his touch. And I got to catch that excess. I got to grab on to Lincoln's extra heart. His abundance of love. I'd never let it go.

That made me think that maybe I was one of those that did a really good job at the choosing.

I closed my eyes, inhaling deeply, three steady breaths in a row. "We can go now. I'm ready to visit my mom."

# THIRTY

*"We're just doing a graveside ceremony, Eppie."*

*The wall in front of me was blank, but I stared at it as though there was an abstract painting adorning it and I was expected to decipher its meaning. I swallowed, processing his words, and then blinked. When I opened my eyes, I tried looking at my dad, but I just couldn't connect. Staring at the nothing before me was so much easier.*

*"They advised against holding an actual funeral service." His voice shook, even though it was quiet in volume. "I can definitely understand the reasoning there. The papers have been vultures. We don't need to give them even more fodder by drawing excess attention to what happened." Dad sighed. "Should I plan for you to attend, or should I see if Phil is able to stay with you?"*

*"I'm not ready to do that," I admitted without pause. "I'm too scared to go to the cemetery. I hate cemeteries." I did. They were full of goblins and spiders and decay and cobwebs. Cemeteries always felt like Halloween, no matter what day of the year it happened to be.*

*"That's okay, Eppie." Dad nodded, too many times in a row. His hands came up to my shoulders, cupping them*

*there. "You don't ever have to go if you don't want to, understood?"*

*I couldn't nod back. "I just don't know why, but I'm so scared to go."*

*"Eppie." Dad never cried. Not even when he got the call about Mom. But now water was spilling onto his cheeks in a soundless emotion that only came out in tears. "It's okay to be scared. This is scary stuff. For as much as I hate all of this, I'm grateful that you're only seeing the scary now, in hindsight. In some twisted way, I'm actually grateful that for most of our lives, we were too ignorant to be scared."*

*"What if I never want to go?" I started, but I had a hard time getting out the words. Somehow they jumbled on my tongue, tripping me up. I'd eaten alphabet soup once and had stacked over two dozen noodle letters together before chomping them down. That's what I imagined my words doing now. They were soupy vowels and consonants, all mixed up.*

*Dad sighed and covered me with a waft of his hot breath. It smelled funny, and I didn't like the smell of it at all, so much so that I covered my nose with the inside of my sleeve to avoid the stench. "Well, I can't imagine you'd ever really want to go. This is a horrible ending, Eppie." He took a drink from his cup and I realized whatever was in it was making his breath smell so bad. Stuff that putrid shouldn't belong in your body. Stuff like that should be considered toxic. "If I were you," he continued, "I'd want to hold off on that ending, too."*

*Dad never gave me much advice in the past, but for some reason, this felt like something I should listen to.*

*So I did. I listened.*

*I'd hold off on that ending for as long as I could.*

# THIRTY-ONE

Had it been necessary to set foot in the actual hospital, it would've been easier, and that was saying a lot because I honestly felt as though they'd have valid reason to have me committed with the amount of nervous pacing I was currently doing. And truth be told, if someone marched down the hall and told me I'd be staying there, I wasn't entirely sure I'd argue. Surrender almost seemed sweeter.

We all harbored varying degrees of insanity within us, I figured. That was just the curse of being human. Some of us hid it better than others. Some managed to tame it out until the rest of the world thought it no longer existed. But none of that was truly ridding ourselves of the nature inherent in our beings. I'd heard too many stories of once domesticated animals bearing their claws and reverting back to the wild creatures they originally were. The creatures they always were.

Maybe that's why places like Serena Vista existed—to tame the wild ones back into submissive captivity. That thought made me sad. So sad. It made me want to run, screaming through their halls, throwing open every door, unlocking the cages. *You're free! You're free! You're wild and free.*

Leaving that building didn't equate to freedom, though. That definitely wasn't the case for people like my mother. That place wasn't the real trap, I knew that much.

Because how could you ever truly escape a trap set up in your very own mind?

I doubted you could.

Was it really so realistic to think we'd be able to coast through existence, toeing around that snare, never thinking it would one day snap down on us? What made us so arrogantly confident to believe we were strong enough, brave enough, wise enough, healthy enough to avoid the trap without a little extra guidance?

That's what we needed. We all needed help. Some with medicine. Some with talking and listening and talking some more. Prayer. We probably needed prayer. And we needed one another. We needed one another to verify our crazy. To see it reflected in another person. To realize it wasn't as scary or hopeless as it seemed. To hold hands and tiptoe together. We were stronger in twos, we had to be. After all, hadn't all of those wild animals boarded into the shelter of that big boat side by side? Hadn't they endured the relentless storm and come out under the sun, still a united front?

We needed something to weather the storm in. An ark to keep us safe.

That hospital, I figured, was that for its residents. Not a trap. Not at all.

I looked across my shoulder to Lincoln, feeling so much stronger with him by my side, paired off together.

"Do you know which one is hers?"

We were leaned up against a decorative pergola positioned in the middle of the grass, our bodies slumped against the concrete wall. Mid-afternoon light twinkled through the cutouts in the trees, the crisscrossing branches creating gaps and holes for amber rays to spill through. It washed across my face, warming my cheeks with its golden warmth, feeling wonderful even though every other part of me hurt. My backbone protruded against the flat surface uncomfortably so I pulled my posture straight, taut like a wire. That didn't help. I curled into myself. That just made the bone on the wall more noticeable. Comfort wouldn't be found.

"She's next to my grandparents. Under that big oak." I nodded up ahead with the tip of my nose toward a craggily tree whose bark was peeling and curling along the base. It had to be practically ancient, and I wondered how many rings were embedded in that thick trunk. Things like that had always fascinated me. How even trees kept track of the years they'd lived.

"Tell me how you want this to go, Eppie." Lincoln's thumb rubbed against my hand in slow, steady circles. "Tell me what you hope to get out of this."

That was a loaded question. I paused for a moment, letting it ruminate in my head. What *did* I want out of this? What was the goal? To make some spiritual connection? To get answers? To understand, once and for all, that she was gone and never coming back?

Yes.

Yes to all of the above. I wanted everything.

"Will you walk with me?" My voice was small, my footsteps smaller as I edged forward, careful not to disrupt the freshly manicured grass on the gravesite immediately in front of us.

"Of course, Eppie." He turned to me, sunlight filtering through his curls of hair. I swear, he looked like an angel. A baseball cap wearing, lopsided-grinning angel. "I'd walk to the ends of the earth with you."

That caused a laugh to burst from my lips, and I felt a bit self-conscious at the whole laughing in a cemetery thing. Pretty sure that wasn't proper etiquette. Slugging him against the shoulder probably wasn't, either, but I did that, too. "Cheesiest line ever."

"Truth is often cheesy, and I speak a lot of the truth. Therefore, I tend to be a bit cheesy. I often ooze cheese, so I'm a kind of the Cheese-Whiz of truth telling. Just the way things roll."

I laughed again, this time not caring at all if it was okay or not to do so.

We strategically guided our way around headstones and plaques, and I tried not to let my eyes make contact with any of the names and dates etched into their marbled surfaces, but they couldn't help but land on them. I really didn't wish to know of Julia Grey who was just fourteen when she passed. Or Alma Morgenstern who lived a hundred and two years and died at the turn of the century. And Ralph Gandy. I didn't need to know about his thirty-nine short years of life.

My brain couldn't comprehend all of the life lived between those small dashes on their tombstones.

It certainly couldn't comprehend the one on my mother's.

"This is her."

I closed my eyes, praying just like my father said he had, but my breathing was so fast I could hardly focus on any one thing without the dizzying delirium that accompanied each unsteady breath. The panic slowly settled in, if panic even settled. More like crawled. Panic crawled through me, scratching at every nerve ending, altering every breath.

"Deep, square breaths, Eppie."

I did some of those. Rise and fall. Rise and fall.

The blackened, blurred edge started to recede, sloughing away from my vision, but white stars filled the gaps where they once were.

Taking my shoulders into his grip, Lincoln moved me around to face him. "Talk to me about what you're feeling," he said, his eyes alight with encouragement. "Tell me what this means to you."

I felt—

I felt...

I felt nothing.

I saw a woman this morning. We'd fleetingly connected stares at a red light. She wore a tattered patch on her navy-colored Dickies shirt that read, "Louise." She was on her way to work, to the only mechanic garage in town, I figured, based on her attire and the thick line of grease in the crescents of her nail. It was like the opposite of a French manicure, as opposite as you could get on the color spectrum.

This woman in the ground was her.

And she was also the man who'd offered me his cart in the parking lot of Winn-Dixie when Lincoln decided a cake was an appropriate thing to bake on one's birthday and that ingredients needed to be purchased immediately. The man wore a toddler on his hip and a curdled trail of spit-up down his back, and our encounter was so brief and momentary that I wasn't sure I'd remember many more details about him once those two descriptions were lost from my short term memory.

She was that man also.

Because she was truly no more than a stranger to me. No more than another once-resident in a town where I happened to live. She could've been anyone, because she was no longer someone to me.

Why hadn't I figured this would be how it would go?

I thought I came here to finally mourn her, but that wasn't it.

I came to mourn the loss of a mom. You would think they'd be one and the same, that the loss of her—that her death—was the truest tragedy. For most daughters, I supposed that's how things went. But for me, the slow tragedy began with that first dose she'd administered. I wondered if she knew that she'd been immunizing me against her with every doctor visit she'd scheduled, every lie she'd fabricated. If mourning was necessary, that should've happened back in the hospital when I found out who she really was. But I didn't fully mourn then. And now, so many years later, it felt like too little too late.

"Are you okay?"

"I don't know. Is it wrong if I say if I am?"

In the few months I'd known him, Lincoln never let me feel guilty for expressing emotions that weren't what would be considered appropriate for the time or place. Now, like all of those consistent situations, was no exception.

"Your feelings are exactly that, *your* feelings. Eppie, there is no right or wrong here." He met my eyes and examined me, probably trying to pull something out. I wasn't sure what emotion clung to my features. I wasn't sure what he would interpret given the look I offered. "I'm going to talk to you a little bit about something I know to be true, okay?"

"More cheese?"

"Maybe." He smiled, head tipped to the side. "But I'm willing to take that chance."

I gave him the go-ahead with a quick nod.

"A whole lot of what we're taught in life is complete, utter crap. Seriously, forget all that you think you know. Blood is not thicker than water. Family is not life's greatest blessing. You know how I know that? Because, like you, I got the short end of the stick when God pieced my relatives together." Lincoln's mouth scowled, waiting while a memory or something played out in his brain, then his lips parted to speak. "But somehow, the fact that I was placed into this loveless familial entity made me a man who knew exactly what love was when I finally got even just a small taste of it. Like that perfect, juicy bite from a fruit that's ready for the picking when all you've ever known was the sourness of an unripe peach. Living without love made me ripe for it."

"You're wrong," I said, a smile playing on my lips. "You're not cheesy. You're totally fruity."

Lincoln didn't bother to disagree with me. "Maybe so. It's just that I see you here, seemingly guilty at your lack of emotion toward your mother, and that's okay, Eppie. Because it's not that you're without feeling. It's not that you don't have love. It's just that she's no longer capable of earning any of yours, not even her memory," he said. "So the fact that you deem me worthy of that love is a huge honor, my little peach. You've saved up all of your love for me."

"Now you're just plain crazy."

"Maybe." He shrugged. "But I think being just a little crazy makes me capable of loving you like crazy, so I'll take it."

"I'll take it, too," I said, then paused a moment. "But I *did* love her once, you know? In the blissfulness of naivety, I loved that mom I thought I had." My chest was tight, a balloon nearly pushing out on my ribcage. With a slow, steady hiss, I forced out the air trapped within me. "I don't know what I was expecting when I came here." I tossed my hands to the sky. "It wasn't like I believed she was still alive, but without seeing this permanent place in the ground—without reading those dates right in front of me—it was like I was free to make up my own ending, not the one where she gave up on herself. Or maybe she gave *in* to herself. I don't know what truly led her there, what made her take those actions." This sounded preposterous, surely. But sometimes even the hard things needed to be spoken. Maybe when it came down to it, they were the only things that needed to be spoken at all. I decided to put on a brave face and speak them. "I would pretend she was just at Vista, really taking her time to get healthy. I'd make up these alternate endings to our life. She's coming home next month. She's doing so well she's teaching classes on overcoming your obstacles and inner demons and she won't be home until Christmas," I explained. "As it turns out, death isn't always an ending."

"Nope, it's definitely not. The dead don't take their memories with them when they go." Then, with his hands around me, he gathered me closer. "You deserve an ending, Eppie. A happy one."

"I don't think I need a happy ending, necessarily. I just want a happy life where the good slightly outweighs the bad. And that's what I have with you, Lincoln. Even in this short amount of time, you've tipped the scales in favor of good. Even this..." I turned a hand toward the tombstones flanking us, their shadows long in the early evening light. "You've managed to make this okay for me."

"You know how concerned I am over every part of you being okay," he smiled, making my mind and heart flit back to the night I found him on my roof. The night of the perfectly awkward kiss and declarations of young, incurable love.

"Well, you've done that," I confirmed. "You've done that remarkably well."

"So did this end up being a good birthday for you then?" he asked, his brow lifted, arms bracketing me in.

"A good birthday," I answered, nuzzled against his chest, my newest favorite place in this world. "A good everything."

# THIRTY-TWO

"Open up the envelope." Lincoln had as big of a grin as the elasticity of his face would allow. And if his overly excited knees didn't stop bouncing, they'd soon slap him in the chin. Nothing about his face or body was settling; it was all cartoony grins and over-exaggerated movements. "Open it, Eppie."

"I'm a little worried that something horrifying is hidden in this, Lincoln. I've got that classic something-is-going-to-jump-out-and-scare-the-ever-loving-crap-out-of-me type jitters. I'm drowning in anxiety."

"You've made your irrational fear of surprises loudly known to me already. Plus, it's an envelope. Folded paper. Nothing scary about it. I promise, this is a good one. Scout's honor."

I decided not to put up a fight, even though I did question the authenticity of his boyscouthood. With my index finger in the flap, I tore the top from the padded envelope and stared directly into it.

"Bungee cord?"

"We're jumping." He grinned, taking the red and black rope from my hands. "Nothing but you, me, and a giant bungee shooting us out of the sky, narrowly missing earth."

"I don't know—"

"Listen." He yanked the cord away from me and snapped it between his hands and one hooked end ricocheted off the driver's side window. That crack of metal against glass really didn't make me feel any more at ease. "I'm a pansy. I hate heights. If you think that you're more scared than I am about this, you're sorely wrong." Yet somehow I doubted that. "This is your birthday gift, Eppie. The chance to finally jump and get someone the help they need. In this instance, that's me getting over my irrational acrophobia."

"I don't think it's all that irrational—"

"We're going to take that leap together."

"To our deaths?"

"To our future!" Lincoln's fist pumped in the air and Trudy swerved erratically to the left. Dropping both hands back onto the wheel, he guided her into our lane like reining in a spooked horse. "Sorry 'bout that."

"I get the gesture, I do. And I'm grateful for it, but I don't think any of this is necessary. I'm good where I'm at, truly good. We don't have to have some grandiose playing out of symbolic jumping for me to be okay. You've already gotten me to that good place."

"Maybe, but *I'm* not in that place yet." Eyes on the road, Lincoln talked through the windshield as though he was holding a conversation with the painted yellow line up ahead. There was a lot of intense brow furrowing currently going on. "This is what's about to happen. I'm going to get up on that ledge and I'm going to panic. My chest will get tight. My breaths will trip upon themselves. The world will spin as though on a merry-go-round. And then we'll jump." That ill-placed speed bump was a sick joke, making me practically shoot through the roof as we bounced over it in his jalopy. "And then I'll realize that the fall isn't nearly as scary as the fear."

"Or you'll realize it's infinitely more so."

"That's certainly a possibility." He shot me his crooked smile. "I plan on jumping today, and it would make the experience all the more pleasurable to have you strapped to me while I do it."

Weighing the incredibleness of being pressed up against Lincoln's body with the horribleness of plummeting to my premature death, I made my swift and easy decision. "Okay. Let's do this."

Another unbalanced smile. "Let's do this."

Evidently the day of my celebration of birth was a popular day for testing immortality, which was a touch morbid since we'd started the earlier portion of it at an actual cemetery. There were two couples already ahead of us in line when we arrived at the *Extreme Activities* tandem bungee jumping facility, just an hour outside of town and into the curving hills and dirt roads that twisted through the mountainsides flanking Masonridge. We were in the literal ridges around Mason, I supposed. And there was this bridge called "Lover's Ledge," suspended one hundred sixty feet above a river that, though flowing with water, didn't look nearly deep enough to swallow our impact had our bungee decided to snap instead of retract. If things went wrong, their only option was to do so terribly.

"It's gonna be a total adrenaline rush." Spike, our Extreme Activities Instructor—or EAI as he acronymed it—used the word *total* the way some people used salt. It flavored practically every sentence out of his mouth. "Like an atmospheric orgasm."

"Not necessarily what we're going for," Lincoln said, adjusting his harness though I'd begged him not to fiddle with it at least fifty times now. "But I'm certain it will be an adventure."

"Totally," Spike, who—fittingly enough—had bleached tipped hair standing straight on end, said in complete monotone over the shrill echo of both a grown man and woman screaming bloody murder that bounced loudly off the canyon walls. I was baffled by the notion that jarring sounds like these were just the background music to Spike's everyday work life. I'd request a different soundtrack if I were him. "Alright. I'm gonna go push this next couple off and then I'll be back for you. All good?"

"All good." Lincoln was speaking for himself only.

"Are you sure you still want to do this?" Sometimes people changed their minds after the eighteenth or nineteenth time of asking, right? That's what it meant to wear someone down, I figured. "No one has to know about our chicken-ness if we back out. Your secret is safe with me."

"Here's the thing, Eppie." Lincoln leaned against the rusty railing, then stepped off from it, then tried leaning once more, but it was so glaringly obvious that he was terrified and couldn't find his confidence up so high on this bridge. "I'm a coward by nature—"

"No—"

"Let me finish. There's a very real possibility that our leap from this post will render you deaf from all of my decibel-shattering wailing, so I feel the need to get this out while you can still hear me, okay?"

"Okay."

"So," he continued. "As I was saying. I'm a coward. That's my go-to. It kept me out of the army and there's every indication it's what killed Charlie as a result."

"That's so not even fair to assert crap like that."

"I could've been there, Eppie. I used to have these dreams that Dan and Charlie and me were all on the front lines together, just like we'd always planned. Then out of nowhere this bomb would go off and I'd throw myself on top of the guys and somehow shield them with my skinny body and we'd all end up completely safe and unharmed and I'd be a regular hero." He fiddled again with his straps and I swatted his hand from the harness. Then I clasped my hands together, staring at them as he spoke, ignoring whatever it was that he was doing with his hooks and straps. "I'd have these visions, Eppie, and man, they felt so real to me. The frustratingly ironic thing is that I'd awake with these panic attacks and they were ultimately what kept me out of the army altogether," he said, his voice pushing out of him quietly. "I've always wondered how things might've been different had I not just envisioned my future, but actually lived it out instead." He closed his eyes, then said softly as a low whisper, "I'll never know if I'm capable of being a hero because I was always too busy being a daydreaming coward."

"Why do I get the idea that no amount of me challenging your position is going to change your faulty self-assessment?"

"Wise woman," he grinned.

"Very. But here's the thing, Lincoln. Our minds play tricks on us. And yours has been tricking you into believing you've somehow failed." Couple Number Two just sprang from the platform. I didn't need to see them fall to confirm that. Their hoots and hollers were evidence enough. "That wasn't your mission, you have to understand that. That just wasn't your mission."

"You've heard of being in the wrong place at the wrong time?" Lincoln asked, his thumbs all the way under his harness now. I'd have to demand that Spike do one final assessment on Lincoln's get-up before taking the jump, because I was sure he'd fiddled his way out of safety. "I think there's such a thing as failing to be in the right place at the right time, too. I'll never stop wondering about that, Eppie—about my epically failed timing. I don't think I'll ever cease to wonder."

"Well, just stop wondering," I demanded abruptly. My hair blew into my face, the dark strands wrapping across my wind-chapped lips. With my hand, I swept them back under my helmet, securing them there.

"Wonderment should only be reserved for the good things. Not the things you can't change."

"That's a good assertion. I get that," he agreed. "You're pretty smart, you know that?"

"Yes, that's one of the things I do know. And you're pretty brave to come all the way up here and throw a perfectly good body off of a perfectly good bridge."

Playful wickedness entered Lincoln's eyes at the same time his brows shot up and down. I liked how animated he could be at times, and by at times, I meant all the time. "You think my body is perfectly good?"

"Yes, well... um, you know what I mean."

"I do, I think," he spoke. "And I think my show of bravery might just be masked stupidity. This really is a terrible idea, isn't it? To trust some guy we just met, these flimsy harnesses, and an oversized rubber band? We're smarter than that, aren't we? Please tell me we are."

The platform was now empty, awaiting our turn. Spike did a very Spike-y thing and waved us over with both flailing hands raised high above his head as he jumped up and down, his over-enthusiasm for thrill evident in his body language. We were obviously up next.

"We *are* smarter than that, yes. But I say we just do it. It's absurd, but it requires absurd amounts of bravery, so I think this could really work for you," I suggested, already making my way over to Spike at the middle portion of the bridge. I could see through the wooden planks below me, and it wasn't like there were these huge, rushing waves threatening to swallow us up or even a dozen angry crocodiles with their jaws unhinged, ready to devour us. The river was peaceful, calm. And suddenly so was I, remarkably.

It was a different story for Lincoln.

"Finding... it... hard... to... breathe." That sounded like five separate sentences, poor guy. Panic had clearly begun its attack. "World. Spinning. Heart. Pounding."

"And now you know what it was like for me during our first kiss," I teased, hoping that saying things like that would help Lincoln focus on anything but his overwhelming fear growing within him.

"Not... fair... to... bring... that... up... now," he panted out breathlessly. Spike began the work of rigging us together as he bound our ankles and instructed us to wrap our arms around one another, our appendages acting as additional harnesses. "I think... my lungs... just cracked... one of my... ribs." Lincoln pulled out from my arms and clawed at his chest with his long fingers.

"You okay, man?" Spike was still at our feet, giving something one last tug. That was reassuring to me. I'm not sure why, but it felt like he was covering his bases. Checking and rechecking and that sort of thing.

"No. Not okay."

"He'll be fine," I interjected. "Hey."

"Yeah?"

"We're doing this together," I assured. Lincoln's head shifted and his eyes traveled to the valley below as he took in the depth or height or whatever distance is was between us as Earth's familiar surface underneath. "Hey. Don't look down."

"I... I, I can't help it." With an Adam's apple jumping so much it looked like it was dancing, Lincoln swallowed the longest, most deliberate—and somewhat painful appearing—swallow. "Down is all there is."

"Until it's all up," Spike said, his voice accented like a Southern California surfer. "Cuz when you jump, down becomes up and up becomes down."

I'd never expected such truth-filled words to come out of someone as unlikely as Spike, but he was absolutely right on more levels than he probably even realized. My world had been so upside-down until Lincoln. And now, even though we'd technically be dangling from the sky, I knew everything would continue to be right side up. Because that's what he did for me, he turned my world back around. He righted my life.

"Here we go." One last squeeze of our shoulders as Spike said, "On the count of three..."

"I've forgotten how to do that," Lincoln yelped. "I don't remember how to do that."

"One," I said, slow and steady. "Two." He joined in for that one, echoing my voice.

Then we said "three" in unison and took the leap together.

# THIRTY-THREE

"Your hickeys are really impressive."

"Shut up," Lincoln said. His hand flew from the steering wheel to his neck to cover the reddish-purple spots that dotted along his collar. "In all of the paperwork riddled with warnings of possible spinal injury, unlikely death, and far-fetched retina damage, they made no mention of the necessity for turtlenecks. I would've come prepared had it at least been brought to my attention."

"Those harness hickeys will get you every time."

"I think," he said, "we can agree that this was the least of my concerns."

Lincoln really had done well, given the circumstances. After making me promise not to think any less of him had he peed his pants, projectile vomited on me, or performed any other involuntary reaction as a result of the impending free fall, we did it. We jumped.

And it wasn't half bad. I mean, after all, I was as close as I'd ever been to Lincoln, physically Velcroed to his body. That was the good half. The bad half was everything else. Come to find out, there's a valid reason for panic. It's your body's way of reminding you that there are limits in this life and sometimes those limits are better left untested.

People are not meant to dangle from bridges; this was a new fact for me. The supporting evidence came to me in the form of an extreme head rush that pushed so hard against my skull, shattering only seemed inevitable, and as a living, breathing human, I really wanted to keep my brains in my head. It was also in the crazy wedgy that I was still attempting to release from my butt cheeks. That was going to take a while to get free. And finally, it was in the fact that I'd hummed the entire time. That, for me, was a sure sign that everything about it was wrong.

We all had coping mechanisms. Humming was mine, and while jumping might've taken a slight edge off of Lincoln's fear of high up places, it didn't do much to keep me from my usual blocking out of reality through vocal chord vibrations. And that was okay, because this wasn't *for* me. Goodness, Lincoln had already done so much in the way of lessening my own fears or facing them head on or whatever it was that happened when we visited my mother's resting place. This was meant for *him.*

I figured I'd follow him to whatever heights necessary in order to help him overcome anything. If he was willing to walk the ends of the Earth with me, it really was the least I could do.

"Oh no." Lincoln's body suddenly pulled taut, rigid in his seat. "Oh no, no, no, no!" He banged his hand on the dash, soft at first, then much harder, like beating a drum. "Trudy, don't fail me now, girl!"

"What's wrong?" Though I had limited knowledge of anything vehicle related, I assumed the croaking sound that came from the engine, coupled with the look cloaking Lincoln's face, only meant bad news for his precious camper.

"No, no! Please, no, Trudy."

And then we sputtered to a stop.

In the middle of a twisty two-lane road in the desolate woods, just an hour shy of home.

At dusk.

And without a cellphone. That, too. Because although Spike had seemingly taken quite good care of us when preparing for launch, one minor detail we'd all overlooked was to remove Lincoln's phone from his pocket prior to the jump. And that resulted in a swim for his smartphone down Rushmount River, only to end in a watery grave. Mine was inconveniently perched on my nightstand at home.

"Dammit!" Lincoln's fist connected with the steering wheel, then suddenly, "I'm sorry, Trudy. I didn't mean to hit you," came out as a quick apology. His hands affectionately stroked the wheel. "Forgive me."

"Okay," I said. "So I haven't spent a whole lot of one on one time with you and Trudy, but I can see you're taking her breakdown unreasonably hard."

Lincoln was out of the camper and at its backside, where, I gathered, the engine was. So much was just absolutely backward about this day. So much.

"Come on, girl, come on," he begged, tweaking some valve with dexterous fingers. His eyes squinted and he stooped down to fiddle with another cord before yanking his hand back quickly. "Ouch! Trudy, that wasn't necessary!" His thumb was in his mouth, soothing whatever burn he'd just received.

"I feel like I should leave you two alone to duke this out." Guys loved their cars, I knew that. Lincoln, though an exception in everything else relating to nineteen-year-old manhood, was not one here.

"We'll be fine," he waved me off. "But sometimes she holds a grudge and refuses to budge for hours at a time. This could be a long night for us, Eppie. Just gotta warn you."

"As in, we won't be able to get her working? And we'll have to stay out here overnight?" I looked around, surveying our surroundings. It was unfathomably gorgeous. Evergreens rose up from the ground, like we were bordered in by hundreds of Christmas trees, minus the decorations and tchotchke ornamentation. A lake peeked out through the branches and reflections of light flickered silver twinkles across its shimmering surface. This was where the term picturesque originated. "Such a shame to be stuck in a place like this with you."

"Is that sarcasm I detect?" With a wink, he gave me one of those smirks that arrested my breathing and made my toes tingle. "If I didn't know any better, I would've thought that you and Trudy orchestrated this little snafu."

"Oh yes, Trudy and I are in cahoots. She knows just how badly I want to be stranded overnight with you."

"Eppie." It was as though Lincoln was a pre-pubescent boy again the way the sound crackled out of him in two different octaves. "Don't say things like that to me. Please."

I gave him a sidelong glance.

"Though I've tried desperately hard to remain a gentleman with you, saying things like that is pure kryptonite to my chivalryness." That was a new term. "Such phrases don't even enter my brain but go directly to other various body parts that I don't have too much control over."

Oh dear Moses, I was blushing so badly it actually hurt my face. Just like that burn on Lincoln's finger, his words singed my cheeks. I was now thinking of said body parts, and that just wasn't right to think those things. At least not yet.

"I'm sorry."

"Don't be." Lunging forward, he hip-checked me as he passed by to fish something out of the backseats of his van. After fumbling around, he whipped out a towel, snapped it at my backside, and took off racing down the hill, dodging trees and shrubs at his feet, looking absolutely, adorably ridiculous. "Last one to the water is an apple fritter!"

...............

"We don't have suits."

It was the time of evening when the sun was nearly all the way down, just hovering over the horizon as though paused in the air. Because of this, velvety light skimmed off of everything in its path, including Lincoln. Including his body. Including his abs. Mostly just on his abs, actually. Or maybe my eyes were fixed on his abs and so that's all I could see. But I swear it was as though Mother Nature was highlighting Lincoln's muscled upper half on purpose, like she really wanted me to appreciate it, too. I wasn't about to pass up that opportunity.

"Who needs a suit?" He was fiddling with his belt at the same time he toed off one shoe, then the other. Despite the highlighting, I couldn't continue staring. This was getting a little too intimate. "Ever heard of skinny dipping?"

"Lincoln! No."

"No, you haven't heard of it? I figured you were sheltered and all, but this kind of activity really is common knowledge. It's when you disrobe, then swim. You haven't lived until you've tried it. Exhilarating on the highest level."

"I feel as though the same could've been said for the bungee jumping. How much living do we really need to do today?" It was rhetorical, but it sort of wasn't. I was not about to get naked in that murky water with Lincoln. Nakedness was *not* going to happen.

"I figure while Trudy's cooling off, we should do the same."

He was about to take his pants off. Lincoln was going to remove his pants. I was not ready for this.

When the leather strip of his belt slid backward, releasing the metal hook from its loop, I did the only thing I could think to do. I launched at him, full force, tackling him to the ground.

Lincoln was instantly leveled, flattened onto his back, and there I was, straddling his bare waist. Unintentionally, of course, because this was not the execution of some planned out football play. This was just me freaking out. Simple as that.

"Whoa there, tiger." It was a whisper, which was worse than anything he could've done because suddenly this felt *way* more intimate than Lincoln only possibly shedding his clothes in front of me. His fingers lifted to my hair, gingerly. "Whoa."

"I... I'm sorry." For the tackle. For freaking out. And mostly for the fact that I was still sitting on him, not budging, seemingly frozen in place.

His face, for the first time that I was aware of, remained expressionless. "Don't be. Don't be sorry. At all."

Had I wanted to stand up and remove myself from his body and this increasingly awkward situation, I wouldn't have been able to since my legs had no feeling in them. They weren't even Jell-O or mush. They just weren't there.

"Eppie, you're stunning." Lincoln's eyes didn't crinkle like they so characteristically did. They were wide open. Saucers even. "The sunlight on you. In your hair. Skimming every part of your body. You're so beautiful."

The ground against my knees was wet and I had to figure that all of the grassy area underneath Lincoln was equally as damp and uncomfortable, but he didn't let on if that was the case. He looked like someone lacking any plans to ever move from where he lay. That made me want to stay in place just a little bit longer, too.

"So beautiful."

I smiled down at him, gazing into his honey brown eyes. I knew that descriptions such as the word *gazing* were so daytime televisionish, but I did exactly that: I gazed. Because he was beautiful, too, and I didn't know if it was okay to say so or if that was an ego-killer or not. So I just gazed—longingly even—and let him stare back up at me with his gorgeous, warm eyes.

"I thought skinny-dipping with you would be something, but this—you on me in a sunset-lit meadow—this is... this is just... Quite honestly, I have no words for what you're doing to me right now, Eppie."

When the wind rushed at my back and along the bending reeds of grass feathered out around us, Lincoln shivered slightly, his stomach muscles clenching against the breeze, although a warm one. And even though I figured he wasn't cold, I couldn't help but lean down to drape myself across his chest. It was instinct. It was instinct to be as close to him as possible.

It was also instinct to slip back up almost as instantly as I'd bent over in order to slide first my right arm, then my left, out of the armholes of my long-sleeved shirt, lifting it slowly up and over my head. Lincoln's hands reached out to assist me as I wiggled the cotton fabric off, and he tossed it to the grass beside us in a ball. Though I still had a thin-strapped tank underneath, something between us changed now that there was more skin than clothing. Some exchange of vulnerability.

His hands, all calloused from work, should've been rough against my skin, but that's not what I felt when Lincoln touched me. When his palms stroked up my bare arms to my shoulders, something fluttered inside. When his fingertip ran along the upper hem of my top, so lightly—maybe not even making actual contact with my skin because at this point I couldn't be held responsible for even verifying if that was the case—my eyelids blinked much more than necessary, so rapidly.

"Every inch of you is artwork," he spoke as his finger traced the lowest dip of my shirt and the shallowest part below my collarbone. No one had ever touched me here, and I wasn't sure if I should consider this a base or not because he wasn't even grabbing my chest or anything like that. Truly, he wasn't even *touching* my chest. He just ran his longest finger slowly, back and forth, over the soft divot of flesh in the *middle* of my chest, in that valley there.

And it was the most sensual thing I'd ever experienced.

"Is this okay?" His eyes were relaxed with that look of desire hooded within them when he nodded up toward what he was doing with my less than impressive cleavage.

"Mmm, hmm," I nodded back, my bottom lip pinned between my teeth. I wasn't especially trying to appear sexy. It was out of necessity that I did this. Otherwise that lower lip would tremble and that couldn't be considered attractive at all. That would just look pathetic.

Lincoln licked his lips. "Tell me what else is okay."

I didn't know how many other steps there were in between this and everything else. I was new to this. I was new to love, and I was painfully new to expressing it.

"What about this?" His finger pulled back across my flushed skin and over toward my shoulder, but it stopped short before getting there and changed up its path, cutting down my side, now on the outer edge of my torso. It was as though Lincoln was outlining my body, careful not to go too far, but going just far enough that I would surely lose it from this game of sensation. "Yes or no?"

"Yes."

He smiled, only in the right corner of his mouth.

"This?" His thumb quickly brushed against the full underside of my breast, more on my ribs than anything. "Yes or no?"

"Yes," I said again, figuring that would likely be my answer for any question he may ask.

Another smile.

Lincoln's other hand mimicked the same slow movements, and he gripped his remaining fingers against my back, his thumbs still teasingly close.

"Eppie, I've slept with two girls in my life."

My body sunk within his grasp. "Oh."

"I want you to know that." His hands didn't let up on their light touch. They sloped their way down to the round curve of my hips and wrapped on there. "Up until now, I thought I knew at least two girls quite intimately."

My heart was sinking just as fast as my posture. I couldn't fit the pieces of his sentences together with the way his hands were resting on my body. It felt like the most ill-placed subject matter—to be talking about his exes when holding me this way.

"Oh," was all I could say again.

Now knowing what path his hands were permitted to travel, Lincoln's fingers followed that line along my body, busying themselves at my heart's expense. I wanted to cry.

"But I was wrong," he said, hands paused in place. "That was just sex. There was no intimacy there. This, Eppie?" His eyes rounded so much, so fully open. This was wonderment. This was wonderment on his face. "Oh man. I mean... touching you? Asking you what you're okay with instead of just assuming and taking it from you? Jeez, Eppie. This... this is truly the most intimate thing I've ever experienced."

I wasn't certain why the sensation to cry still lingered, but it held on, gripping me. "Me, too."

"Your body—I mean, I know I'm a guy—but your body is off the charts. And here you are, letting me explore it. Trusting me to explore it. Trusting me to know what pace to take. I can't even... I just... Thank you, Eppie."

I laughed a little. "For what?"

"Thank you for letting me earn your trust."

"I trusted you enough to jump off a bridge with you, Lincoln. This doesn't seem like nearly as much."

"No," he stammered. "I mean, yes—thank you for that—but this is different. This is your body, Eppie. This is such a big deal." His words were racing at the same speed as my heart. "I know you probably figure since I've slept with someone before, that this wouldn't be a big thing to me, but it is, Eppie. So much."

I was grateful to hear that, because for a novice like me, this did seem like a big deal. Having Lincoln validate that I wasn't in the same category—that *this* wasn't in the same category—was overwhelming on all levels. No one before had ever really respected the fact that this body belonged to me. My mother certainly hadn't when she'd sickened it to meet her own need for attention. The doctors didn't when they'd tested and poked and prodded at her request. But it was mine, it always had been, and now I really felt like I might finally be okay with giving pieces of it to someone else.

"I'm going to take my time with you, with this body of yours, with this heart of yours," Lincoln said, so much thoughtfulness in his gentle tone.

His hair slipped across his forehead and his curls lifted in the breeze. I couldn't stop looking at him. I wanted to memorize this moment. Memorize that way his smile pulled up more on one side than the other. Memorize the exact shade of his amber eyes and all of the golden flecks strewn through them. But I already had. When I closed my eyes briefly, I could see an exact representation of Lincoln in my head, in my heart.

Because it was my heart that had memorized him so long ago.

"I'm going to kiss you now."

"Yes. Please."

Shimmying my body down, I met Lincoln halfway, his shoulders straining up toward me. But he didn't appear strained. His right hand cupped the back of my head while his left supported our weight behind him, pushing on the ground.

"I'm seriously overwhelmed by you, Eppie."

Our mouths met slowly, like the first time. With connected lips, Lincoln straightened fully up, grabbing onto my backside to tug me closer. I wrapped my legs around his waist, and crossed my ankles to keep him pinned there. His hair coiled perfectly around each individual finger, looping within my grip. I ran my hands along his shoulders and I pulled my mouth from his to bury my nose in his neck, wanting to inhale his musky scent from the damp sheen of sweat that clung to his skin. He'd already gotten an unfortunate hickey from our earlier adventure, so I chose to forgo that area and instead worked my way up to his ear, leaving small kisses along his neck and jaw the whole way. When I sucked his perfect earlobe into my mouth, I think I just about did poor Lincoln in.

"Uhh," he groaned, and then with an audible smile he said, "Wow. You can keep doing that all you like. Please, in fact. Yeah, please keep doing that."

Playing a little, I bit down with my teeth and Lincoln went wild.

"How did you learn to do that?" he breathed, pulling my face from his ear and palming it between his hands. His eyes looked shocked and equally excited. "Where did you learn that, Eppie?"

"I didn't learn it anywhere." It made me shy to talk about what I was doing—what I was doing to him and what he appeared to like so much. "I'm learning with you."

"What a lucky teacher I am." I felt his smirk spread against my lips as he came in for another kiss. "Anything else you care to learn?"

# THIRTY-FOUR

*Kyle Strauss killed the engine and fidgeted in his bucket seat like his corduroy pants were about three sizes too small. He'd been doing that all evening, shifting his weight around nervously in a manner that made me think his brain and his body weren't quite on the same page. Like they hadn't talked things over prior to the date and so now they were all discombobulated and out of sync, not knowing what to expect from the other.*

*"I had a really good time with you tonight, Eponine." Kyle had a gap in between his upper teeth that was slightly larger than what would be deemed acceptable in opting to forgo the customary ritual of teenage braces. During dinner, a grilled piece of asparagus lodged in between the two, and when he talked—his mouth full of food, mind you—it stuck out like a mini tree, planted in his goofy grin. Even though it wasn't in there now, I could still envision it every time his lips parted.*

*"Yeah," I stammered, lying through my teeth. Apparently I had something of my own lodged in there, as well. "Me, too. Lots of fun."*

*"Really? Cuz you hardly touched your meal. I was hoping the waiter wouldn't charge me for the whole thing.*

*That set me back like twelve dollars. That's like nearly two hours working down at the yard."*

*He was fishing for an apology with his blunt, guilt-inducing assessment of our evening and my leftover plate contents. Sam had lied when she'd said dating older guys was the only way to go. Though Kyle was a junior and I just a sophomore, I could name at least a dozen freshman boys I would much rather be out with at the moment. All of which could have an entire garden full of veggies fit between their chompers and it wouldn't bother me one iota.*

*"Wait. You're not sick, are you?" Kyle said it as some sort of revelation, like this would all make sense had I been feeling under the weather or been suffering the lingering effects of some stomach bug. "I mean, that's not why you didn't eat, is it?" I shook my head in answer. I just hadn't been all that hungry. "She didn't like completely ruin you, did she?"*

*"She?" I unclicked my seatbelt, readying to go, but the strap stayed paused in my grasp as I asked him to clarify his statement.*

*"Your mom. I mean, you're not like terminally ill now, are you? Cuz I've heard things, and I just wasn't sure."*

*"You've heard things."*

*My house was just a lit pathway away. All I had to do was unlock the car door and race up the walk, bolting the door shut behind me. It would be so easy to run from Kyle and his ignorant remarks, but I didn't want to do that tonight. I wanted to set the record straight. Maybe it was finally time to set* everyone *straight.*

*"I'm not sick, no." In fact, I'd been healthy for so long now that I couldn't even remember that sensation of feeling as though you'd never be well again. That part of me was just fine. My physical health was no longer a concern.*

*"Good," Kyle nearly cheered. He raked his stubby hands into blond hair, cut too short to possibly style in any way other than up. "Cuz I don't want to catch anything when I do this."*

*And then, suddenly, Kyle's overly-large-for-his-face lips came careening toward me, the way things seemed in movies when the camera zoomed in super close with a fish-eye lens. Objects in mirror are closer than they appear and all that. I had to duck out of his way to avoid the post asparagus onslaught of his mouth, and even still his lips slammed onto my cheek, sloppy and wet with what I could only figure was drool.*

*I would never kiss another guy again.*

*Kyle ruined it for me, and if he didn't peel his lip-suction from my skin quickly, he'd ruin the male gender altogether.*

*"What the hell, Eponine?"*

*Using my shoulder, I wiped everything from my jaw up to my temple with the fabric of my sweatshirt. I'd burn that shirt once inside my house.*

*"What's wrong with you?"*

*"Nothing's wrong with me." I pulled my hand into my sleeve like a turtle ducking into its shell and used that cloth to do another vigorous face wiping. "I'm fine."*

*"You are not. I was just trying to, you know, kiss you. Because I thought that's what you wanted." Kyle dropped*

*two frustrated hands onto the steering wheel and strangled it. "It's what most normal girls want."*

*"I don't think I'm like most girls." I knit my hands in my lap, keeping them securely there because if I didn't, they'd continue scrubbing my skin until my cheeks were nothing more than raw strips of flesh.*

*Annoyed, Kyle huffed so loud I assumed all of my neighbors heard it. Maybe even the whole county. "No, you're definitely not," he said with rolling eyes. And then, "Maybe you should work on that."*

*Disappointment sank deep in my gut. It wasn't that I sought approval from the likes of ill-mannered boys such as Kyle, it was just the growing knowledge that stigmas weren't easily shaken that did that to me. I'd been branded by her choices, and I wondered when I'd ever get the chance to do my own choosing. Maybe I never would. Sometimes it felt as though she'd determined my path the day I was born and solidified it the day she died. The problem was, none of my peers would ever let me change direction. Their whispered rumors kept me hemmed in on all sides. I felt destined to remain on this broken road, especially if I kept hanging around with Kyle-like adolescents.*

*I'd have to find someone already on their own path. Someone taking a different direction. That's the only way I'd ever be able to change my course.*

*The problem was, I doubted any guys like that existed in Masonridge.*

*I doubted they existed anywhere.*

# THIRTY-FIVE

"Cowabungaaaaaaaaa!"

Lincoln was able to drag out that last vowel in an impressively long manner before it was swallowed up by the rush of water that sucked him under the surface with a big "gulp." He was gone for several seconds, and when he ultimately crested, he sprung up quickly, shaking his hair back and forth like a sprinkler. Or like a dog. Actually, like a dog having just run through a sprinkler. A dog like Herb/Ralph. Oh, that made me so sad.

"You seriously have to try that, Eppie," Lincoln breathed. His eyes darted toward the rope swing hung crudely from a tree at the water's perimeter. Even from this distance, I could see the frayed edge of the twisted knot at its bottom, along with the thinned out midsection that threatened to snap with any amount of weight pulling it down. "I liken it to the bungee experience, only more horizontal than vertical. Swinging versus springing, I suppose."

Water slipped down his naked torso in beads as he waded closer my direction. Beads I wanted to lick off. Never before had the thought of lapping up possibly parasitic water droplets from someone's body ever crossed my mind. Lincoln was definitely challenging me to think outside of my well-secured box.

"I'll pass," I giggled. "Though it does look like you're having an unreasonably good time without me. I could use a little excitement tonight, too."

Walking through water was a slow-motion task, which only added to the subtle drama as we made our way to one another, arms outstretched.

"We can't have any of that. I say we find something else to satisfy both of our needs for a good time then, shall we?"

Oh man, that idea made me buzz with nerves. Though we technically weren't skinny-dipping, we both had on significantly fewer layers of clothing than during our earlier make-out session. Lincoln was down to his boxer briefs, and I still had my tank top, as well as my boy short underwear, which had been a completely random, yet convenient, choice when dressing this morning. So no, it wasn't quite skinny-dipping. More like fat-dipping or whatever skinny-dipping's more-clothed counterpart would be called.

"Ever kissed underwater?" A light sparked in his eyes, even though the sun was nearly completely tucked away for the evening, already having put herself to bed. Apparently, Lincoln's own aura was enough to illuminate things all on its own.

"No. In fact, I've had enough on-land disasters to steer clear of any submerged smooching."

"Eppie!" Lincoln was a kid on Christmas morning as he bounced with excitement. Rings of water rippled out from him. "I've always wanted to try this! I used to have a serious thing for Ariel."

"That's so very creepy."

"Oh, please. Don't tell me you've never crushed on an animated character."

"Can't say that I have."

He thumbed his chin quizzically, disbelief in his devious smirk. "What about Tarzan? I mean, he's kinda hot, what with all the bulging muscles and the loincloth that never once shifts out of place. Seriously, not even when swinging from trees. Those are some impressive undergarments right there. Though I suppose they are technically his outer garments. Either way, Tarzan is one sexy beast."

Treading the water, I fluttered my hands back and forth at my sides. It was shallow enough that I could stand fully upright here, but the chill in the air was colder than the water's temperature, so I stayed under in an effort to keep warm. "Why do I get the feeling you were channeling your inner Tarzan when trapezing from that rope just now?"

"Me Tarzan, you Ariel."

"You're getting your story lines crossed."

Lincoln dipped under the water right as I said that, and when he came back up for air, his hands slicked through his hair to push it all to the back of his head, his curls clumped just at the nape of his neck. "What about my loin cloth?"

"I said *lines crossed.*"

"Oh, that's unfortunate." He shook his head down and to the left like he was attempting to free water from inside his ear. “For a moment I thought both this conversation and evening were about to get really exciting.”

I popped my eyebrows up and down as a challenge. “But they are, right? Unless you were just tossing around false promises with all that underwater make-out talk.”

“Nothing false there. But the truth of the matter is that it involves the unfortunate risk of death, what with the not breathing and all.”

“A growing trend with you as of late. Now even your kisses have to be death-defying.”

“In fairness,” he said, tapping the side of his head with the broad heel of his hand as he shook his ear again. “This level of risk taking is new for me.”

An owl hooted in a nearby tree, reminding me that we really were in the middle of the wilderness, among woodland creatures and those sorts of feathered and furry inhabitants in this dark setting. That also called to mind the likelihood of fish swimming around us, though undetected. I never liked the idea of sharing water space with creatures you couldn’t see. Kind of like the notorious legends of spiders crawling into your open mouth while you slept. I’d studied the odds of sleep-swallowing insects before and knew that the ingestion of five arachnids per year was five too many for me. So the thought of even one fish bumping up against my bare thigh just about made me hightail it out of the lake right then and there.

But then there was that kiss offer still dangling in front of me.

"How do we do this?" Based on the narrow size of my ribcage, I assumed my lungs couldn't be all too big. Their capacity for holding air would be no longer than seven seconds, max. I'd played seven minutes in heaven once my freshman year at a coed party, and based on how that went, I knew that even just seven underwater seconds with Lincoln would be so much more heavenly than anything that happened (or didn't happen) in the birthday boy's coat closet in seven minutes time.

"I'm going to dip under the water first," Lincoln explained, his index finger pointing to the lake below. "I'll keep my hands on your hips and then tug you down with me." He'd thought this through. "We can't do open mouthed or anything, just lips."

"Got it. Just lips."

He nodded. "And don't open your eyes. The water's all murky. We don't want to contract some scary eye infection as a result. There's no real evidence that this lake isn't some toxic dumping ground for local nuclear plants."

"Right. Okay. No eye opening."

"But that's pretty much the norm with kissing anyway, so it should come naturally." Lincoln's chest puffed out in a barrel shape. This must've been the practice round, since he held his air for an impressively long time, then hissed it out slowly between parted, pink lips. "Okay. I'm all set. You?"

"Yeah. Ready."

"Spread your legs a little," he said, giving a final instruction that made me shudder with embarrassment.

"Wha—?"

"This is super shallow right here and I won't have anywhere to go once I'm under. I haven't mastered the acrobatic art of folding up into a human accordion, so I'm gonna have to stretch all the way out along the bottom. You'll have to basically straddle and sit on my lap to make this work."

I came back down to earth. "Right. Of course."

Lincoln smiled. I figured he'd discovered my unwarranted embarrassment based on the sweet look he offered. "Here we go, my little mermaid."

"Don't call me that."

"My little fishy."

"This is getting weirder and weirder by the minute."

He laughed. "Okay. Let's just do it. Ready, set..." Then his mouth made a huge gasping sound as it stored up the available night air and he slunk into the water. Bubbles rose to the surface where he submerged and popped like little balloons. *Pop, pop, pop.*

His hand on my hips squeezed once as a warning and yanked me swiftly down. Before my face was completely covered with water I managed to suck in a large pocket of air to last me for what I hoped would be long enough. Or at least I felt like it was an Olympian-sized breath, based on the searing pain of it.

It was disorienting under the water, like floating through space. Similar to earlier in the day, the terms up and down lost their definitions and it all just became surroundings. I tried not to think about the things that could *possibly* surround us, and instead focused on what I was certain of. Lincoln's hands. They were tight on my waist, dragging me down on top of him. He was right, the shallowness of the lake didn't allow for him to do much other than lay nearly flat on the bottom, so he had to pull me down in a way that forced my knees to the ground on either side. Stones and smoothed rocks and underwater plants grazed my legs, but the inside of my thighs pressing against his hipbones served as a much more pleasant feeling, so I focused my attention there.

The water took away every last one of my senses but touch. I couldn't see Lincoln in front of me, couldn't smell his familiar scent that usually wafted into my nose when he edged in for a kiss. I couldn't taste anything yet. And I couldn't hear—my ears plugged with pressure from the water quickly filling them up.

Only touch could guide me. A hand jutted out and palmed my jaw, languidly dragging my face forward with fingers wrapped around my neck. I bobbled a bit until I could reach out enough to find Lincoln's face, too. My finger recognized the softness of his lips as I searched to locate him in the darkness of closed eyelids and opaque water. I thumbed at his bottom lip, feeling a bubble escape against my skin as he let air out through what I knew must be a grin.

There couldn't be much time left. I was already feeling the effects from the lack of oxygen in my spinning head and aching muscles. Lincoln sensed the immediacy, too, because he drew me toward him, a quick pull of my neck, and our lips brushed together, not lined up quite right. My mouth pressed more onto his chin, so I adjusted my angle to lift my lips back up to his. They were still smiling. I could feel the curved tautness of them against my own. When they relaxed, they felt soft, plush and slack.

My hair swirled around us, tickling my skin like feathers. He brushed it away with one hand, but clung tightly to my neck with the other like there was the possibility of me floating away from him without being tethered down securely. But this floating sensation was familiar. It was how I felt every time our lips touched. Being under the waves and the water only increased that tenfold.

Lincoln's other hand stroked against my bare arm, and that, coupled with the bubbles that rose up around us like fizz, caused every part of me to prickle with sensation. Our mouths met once more, briefly, just as the need for air took over and Lincoln pulled me up and we burst through the still surface, gasping the cold air into our begging lungs.

I shivered against his skin and he gripped my body, dipping back under until the water covered our shoulders.

"That was all kinds of awesome," he smiled knowingly.

"Took my breath away."

"Well, that was a given."

Water dripped through my hair, dotting my face. Lincoln swept his thumbs across my cheeks to blot them away, though they came spilling down faster than he could dry them. It was such a nice alternative to crying, how he typically wiped away my tears.

I could get used to this whole underwater kissing thing.

But then, when he wrapped his arms around my shoulders, folding me into his slick chest as his arms curled around me nearly twice, he brought his head down, about meet my lips again, and I realized that out of water kissing was just as incredible.

He was tentative as he lowered his mouth to mine. The frigid air had chilled my lips, so when his mouth finally pressed down, shockwaves of heat spread throughout my body. My eyelids slipped shut in response, my eager lips surrendered, and a groan escaped from deep within my throat, an uncontrollable rasp working its way out.

I don't know how I sensed it—maybe I was just that in tune with Lincoln—but I could feel his eyes on me, even with mine shut. It had been instinct to close them initially, just like he'd said, but it was curiosity that pulled them apart. Our eyes met at once, and he gave me a shy look that made the pit of my stomach warm and tingly. He closed his eyes briefly—slowly—as though to trick me into thinking he'd actually keep them that way, but when he opened them again after just a few seconds, my gaze was still locked on to his.

"I like watching you when I kiss you," his whispered against my mouth. His words were hot and damp on my lips. "I like the way your eyelids flutter, even when they're closed."

Saying that left me no options. I couldn't close them for fear that they'd do nothing but twitch, and I couldn't keep them open because all they begged to do was to slip shut and slip further into the moment.

But then I saw stars, which threw me because although everything about this was intense, I really hoped I wasn't about to pass out. I needed to stay in this and soak it all up.

But then those bright, startling lights shot across my vision again, blinding and brilliant.

"What was that?" Lincoln whispered. His arms straightened out as his hands clamped down on my shoulders, tossing me back from him. Wind rushed through the open space between our bodies. I shivered and my scalp stung at the roots of my hair. The whites around Lincoln's eyes grew wider, encasing his irises with panic. "Did you see that?"

"The lights?"

"Yeah. What was that?"

His breath puffed out in suspended clouds, and suddenly another glaring stream flooded the wilderness, illuminating everything in a stark wash of light. It swung back and forth like a pendulum and pulsed like a strobe, and it played tricks on my eyes and my brain.

"A flashlight," Lincoln murmured loudly. "Someone's here. Come on, we gotta go."

With our hands gripped together, we raced through the water to the shallow bank, stumbling and splashing all the way. My knee hit a fallen log as we fumbled in the dark, trying to locate our clothes under the tree where we'd left them, and I felt the hot spill of blood trickling down my leg. I bit my bottom lip to dull the pain as more stars shot through my eyes.

"Who's out there?" A voice, deep and commanding called down the ravine. It echoed against the trees and crater of the lake. "Come out and show your face!"

Lincoln shoved my balled up shirt and pants into my chest. "Put these on. Quickly."

Then he hurriedly unfolded them and held out each leg for me to step into like I was a toddler, but I crashed to the ground, unable to secure my footing or balance. Not caring that he was still standing in his underwear, drenched and equally disheveled, Lincoln slunk my shirt over my head and then rushed to yank my pants up and onto my hips while I still sat crouched on the ground as I struggled with the zipper and button.

"Who do you think it is?" I panicked, my voice unstable with worry.

"Not sure." His hands felt around for his own pants and shirt and he made quick work of pulling them on. "Whoever it is, they don't seem very happy about us being here." He rummaged around some more. "Shoes... shoes. I definitely had some of those."

A dog barked loudly, followed by a bone-chilling, predatory growl that scraped down my spine and pulled up the fine hairs on my neck.

"What the—?" Lincoln breathed. His mouth was inches from me as we cowered behind the log that split my knee open just moments earlier. He pressed his index finger to his lips, then swiveled around to peer over our barricade, indicating that I stay hunkered down.

"Come out with your hands up!"

My mouth dropped open. "The police?"

"You have to the count of three!" the voice boomed.

"In fairness, you said you wanted a little fun tonight."

I scowled. "This is not at all what I was envisioning."

"This is your final warning!"

"I don't think we really have much of a choice." Lincoln's palms were pressed to the bark like he was readying to stand. Or run. I couldn't figure out which. This was too unbelievable to comprehend. "Things are about to get exciting, Eppie. Hands up."

# THIRTY-SIX

Metal gripped against Lincoln's wrists, braceleting them in two shiny handcuffs.

"Officer Marlin, there has obviously been a gross misunderstanding."

Like they do on those cop shows, the police officer—a big bear of a man with a uniform that looked too similar to a superhero's costume with all of his bulging muscles bound underneath—patted the top of Lincoln's head before roughly ushering him down and into the back seat of the patrol car.

"I honestly hope so, kid." He sounded sincere enough. Much less gruff and alarming than earlier when he was yelling at us in the forest. "I really do."

"I promise you, Trudy's all mine."

I stood outside the cruiser, wishing for the first time in my life that I could be the one sitting behind that partition.

"Unfortunately, a stolen vehicle report has been filed, and because of that I have to take you in."

Lincoln leaned forward. His head dropped onto the barrier in front of him, his eyes slowly closing.

Exhaustion draped across his face. "This makes no sense."

"Eponine, you can have the passenger's seat."

The ride back into town was practically unbearable, what with the soaking undergarments that made it appear as though I'd peed my pants and was possibly lactating, too, and the fact that Lincoln was about to be arrested while Officer Marlin continued to make small talk with me in the front, mildly less criminal-feeling, space of the vehicle.

"Marty and Cujo will wait for the tow truck, then head back into the station."

My brows shot up to my hairline. "Cujo? Seriously?"

"He's more bark than bite. Promise. Sweetest canine we have on the force."

I groaned. "How was it even necessary to bring him out there? What kind of threat are two kids and a VW camper? I don't get any of this." I knew that rolling your eyes at the authorities was cliché teenage rebellion, but I couldn't help it. They somersaulted in my head freely. I was fed up with this insane run-around and the fact that he didn't seem to be listening to Lincoln and his assertions, and I couldn't keep my body from expressing that, even if I'd wanted it to, which I didn't. I was all about the angst.

"What's going to happen?"

I turned around to see Lincoln, slumped in his seat, head still downcast, murmuring into his shoulder.

Officer Marlin eyed him in the rearview mirror. "You'll stay overnight. They'll set bail and hopefully you have someone that loves you enough to post it tomorrow."

My empty wallet mocked me.

"I don't know anyone with any kind of money." Frustration was heavy in Lincoln's tone. He let his hair fall over his eyes, hiding him like a curtain. "This is literally the craziest thing that's ever happened to me."

I nodded over to the officer, validating Lincoln's comment. "It's true. Lincoln and I are well acquainted with crazy and this easily takes the cake."

Officer Marlin's head swiveled on his thick neck. Pretty sure steroids had a little something to do with his glaringly ill-proportioned body type. "I'm just doing my job, kids. I can name about forty other things I'd rather be doing tonight than chasing down two skinny dipping teens."

"Oh." I shook my head fast. "We weren't skinny dipping. Just in our underwear."

The policeman shot me an incredulous look. "O-*kay*," he drew out into two separate words. "That's different."

"I care too much about her virtue to thrust my nakedness upon her just yet," Lincoln said.

It actually required me biting down on my knuckle to keep from bursting out with laughter. Lincoln had just used both thrust and naked in the same sentence, and that was too much for me to handle. My poor finger was definitely left with a mark.

"Strange," Officer Marlin noted. He had a wide, dark brow that lacked any arch, and when it seemed like he was thinking hard, it lowered over his deep-set blue eyes. "But you don't care enough to keep from running around in stolen vehicles with her."

An annoyed huff flew from Lincoln's lips. "Like I said, it's not stolen. I've paid for Trudy in full, every last penny."

"Kid, I don't make the rules, I just enforce them."

We were paused at a traffic light, just two blocks from the jailhouse. I remembered my mornings on the way to school—how exposed I'd felt as I trudged that familiar path, when all of my other peers drove. This was slightly worse for Lincoln, I assumed. Being paraded around town in the back of a cop car was definitely more of an exposition. Thankfully, Officer Marlin had been kind enough to keep the lights and sirens off. Still, humiliation was the only appropriate response here.

"One night in the slammer isn't going to ruin you," Officer Marlin said. And I knew that to be true. In this life, I figured, it took a hell of a lot to actually be ruined. I'd had my share of attempts, but nothing ever got me to that point. Being damaged wasn't the same as being ruined. Damaged things healed. Ruined things were just, well, destroyed. Neither Lincoln, nor I, would ever be in that category. We were not the easily destroyed type.

Officer Marlin was right. Twenty-four hours from now, Lincoln's bail would be met and this weird misunderstanding would be behind us. On to other things.

"Your dad can get you out," I asserted after racking my brain for options to help us out of this predicament. "Your parents must have the money."

If Lincoln had appeared defeated before, this look was one step further than that. What was worse than defeat? Surrender, maybe.

"I really don't want to involve them in this," he sighed heavily. He looked out the car window, a blank expression held on his face. "It's better if we leave them out."

"Well," Officer Marlin interrupted, apparently feeling like he was a welcome contributor to the conversation. Wasn't sure where he'd gotten that impression. "I think you'll have a difficult time leaving them out since they're the ones who filed the report."

..............

"Is someone coming to get you?"

My head sprang up. Officer Marlin stood in the doorway, the glow from inside the station backlighting him. I could see gnats swirling around in the cool night air as they flew in disoriented patterns, bumping into one another like flecks of dust in the sky. I felt like those stupid bugs. They were completely out of sorts, just like me.

"Um, yeah," I answered, finally. "I have a friend picking me up."

As if on perfect cue, that old, black Datsun turned into the lot from the main thoroughfare in town. It crept close, hugging the edge of the sidewalk with its whitewall tires, until it lined up with the bench I sat upon.

"That's him," I motioned as I stood up and the vehicle slowed to a stop.

Phil got out of the car and walked its perimeter with quick strides to unlock and open my door. I never figured he was capable of transparently disclosing his true, inner assessment of a situation, but the glare he shot Officer Marlin was anything but inconspicuous. *Go Philly.*

"Goodnight, Eppie," Officer Marlin tipped his head my direction. "Sir."

Phil was having no part in the pleasantries. Barely before he even got the door closed again after returning to his driver's seat, he peeled out of that parking lot, wheels screaming against the uneven asphalt.

"Calm down there, Philly," I teased, but my knuckles were white as they gripped the dash to steady myself. I expected to see rubber physically burning when I glanced out the window.

He glowered at me. "Do you mind explaining what in Sam Hill is going on here?"

My throat tightened. "Are you upset with me?" This was an unwelcome first. I was used to my dad's escalating anger, but this wasn't something I was accustomed to when it came to Phil. He was always so steady, always so consistent in temper and tone.

"No." Phil's mouth cinched, then relaxed. "Of course not with you. No, Eppie." He let his heavy foot fall off the accelerator to ease up speed as we approached a red light. His frame slouched, mostly in the shoulders. "I just want to know what sort of parent intentionally sends their own son to prison? A son like Lincoln. I just don't get it." He swung his head my direction to offer a sympathetic look that made his eyes appear wet with moisture. Phil's stormy mood was so unpredictable that I was tempted to ask if he was possibly menstruating. He was that out of sorts. "I'm sorry, Eppie. I didn't mean to make you think you did anything wrong. I'm just so damned sick and so damned tired of all of these irresponsible parents who don't understand how damn lucky they are to have such great kids. To have *any* kids, at that. It's a damn shame."

"And that's a lot of damns."

The light flickered green and the car began to move.

"The way I feel right now is worthy of a lot of damns."

There are people in this world who are the askers: the ones who excel in questioning and digging deep. They enter a conversation with a readied icebreaker and follow up comment. They draw out of people, where others drain. These are the types of people you want to be surrounded with because it simply feels good to be in their presence. Even the most humble of persons would admit to the swell of pride when in the center of their attention. You leave feeling better about yourself, and about the world in general.

Phil is that person, by nature and occupation.

The complicated thing about people such as Phil is that while they fill entire conversations with questions and inquiries, the end results in little knowledge of just how Phil, the man, might be doing. In a relationship, when one person is often the asker, the other is typically the answerer.

It was time for me to start asking the questions.

"Hey." I reached over to swivel the volume control down to zero. Quiet blanketed the small car. "You okay?"

I knew it wasn't much, but figured it was all I needed.

"No." Phil's bottom teeth tugged his mustache into his mouth. "No, Eppie. I'm not."

I knew little of Phil's personal life. I mean, I knew he was a middle-aged bachelor, but that he once desired a family. He spoke of this on rare occasion. But his reaction to Lincoln's arrest? His accusations and assertions about undeserving parents? This was different. This was a glimpse into a part of Phil's life that had been hidden under a professional surface and a *let's talk about you* glaze.

I was going to get past that. "Do you want to talk about it?"

The role reversal felt strange, odd and unnatural. But this was consistent with the day's events, so I wasn't certain why I expected anything different, truly.

The jailhouse was only a few miles from Lincoln's duplex, and though we'd completed our drive, I'd just initiated our conversation. I wouldn't be exiting the vehicle any time soon and Phil knew that. His thick hands clicked the key out of the ignition and the car hissed when it shut down in the driveway, and creaks and pops followed every few seconds as the engine cooled off. Fumbling with his aviator glasses tucked into the collar of his Hawaiian shirt—unbuttoned two more buttons than was necessary so that wiry gray tufts of hair peeked out—Phil busied himself, but only temporarily.

Then he took a breath and told me his story.

"We'd only been married two years," he began, his gaze forward. "Tabitha." He looked at me suddenly, startlingly. "That was my girl's name—"

I nodded, encouraging more out of him. "Your wife's."

"No," he quickly corrected. "My daughter's." He played with the arms on his sunglasses, snapping them open and closed alternately. "She was just six months old. Cora—that was my wife's name—she'd taken her to the store that morning to pick up more diapers. I was supposed to get them on the way home the night before, but I'd just been assigned to this new case and had been doing research and left the office much too late to remember anything other than the familiar route from my building to my front door. Diapers weren't on the agenda." I couldn't believe I'd never known. Even worse, I couldn't believe I'd never even asked—that I'd never asked about the life Phil led apart from the segments that intertwined with mine. Why had I just assumed that I'd always been at the center of it when he'd obviously had his own story?

"They were broadsided by an SUV that barreled through a red light, so I guess that was the best case scenario, because from what the first responders said, it was fast and painless." A lone tear skimmed down the rough terrain of Phil's face, catching on his beard. He ignored it, continuing, "But I always thought that was odd, to assume to have any notion of someone else's pain. Who's to honestly say they didn't feel pain? What? Is it just because they couldn't speak of it? Because no one heard their cries?" Phil sniffed loudly and shuddered, which seamlessly led to him shaking his head back and forth. "I can guarantee you, unspoken pain doesn't hurt any less."

The pieces clicked into place.

"That's why you get people to talk about it," I said, making sense of his words. "That's why you do what you do. Help people process their pain."

He was stoic as he offered me a smile meant to be kind, but one that carried the heavy weight of sorrow within those two lips. "No, Eppie. I don't think so necessarily. I think maybe that's why I was dealt the pain, because I'd been preparing for it for so long."

"What an unfair world you believe in." I sighed.

"It's not a matter of me believing in it or not, it's just what exists." Phil tossed his glasses to the dashboard and reached across his body to unclasp my seatbelt. "Pain exists. And horrible people who don't realize the gifts they've been given—those people exist, too."

"Like Lincoln's parents," I said.

"Like Lincoln's parents. Like *your* parents." He rubbed his eyes with two balled up fists, then pushed his hands through his hair before waving toward me, shooing me from the car. "Go on inside. Get some sleep. I'll be by to take you back to the station in the morning." A yawn tacked on to his gesture indicated that this night should be over, for all of us. I was so done with this day. With my birthday. "You remember where Lincoln said to look for the money?"

"Yeah. Under his bed."

Phil laughed gruffly. "Be careful what you find there, my dear. The space between a teenage boy's mattress is a very sacred place."

I chuckled, too, grateful for the relief, but nervous by the statement.

"I'll proceed with caution then." Just before I exited the vehicle, I turned back to Phil, waiting until he looked back over at me and I had his attention. "Thank you," I said in a quiet, almost apologetic, voice. "For coming to our rescue tonight. I really appreciate it. I mean, it's late and I'm sure you're tired and—"

"It's nothing, Eponine," he assured.

"That's absolutely as far from the truth as you can get. It's something, Phil. Really something."

All he did was smile, and there was no sorrow masked within it this time. It felt warm, like a hug. A hug from someone who loved you completely. "In that case," he said, lips still upturned, "You are most welcome."

# THIRTY-SEVEN

"Hey." Dan stopped just outside of Lincoln's bedroom door, his fingers on the gripped hand rim of his chair. "Hey, Eppie. I didn't know you were here." He backed up enough to rotate directions and pushed forward a cautious foot or so, waiting in the doorframe. "Mind if I come in?"

"Oh, yeah. Hey, Dan." I propped up on my elbows. I must've fallen asleep because my heart raced as though suddenly stirred from a dream and my mouth was tacky and dry. Rubbing my eyes and glaring against the overhead light I'd left on, I said, "Of course, come on in."

"Sucky birthday, huh?"

"Not all of it." I shrugged as I pulled down Lincoln's covers and swung my legs over the side of his bed. My bare feet hit the hardwood and I toed at the worn divots in the flooring with a chipped pink toenail. "Most of it was really great, actually. Just the whole boyfriend-turned-felon thing. That's kind of a bummer."

Dan's smirk was a good one with two pouty lips that made his face permanently look flirtatious. He threw his head back a little, causing his sandy hair to flick across his forehead and drop into his light eyes. He shook it out quickly. "Yeah," he laughed. "I can see how that could be the case."

"I don't know, though," I started. "Kinda makes him seem hardcore, you know? I think we can work with that."

"Hardcore and Lincoln don't even belong in the same sentence. He's a softy through and through."

I thought of Lincoln—of his perpetual smile and penchant for anxiety over worries legitimate and unfounded. Maybe he was a softy, but that was okay. Being hardened by this world, I figured, was a true tragedy, and Lincoln didn't belong in a tragedy. A comedy of errors, possibly, but not a tragedy. For as long as I was in his life, I wouldn't let that be the outcome.

"Did they set bail?"

"I don't think so. Officer Marlin said it would be morning before we'd know the amount, and I have no clue how we're even going to come up with the cash."

That wasn't entirely true. From the time of Herb's accident, I knew that Lincoln had been setting aside his paychecks to cover the cost of our dog's surgery. Those savings—he'd said—were located directly underneath me at the moment, sandwiched between box springs. All I had to do was flip the mattress back to retrieve it.

"Can I enlist your help with something?" I asked Dan and he nodded before the full sentence was even out.

"Of course."

"Lift this up?" I pointed to the bed. "He's got money under here. I don't know—it feels kinda personal for me to go rummaging through Lincoln's stuff like this. I'd rather have an accomplice."

"Certainly. Glad to help," Dan said. His hands were already heaving the pillow-top upward before I had a chance to hop from my perch. "Though I can't unsee anything I may find under there. I'm charging you for any therapy I may have to enroll in as a result of whatever horrors I may uncover."

"No worries," I laughed. "I happen to know a guy."

Dan gasped. "Oh dear."

"What?" My heart picked up speed and my fingernails were between my teeth instantly. "What is it?"

"Oh no. This is awful."

"What?"

"Your boyfriend has a real problem."

Porn. It was certainly porn. All guys struggled with it, right? I mean, of course a nineteen-year-old kid would have stacks and stacks of pinup-worthy women wedged under his bed. But wait, wasn't that what the Internet was for? I couldn't figure why he'd have physical copies when silicon enhanced images were just a mouse-click away. My skin clammed up and I tried not to let it bother me, but insecurity swept in and I unintentionally folded my arms across my own chest, hiding within myself.

"What kind of problem?" I asked slowly, not wanting the real answer.

"Yuck," Dan grimaced with a dramatic shudder. "A truly awful one."

Okay, so maybe it wasn't pornography. I couldn't imagine that Dan would be so disgusted when I assumed his own Internet history would point to the same sorts of vices.

"How awful?"

"Your boyfriend... Wow." Dan swiveled around, a stack of some unidentifiable magazine upside-down in his lap. "You've heard of bestiality, yeah?"

Oh, hell. I was getting nauseous just at the thought, and I had no idea *what* to even think.

"Yeah, I guess." My stomach tumbled.

"Well, this is so, so much worse."

What on earth could be worse than the sort of perversion Dan was hinting at? I couldn't handle it anymore. Just as I was about to rip the magazine from Dan's grasp, he flipped it around and cocked his head devilishly, his blue eyes slivered into thin, teasing lines. "Mechanophilia, sick bastard."

An image of a very Trudy-like camper graced the cover of *Vintage VW*. Dan shuffled about five more similar periodicals through his fingers, groaning at the sight of each one like the next was worse than the last.

"What are you doing?"

My hands dropped to my side and I spun around. "Lincoln!"

"Hey buddy!" Dan cheered, tossing the magazines into the air like the celebratory release of a graduation cap. They fluttered down around us and I could feel the soft breeze from the pages against my skin.

Lincoln immediately dropped to the ground to recover his precious stash. "Hey, man! Be careful with those. They're vintage!"

"Yeah. I kinda picked up on that from the title."

Lincoln was tending to the disarray when I tackled him for the second time today.

"What are you doing here?" His shirt twisted within my fingers and I wrung it tighter as I pulled him up to me. Disbelief filled my tone and my expression. I shook my head, not quite convinced he was truly here in front of me. "How did you get out?"

"My parents dropped the charges." Like I didn't weigh a thing, Lincoln lifted me by the hips and placed me to the side. His knees crackled as he rose to stand, collected magazines in hand. "They still claim they own Trudy, but they're willing to talk it out tomorrow at their house instead of next week in the courtroom."

My mouth quirked into a frown. "How very generous of them."

"I know, right?" Lincoln smiled and swiped his finger across my nose. "Anyway, I'm gonna go wash the prison smell off of me. I've got criminal funk deep in my pores." He leaned down to drop a chaste kiss on my forehead, yet Dan still audibly groaned.

"Don't drop the soap!" With his hands cupped around his mouth, Dan taunted a very exhausted, very drained Lincoln. Even though he was both of those things, he managed to eke out a feisty, "Hardy, har," before heading to the bathroom.

For the next half hour, Dan and I talked while Lincoln spent a well-deserved break showering off the day's events. We spoke of Lincoln's parents, of Dan's deep-seated dislike for the entire Ross family—Lincoln excluded—and the many ways in which this sudden and unexpected occurrence wasn't quite so sudden and unexpected.

"They've always been horrible," Dan had said, his jaw set and teeth gritting down tight. "I was two years older than Lincoln in school and much closer in age to his older brothers. I think his parents thought that was weird—that I'd choose to hang out with someone younger when Tommy and I were peers. But the truth was that Lincoln was the only likable person in that family. All they ever did was criticize him and put him down." The water had shut off in the adjoining bathroom, but Dan kept talking, pulled deep into the memory. "I stood up to his dad once. Didn't end well. He'd been giving Lincoln grief about some ball cap he wanted to wear. Said it made him look uncivilized or some senseless shit like that. Said he was always hiding under the brim of a hat because he was too much of a coward to look people in the eye."

My heart stuttered in my chest and I unintentionally clawed at my skin like that could get it beating on track again. But it just hurt. My heart hurt for Lincoln.

"I told his dad to suck it and that landed me out the door and on my ass, but I didn't leave before telling Lincoln what I really thought."

My eyes were wide and my mouth gaping. "And what was that?"

"That wearing a damn hat didn't make him a coward. That people took off their hats as a show of respect, and his father didn't deserve any of his."

I'd heard the blow-dryer click on and smiled inwardly at the adorable fact that Lincoln dried his hair. He really was just too much sometimes.

Dan continued. "I told him to let that hat be a reminder that there are choices in this life, and you get to choose whose opinion you value. I said, 'Wear your cap every time you need a little confidence, and know that it's pretty much the same as giving your dad the finger.'" His shoulders rolled with the chuckle that escaped and he shook his head in a way that indicated a sense of accomplishment. "I'm not even sure if he remembers the conversation, but I haven't seem him go a day without it on his head since."

After that, a freshly-cleaned Lincoln joined us back in the room and Dan excused himself, saying he planned to wait up for Sam while watching ESPN highlights and eating an entire carton of cookie dough ice cream all on his own. He'd offered for us to join him, but Lincoln politely declined, while at the same time giving me a look that made my insides mush.

"So," I said as soon as the door shut behind Dan and we were alone. "You dry your hair, huh? Didn't take you for much of a primper, to be honest."

If the way a guy's mouth curled could be considered sexy, Lincoln's was exactly that. I was beginning to think the corners of his mouth were the most sensual parts on his body.

"I don't typically dry my hair, no. But I didn't really want it dripping on you."

"And why would it drip on me?"

"Um, I don't know," Lincoln smirked. "Maybe when I did something like this?"

His hand reached forward and he swung an arm around my waist. Then, like we were dancing, he waltzed me backward to the edge of the bed until my knees buckled against the solid mattress. We dropped down together in a pile of laughter and racing hearts and hormones.

"Doing time has made you a bit horny, huh?" I giggled against his mouth as it collided with mine for a kiss.

"Well that just makes it sound creepy." Lincoln popped up and shook out his hair, demonstrating the effectiveness of his thorough drying. I laughed into his solid chest. "But truthfully, the thought of being apart from you—unable to talk to you or even touch you—makes me want to do nothing but absolutely that."

I pressed up for another kiss, and my tongue darted into his open mouth. Delving in deeper, Lincoln's traced mine and our bodies meshed together like even though he stood a good foot taller than I did when we were vertical, we were always meant to go with one another. Like there was no difference between us. Like together, everything just fit. He hooked one lanky leg around my hip and snuggled down close and we became one as much as our clothes and hearts would allow.

We kissed for at least an hour, until the clock read nearly 2:00 a.m., and we traded positions and breath as we found new places to tease and explore. All the while Lincoln remained a true gentleman, even when my body tempted him otherwise. He was cautious and courteous, and when he lifted up to look me in the eyes and murmur with raspy words, "Stay with me a little while longer?" I didn't even have to speak my answer.

Of course I would. Of course I'd stay. I couldn't imagine ever leaving.

# THIRTY-EIGHT

In the morning, Lincoln got me up to speed on why he thought his parents would do such a thing as jump to stolen vehicle conclusions when they clearly knew its whereabouts and in whose garage it resided. We sat at the round kitchen table and ate a breakfast he'd prepared (which included what I figured was an entire pig's worth of meat), and it almost felt like playing house, except for the fact that I'd stayed with Sam in her room last night, rather than curled up close in Lincoln's arms. He'd said he wanted to save our firsts, and waking up next to me was one he wanted to hold out on for just a bit longer.

"So when I turned sixteen," he spoke as he snapped a piece of crunchy bacon between his teeth, "I needed a car, or at least I figured I did. Kind of that whole rite of passage thing. Anyway, my dad had an old run-down VW camper just sitting in the garage. It had been his when he was my age and I'd had my eye on it since I was eight." He shoveled another heaping forkful of eggs into his mouth and I was suddenly reminded of our first date back at the diner months ago. Something in my gut fluttered at the thought, those butterflies still in there, reawakened. "I figured it would be the ultimate father-son bonding experience, you know? All the movies and TV shows depict it like the best conversations about life and love occur under the hood of a restored vehicle."

I took a sip of my orange juice, quieting my swallow because the kitchen was silent and his words were intense. "And that's not what happened," I inferred based on his expression.

"No, no it wasn't. We didn't work well together, when we did work together at all. He'd promise me a Saturday, but would end up going into the office. Or he'd come out at night when I was tinkering around in the garage, and instead of offering help, he'd tell me I was breaking curfew. How is it even possible to break curfew in your own home?" He shrugged indifferently. "Anyway, I did my best with what I could and I managed to work enough odd construction jobs to pay for the parts to get her up and running. It took nearly three years, but by graduation, Trudy was a pretty impressive piece of metal."

Though I never related to a guy's love for his car, I could understand the sense of fulfillment Lincoln must've felt by giving life to something that once had none. When I really thought about it, that seemed to be a common theme with Lincoln.

"So we had this huge graduation party at our house with Mom and Dad's elite circle and all I wanted to do was show Trudy off. I'd take each guest into the garage and provide them with more details about her improvements than they probably cared to hear. But I couldn't shut up about her. I was immensely proud. And my dad? I thought maybe after seeing all that I put into it that he'd feel that, too."

Even from what little I knew of Lincoln Senior, I doubted that would be the case.

"So he comes out and starts pointing to all the things I did wrong. The missing piece here. The skipped over step there. He's laughing and whispering to his suit-clad cohorts like I should be pitied for the shoddy job I did. So I kinda lose it. I start yelling and throwing wrenches and bolts and things like I'm a toddler. I'm telling him that I didn't want to have to do it on my own—that I *wanted* his help—but he just stands there, smirking. He takes another swig of his drink, shakes his head at me as he turns around, elbowing his friends in camaraderie, and then says over his shoulder that he has no interest in wasting his time with things that can never be fully fixed."

I pushed my plate away, hunger something that couldn't be farther from my mind or stomach.

"I can only assume now that Trudy's restored, he wants a piece of the credit," Lincoln said. "That's all I can figure. I mean, I suppose he still has the pink slip, but for years he's never given that vehicle a second thought. Unfortunately, as we found out last night, Trudy still needs a little work, so he's in for a rude awakening."

A horn sounded from outside the window, muffled through the glass panes in the kitchen, making it seem distant and further away. I swung my gaze around to see a waving Phil in his seat, ready to drive us to get the answers we so needed.

Maybe those asker/answerer roles I'd assumed earlier were more fluid than I'd originally thought.

Maybe the parent/child ones were, too.

As could be expected, Lincoln's family wasn't entirely thrilled with the entourage that rolled up to their expansive home. Phil offered to wait out front, saying he didn't want to impose either his presence or profession upon Lincoln's parents, but part of me wished he came inside. It would've been nice to have just one more backer in our court.

"Your mother and I were pleased that you surrendered the vehicle without much resistance," Mr. Ross said, a cool glass of lemonade pressed to his lips. This guy always seemed to speak with a drink in hand. The only reason I could figure he did this was so in the off-chance he desired to toss said drink into someone's face, it was readily available. Maybe it actually wasn't that off to assume that, though.

"I didn't really surrender it," Lincoln said. "She just sorta stopped."

The Ross's were all about the runaround. Twenty minutes or more had ticked by, and I still couldn't make heads or tails of their rash decision to incarcerate their youngest son. They weren't offering information freely, like every little piece needed to be pulled and coaxed out of them, word by word. This was going to be exhausting.

"Listen," Lincoln finally initiated. We were outside in the brick courtyard and the morning sun streaked down on us in lines of soft light. A wind chime clinked in the distance as it composed a song and I could see the curtains inside the house dancing from the breeze the open windows provided. In another place and time, this moment would've been beautiful, but looks were so very deceiving.

"Let's cut the crap, okay?" he continued. "I obviously did something wrong, and you were trying to punish me for it. Message received." He leaned forward in his wicker seat, his hands held in a fist and elbows pressed into the knees of his khaki shorts. "Now if only I was able to interpret that message."

"Your evening in a jail cell wasn't interpretation enough?" his dad nearly cooed, his voice dripping with snideness.

"I don't know what you want from me!" Lincoln's hands flew out in front of him in a fast, jerky motion. His mother cowered in her chair and her hand went to her chest as though utterly taken aback by her son's sudden gesture. "If you wanted the damn car back, you should've just said something!"

Based on the length of the elder Lincoln's sigh, you'd have thought he'd depleted all oxygen in his body and was starting from scratch to fill it back up. Hissing between his teeth, he expelled his pent up air and said, "We were under the impression that you two were running off."

"What?" Though I'd vowed to keep silent, that just wasn't going to happen.

"Your relationship has moved unreasonably fast, at a level we are not at all comfortable with."

Lincoln's jaw set and his eyes narrowed. "Seriously? Seriously? I moved a hell of a lot faster with Sage and neither of you had a problem with that."

I couldn't lie, no amount of confidence in a relationship guarded your heart against the hurt in hearing an ex's actual name. Names belonged to real, tangible people, and I'd rather not acknowledge those sorts of people in Lincoln's life. Steeling myself for more undesirable past girlfriend information, I took a breath.

"That's because she was a Patterson."

"What?" Lincoln jumped to his feet. I pressed my palm to his thigh to calm him, but he just shook me off. "What? Eppie isn't the right *breed* for you?"

"Lincoln James!" Mrs. Ross scolded in a way that only mothers could do.

"That's essentially what he's saying, Mom! That she doesn't come from a prestigious enough family, right? That *is* what you're saying, Dad, isn't it?"

Margot's mouth crinkled tightly and I could see her deep red lipstick that had escaped from her lips, feathering out in slivers as it bled onto her face in tributaries of wrinkles. She looked so much more haggard than the first time we'd met. Still a beauty, but one with pain hidden underneath the mask of makeup. What had changed between then and now?

"Lincoln," his father said upon a clearing of his throat. "You need to calm down."

"Calm down?" I feared the panic would creep in and rob the breath and the momentum from Lincoln, but it didn't. He was in absolute control. "You're sitting here, insulting the person I love with my whole heart, and you just expect me to take that in stride and go along with your games? I'm sick and tired of catering to this family's ridiculousness. Completely sick of it."

"And you think we're not?" Mr. Ross roared. He crashed his glass to the table, shattering it into pieces. He was up on his feet with face-off readiness. "You think I'm not exhausted with this game? You think that it's been easy to play along for nineteen years? Damn you, Lincoln. Damn you for thinking you've been anything but a nuisance to this entire family."

"Lincoln!" Margot yelled, but she didn't have the same power in saying her husband's name as she did her son's, even though they were identical in letters and syllables.

"Oh, please, Margot! Don't even attempt to convince me that it isn't the truth."

Lincoln's chest puffed in challenge and he stepped one foot closer toward his father. The space of air between them radiated with charged energy and I feared what would happen if either of them entered into that gap. "You bastard," Lincoln seethed.

"That, dear boy, is a term only *I* reserve the right to utter."

"Lincoln!" Margot was hysterical at this point, clawing at her husband's arms, trying to drag him back into his seat. Her eyes flooded with tears. "Lincoln, stop!"

Where Lincoln had only nudged me aside earlier, his father all but backhanded Margot into position and she landed on her knees against the brick patio with a sickening smack. Even when lying prone on the ground, she still bat at his feet, literally begging him to cease as though maintaining one's dignity was no longer even an option.

"I took the camper back because I'm done sharing with you," Lincoln's father said. "Finished. It started with my name and it's been nothing but more of the same every day of your entire existence."

"That's the burden of being a parent," Lincoln reasoned, though his tone was still infused with equal parts anger and confusion. He tossed his head back and forth. "That's what you do. If you were tired of that responsibility after Ricky and Tommy, then why did you even choose to have me?"

Lincoln Senior's hand sliced the air, coming within inches of his son's face. "I *didn't* choose you, Lincoln! None of us did!" he screamed. "Dammit, Lincoln. You're not even mine!"

My breath escaped me. The chimes continued their song, coupling with the ringing that trilled in my ears. I could see Lincoln's frame sway side-to-side, see his broad shoulders jump up and down. Life blurred into a haze.

"What the hell are you talking about?" Lincoln muttered. His fingers drug through his dark hair.

Even though seated, I could still reach out and take hold of his other hand, so I just did that and gripped on tightly, running my thumb across his skin in comforting circles. I couldn't leave him alone standing there, alone with his thoughts and fears. Alone with these monsters.

"You. Are. Not. Mine," Mr. Ross answered, his voice punctuating each word. "You are a bastard child—"

"Lincoln!"

He raised a quick hand, halting Margot's constant pleas.

"You are the result of a very stupid woman making a very stupid mistake. One that we've all had to live with."

"Stop." She wasn't even yelling anymore, her strength to fight exchanged with nothing but the silent tears sweeping down her face. "Just stop."

"You were never wanted, boy. Not by your mother, not by me." Lincoln's mouth was slack, his eyes hollow and vacant. "The only person to ever truly want you was your biological father."

As though snapped from his daze, Lincoln yelled, "Then why didn't you just let him have me?"

Mr. Ross made a tsk-tsk sound with his clucking tongue and teeth, and he swayed his head back and forth so slowly, condescension present in every single one of his mannerisms. "Now how would that look? A man running for council with an adulterous wife? Oh, no. We couldn't have any of that. No, you would become my namesake, we'd be sure to convince everyone of that."

"You're sick," I uttered, unaware when the words left my mouth.

"My dear," he said, turning his head slowly my direction. "Based on your familial history, judgment is not yours to hold."

"Who is he?" Lincoln bulldozed over him. His voice croaked with emotion as he threw his gaze over to his mother. "Who is he, Mom?"

Margot knew her place, so she remained silent, looking only to her husband as though requesting permission to speak. He didn't grant it.

"Who *was* he is the correct tense," Mr. Ross corrected. "You've never met him."

Whether permitted to or not, Margot spoke up. "That's not true." Her tears were audible in her hiccupped words. Her whole body shuddered violently. "He came to the hospital the day you were born. Your father—," her eyes flashed at her mistake, "Lincoln," she corrected, "sent him away."

"Where is he now?"

The older Lincoln practically cackled. "Residing in the same place as your dear girlfriend's mother."

"You killed him?" Lincoln's palms slammed into his father's chest, making him stumble to regain his footing. He pushed harder into his body, shoving him nearly against the siding of the house.

"Of course not. Murder would tarnish our family's reputation so much more than adultery. No, thankfully, he took care of that himself." My stomach tumbled and acid crept into my throat. This was sickening, to listen to this man confess to his sins without any shred of remorse. I don't think I'd ever felt sicker in my entire life. I couldn't handle it. Any of it. "He left the hospital that day in a fit of rage. Ran a red light and slammed his truck into a mother and her infant daughter." I bit back the vomit that threatened, covering my mouth with my hand to hold it in. "Everyone was obliterated instantly, along with the secret he'd sworn to keep. It's so convenient the way the world works sometimes, orchestrating everything so perfectly for you."

I almost didn't see it happen with my head hung so low, but the blow against Lincoln Senior's jaw snapped my eyes up instantly like the crack of a whip. And that's when I noticed him, his hand wrapped around his throat, fingers curling in as they shoved him repeatedly into the wall with blunt force.

Phil wasn't about to back down, even when Lincoln's arms came around to pull him off Mr. Ross's limp body. He'd surely bludgeon the man had we not stopped him, and in truth, I wasn't sure why we did.

"Phil!" I cried, pulling at his free arm. It was as though my voice snapped him from his anger and he shook off his stare and backed away quickly, arms raised in the air, chest heaving.

"Oh my God," he gasped. Lincoln Senior cupped his nose with his palm, blood dripping into it like a faucet turned on. "Oh my God."

Lincoln's hands were at his shoulders. "It's okay. This is okay."

"But it's not," Phil groaned. "Not one single part of this is okay." He looked down at his cracked hands, at the red spilling from his split knuckles. "Oh God." His eyes were wide. "What have I done?"

"It's okay, Philly," I soothed again. "It is."

"No, Eponine." His eyes pierced mine and they were shrouded with pain and concern. "I've made a huge mistake." He cast his gaze toward Mr. Ross, eyes darting all over. "And unlike some others here, I am willing to accept that responsibility."

"What dog do you even have in this fight?" Lincoln Senior forced out. Crimson crept quickly into his cheek, the fresh bruising taking no time at all. He spit blood against the ground and rubbed at his jaw.

"It was his family!" I screamed, unable to hold back. The world spun at double time. Lincoln dropped his hands from Phil and quickly wrapped them around me. No longer able to keep my frame upright, I slumped against his chest, my muscles and bones betraying every part of my being.

Phil was shaking his head, steady at first, then picking up speed the way a train does on its tracks. "It *is* my family," he corrected with unnatural grit and malice in his voice. "*They* are my family." He waved his hand toward Lincoln and me. "They are."

Like a villain in a movie, Mr. Ross spun toward us, painstakingly slow. His head lifted slightly, and his eyes slivered, taking on the same flat line as his tight mouth. "Then I suggest you take this so-called family of yours out of here and leave me and *my* family the hell alone."

I couldn't even process the movements and actions that led to all three of us seated back in Phil's car and back on the highway, but somehow we made it out without any customary humming or panic. There was no room for coping, no room for fear.

We made it out—me, Lincoln, and Phil—and in that moment, for the first true time in my life, I knew what it was to be a family. Through the breakdown of one, I experienced the building up of another. And this family—this mismatching of lost and lonely souls—this was the only family I'd ever want to be a part of.

In reality, maybe it was the only family we were ever meant to be a part of to begin with.

# THIRTY-NINE

You're not like most girls.

*Though I didn't want to give Kyle's voice any power, there was underlying truth in that statement. No, I wasn't like most girls. Circumstances hadn't allowed me that comfort.*

*My life had been altered, by no fault of my own.*

*But what was my fault? Thinking that just because I wasn't born into something most everyone else had, that I was any less worthy of receiving it.*

*A love so unconditional that nothing could destroy it, that was still in my cards. I had to believe that. Because if I didn't, then who would believe it for me?*

*"I'm going out," Dad called from downstairs. I could hear him retrieve his keys off the metal hook in the entryway. We were supposed to go dress shopping for homecoming. That was tonight's plan. But without his car and credit card, I was out of luck. Though I should've been disappointed, relief fell over me.*

*Of course I'd wanted to go to the dance, but the lack of a date with just four days to go made those hopes feel more like far off dreams.*

*It was good to have an excuse. 'I can't get a dress in time.' 'I don't have a ride.' 'There's no money to pay for it.' I became an expert at the excuse game. It was easy to verbally account for my situation when I placed the blame on my circumstance.*

*My mother would always be my excuse. That was the default she'd earned when she used me as her own means for attention and fulfillment. Her sick behavior excused me from living a healthy, love-filled life.*

*But I was tired. Tired of reasoning my existence away. Just because someone chose to take a significant portion of it didn't mean that I needed to forfeit the remainder.*

*I still had a lot of living left to do. At some point, I'd need to shed the excuses and take ownership. That's what I'd been trying to do all this time, however unsuccessfully. Sometimes it was just easier to do things in pairs. I mean, teenage girls couldn't even travel to the bathroom alone. Walking solitarily through life was an infinitely larger feat.*

*I thought that made me a bad person, though, to desire a companion in this twisted life I led. Because no sane person would want to join me and my mess. That would take true, unconditional love—to look beyond the surface and see the potential underneath. Someone would have to really adore me to want any part of that. They'd have to love me like crazy.*

# FORTY

As one would expect, the Ross's pressed charges against Phil and that money we'd intended for Herb and then Lincoln ended up going toward attorney fees, in conjunction with a hefty portion of Phil's nest egg. I'd apologized over and over, unable to let go of the guilt in knowing that somehow, my association with Phil and with Lincoln culminated in two of the men closest to me behind bars, if only for a short while.

"I can't shake the notion that anyone who gets remotely close to me ends up ruining their life in one form or other," I'd said the day Phil's case was dropped due to lack of supporting evidence on the Ross's part. Apparently a bruised chin and ego wasn't enough to convict another man of criminal wrongdoing in this particular instance. "If you cross my path, you're destined to encounter tragedy."

"Eppie." Phil's voice was soft and even though his aviators hid his eyes, I could still sense the sincerity in them. "Perhaps it was our tragedies that aligned our paths in such a way that they would even be capable of crossing."

I'd been mulling over that phrase for the past several weeks, coming at it from all angles, trying to find the flaw in it. But I couldn't. No single sentence uttered into my life ever rang truer. This broken road I'd been on—this lone path I'd blamed my mother for all this time—this is what led me to love. This is what led me to life.

It's easier for those on the broadened path. They have the multitudes to keep them company. When they tire of one relationship, they move on to the next. Attachments are easily formed based on the sheer vastness of possibilities, but when things get tough, I'm not sure how strong those ties remain.

The relationships you form in the trenches, though? The people who intersect your life during your moments of brokenness and stay around to fight with you and for you, I think those are the sticking types of relationships. It's called a band of brothers for a reason. If I were to take my advice from anyone, Shakespeare seemed like a reasonable enough guy.

"From this day to the ending of the world,
But we in it shall be remember'd;
We few, we happy few, we band of brothers;
For he to-day that sheds his blood with me
Shall be my brother."
-Henry V

Maybe it wasn't the sharing of blood that made you family, but the willingness to shed it for one another. I knew of at least two people in my life that met that requirement. I considered myself one of the lucky ones. I figured that was probably two more than most people ever got.

...............

"You look gorgeous in that gown, Eppie." Lincoln surveyed my reflection from over my shoulder. He'd just arrived from his latest session with Phil, and while coming to terms with the lies that coated his past would be a lifetime sort of processing thing, he was doing remarkably well. Sometimes truth, no matter how hard to hear, healed you all on its own.

I smoothed my hair once more, pinning the cap down with two thin bobby pins.

"Brings out your eyes," he teased.

"Not sure I can take that as a compliment considering it's a formless black gown," I laughed. "You must think I've got hollow, lifeless eyes."

He crept close, wrapping his arms around me from behind. His chin pressed into my shoulder, and I could feel the point of it push in and out as he spoke.

"Not anymore," he said, connecting with my gaze in the full-length mirror hung on the back of my bedroom door. "Maybe when I first met you, yeah, a little. But you were toting around a half-dead dog, so I wouldn't imagine you would have smiley and happy eyes. That wouldn't be right."

Never before had I understood the phrase 'that was a lifetime ago' when referencing a short period of time. Time was just time. It all ticked down the same. But now I got it. In the past several months, I'd experienced a new sort of life, one so very different from the kind I led before. So yeah, it was a lifetime ago back at that veterinarian's office. The day when I tried to save someone else, but ultimately ended up saving myself. Or maybe, all of us together wound up saving each other. I think that's what really happened.

That's how life actually worked. Just how certain people fell into certain roles—the askers/askees, etc. — there were the life givers and the life takers. Those who lifted your spirit and those who killed it. To have figured that out at just eighteen years old had to mean something. All of that missing childhood and forgotten adolescence—it felt like I got some of that back just in knowing a little more about the way the world operated. That was a gift. And so was the boy who stood beside me.

"Are you nervous?"

"To walk across a stage and receive my diploma?" I straightened the cap again, not able to get it quite right. Lincoln slipped his hand up to help with the adjusting. "No way. I've been ready for this for so long. This is the ticket I've been waiting forever for. I'm beyond eager to start the first day of the rest of my life."

He smiled tenderly at my mirrored self. "I think you started it long ago, Eppie. I know I did, at least. The moment I started loving you—our beginning was a new beginning for me."

I spun around in his arms. His eyes were shadowed by the brim of his worn hat, but there was so much life in them. The wrinkles in their corners weren't indicative of a tired existence. They gave evidence to the smiling and the laughter and the love that emanated through him. I'd always known Lincoln had a secret. And I was eternally grateful that he chose to share it with me.

"I'm so proud of you, Eppie. Of us." His nose nuzzled mine and I pressed into the cool cloth of his blue V-neck shirt. "We've come a long way, baby."

I could almost hear Loretta Lynn's twang in Lincoln's voice and laughed. "I was worried you were going to start singing for a moment there."

"Nah," he chuckled. "I'll leave the singing to you. Honestly, I really wish you'd do more of it."

I shrugged, feeling the silky sleeves of my graduation robe rub against my shoulders. "I don't know. I mean, I always sang before as a way of coping, you know? Like a distraction. I don't need distractions anymore."

"All the more reason to compose a new tune."

"That's exactly what we've been doing, I think." Lincoln rested his chin on the top of my head and I drew closer to him to press my ear to his chest. This was home. Right here with Lincoln's heart. Nothing felt more welcome. "I think before it was all broken chords. But now? With you? Now I've found my melody."

Bending down to me, Lincoln swept his lips across mine, so gently that it took a moment for me to even feel it. I pressed in and kissed back with all I had, all of the love within me that was only for him.

"I was wrong when I said that whole thing about failing to be in the right place at the right time," he murmured quietly against my mouth as he pulled away. "I think wherever you are at any given time, that's where you're meant to be. Because who would've thought that being stuck with Dan's sick hamster would ultimately land me here, in your arms."

"That hamster was Dan's?" I laughed, never knowing what lead to Lincoln's veterinarian visit that day.

"Yeah," he nodded, his brown hair flopping around his ears. I reached up to tuck it back, realizing he hadn't cut it since the day we met. I ran a few strands within my fingertips, holding it there. "He was supposed to take the little guy in for an appointment, but he actually had to attend a last minute ceremony to get some medal from local veterans for his bravery and patriotism." Lincoln smiled proudly, thinking of his heroic friend. He leaned in a little and said, "So I guess we ultimately have Dan to thank for our chance encounter."

"I think we have so many more than just him," I said, glancing to the clock. It was nearly time to go. I turned back to the mirror again, giving myself another quick once over. "I'm not sure we'll ever even know all of the people and actions responsible for bringing us to together."

"You're probably right," Lincoln said with a decisive nod. "That thank-you list would likely be quite long, and I don't know about you, but I've got awful penmanship."

I laughed, figuring he was probably right.

"So since I can't thank each individual person, I'm going to start with just one." With his eyes open wide, so transparent and vulnerable, Lincoln stared directly into my own. His purposeful intensity caused my heart to thrum just a little faster than normal. "Thank you, Eppie," he said in a firm voice, rich with sincerity. "Thank you for this life and this love, the likes of which I never knew possible. You took a leap with me, and I'll forever be grateful that you trusted me to fall with you."

The tears had no other option than to trickle down my cheeks, triggered by so much more than just his words. They were triggered by his love, and if ever I had a reason to weep, it was over this beautiful boy standing right in front of me.

He scooped me into his chest and we held one another until it was time to leave for the ceremony. And as I walked across that stage and accepted my graduation diploma, I wasn't walking into my future. Sure, it was another necessary step in the direction of adulthood, but my real future was the tall boy sitting in the front row with a lopsided grin and a frayed and tattered hat.

"Congratulations," he said as I made my way back to my seat. "You did it, Eppie!"

"I did," I agreed proudly, finding my place back at his side as the principal continued calling out names. "It almost feels surreal."

"It always does," Lincoln agreed. His hand found my bare knee and squeezed slightly. "The best parts of life are the sometimes hardest to comprehend."

We sat for the rest of the graduation with his arm draped across my shoulders and my body fitted close against his side. When the time came, I tossed my hat into the air along with my peers, celebrating our successes and our journeys and the new ventures we expected to encounter. While many things were still undecided about my future when it came to schooling and degrees and possible careers, nothing was undecided about the way I felt for Lincoln or how I wanted to always have him in the center of my life.

As we left the auditorium and walked to the parking lot, hand in hand, he turned to me, a smile in his eyes and on his mouth. "Have I told you lately that I'm still incurably in love with you, Eppie? Because I am, since it's incurable and all."

I gripped his hand tighter, confident in knowing they'd hold one another like this for many years to come. Then I lifted my head to his with a nod and said, "You have. And when it all comes down to it, I think it's that love that ultimately cured me."

"I think love cured me, too," Lincoln agreed. Then he kissed me like it was both our first and last kiss at once, the emotion climbing from those initial fluttering butterflies to the solid, steadfast confidence in knowing you were completely loved in loving completely.

And he held me in his arms, my ear to his chest, and our hearts beat together in time and tune, just liked they'd learned to so many months ago.

# ABOUT MEGAN

I'm a writer.

I'm a photographer.

I love to photograph about what I write and write about what I photograph.

I'm fueled by Diet Coke and an overactive imagination.

I can't do without the S.F. Giants, my mini iPad with the kindle app, and a daily dose of snuggles with my hundred pound Golden Retriever.

And I love *LOVE*.

Like seriously adore those butterflies you get when you think about that first kiss or when you held hands with someone you'd been crushing on for years. Even if it was cringeworthy and terrible, there's just nothing quite like connecting with another human being on that nervous, hesitant level. Relationships are complex and wonderful and scary, and I get a rush each time I have a chance to write about them and all of their layers.

I get to document life with my keyboard and my camera, and I'm blessed beyond belief that I can do both for a living.

You can connect with me at:

www.facebook.com/MeganSquiresAuthor
www.megansquiresauthor.com

Made in the USA
Lexington, KY
01 December 2015